# Five Score and Ten

*"END OF THE SIXTH AGE"* BOOK ONE

W. Best Publishing
1114 Highway 96
Suite C-1 #120
Kathleen, GA 31047

Bill@BillBest.net

# Contents

# 1. 2,300 B.C.

## Somewhere in the Middle East . . .

Noella understood that it was a risk. But she did not want ever again to be the victim of a rape mob. Unlike most of her girlfriends, she no longer wanted to take part in one, either. The pain of what teenage boys, girls, and even adult men and women did to her on several occasions, when they caught her alone?

She shuddered. No, she would risk everything to convince Raim to be her Protector. She would give him whatever he wanted, whenever and as often as he wanted it—if he would just stand up for her and against any others who would harm her.

Of course, that didn't mean he wouldn't go on rape mobs himself. That would be too much to ask.

Such were the days of Noella's youth. Some regions, like hers, where several Nephilim lived, were worse than others. But according to the traders, it was bad everywhere.

Her Uncle Noah talked about a God and His coming judgment against the whole Earth, that He was angry at the violence and corruption. Noah talked, he preached, and he and his sons kept building—what did they call it? An ark. They kept building an ark and telling people to repent. Everyone laughed at them. The violence, theft, and the rape mobs continued. Noella thought they were getting worse, now also involving incest and increasingly directed against young boys.

But good old Uncle Noah? He must be around 600 years old by now. What an embarrassment. Who ever heard of water falling from the sky, Noella thought as she finished the picnic basket. She was oblivious to the confusion, and even the fear that had spread steadily outward from the strange vessel just over three days' journey from her. Seven days earlier, Noah and his family had entered his Ark, and the door had been closed. Some said it closed on its own, as the last person entered. Days before, animals of all kinds, including many predators, peacefully came to the ark and went aboard. Like the door closing, it seemed they were led by an unseen hand. They came in pairs, young and small, most of them just weaned from their mothers. Birds of all kinds came, also in pairs. For some strange reason, certain animals and birds came in larger numbers. And then Noah and his family . . .

"So, you're going to make this a special day for me, huh?"

The man's sudden presence startled her. He grabbed her from behind and pulled her close, wrapping one arm across her breasts to grab her left arm. His other arm went across her flat stomach to her right hip.

"Oh, yes, my love." She leaned her head back against his muscular chest. "Very special. A preview of what's to come." If you accept my proposal, that is, she thought.

Women had no rights, no privileges. Except one. And today Noella would exercise that right. She was sixteen, half of his thirty-two years. Maybe he could be her Protector for several dozen years, maybe even a few hundred years, if he would accept. She had to convince him that it would be well worth his while. He was one of the strongest men in the village. Once they had their ceremony, no one would dare assault her, as he and his friends would be honor-bound to avenge her. Such a person would never attack anyone again, even if he survived. Most didn't.

## 2. *WRONG PLACE*

*June 1991*

"Oh, crap!" Still breathing hard from her hurried walk to the ten-story office building, Jennifer Lane dropped her tote and snatched a mirror from her purse. She wasn't concerned about the slight flush on her cheeks. The morning was cool for Atlanta in early June, thanks to the overcast skies and gentle breeze. She felt invigorated and, if anything, even more presentable. But . . .

"Tony might be a woman," she mumbled, as she glanced down at her too-open blouse. She quickly put the mirror back in her purse, which she set down on the elevator floor beside her tote, and then fastened the next button up. "Don't need to piss off some older Alpha Female," she muttered. Then she smiled, *at least, not right away*. Throwing open her tote, she replaced her sneakers with less-comfortable pumps that complemented her form-fitting suit. She leaned against the elevator wall and finished putting the pumps on just as the elevator door opened.

The twenty-two-year-old blonde was closer to full-figured than slender. Her five-foot, six-inch frame supported 150 pounds, and her body-fat-index suggested more party girl than fitness freak. She appeared slightly shorter at the moment, bending over to grab her tote and purse. Jennifer straightened and took a final glance down her front, and then at the hand-written notes on the back of her agent's business card.

"Tony Mendenhall . . . room 612 . . . past the water fountain and turn right . . . third door on left."

The elevator door opened, and she stepped into the hallway. She didn't notice that the ornate, bronze plaque across from the elevator read "Fifth Floor," just as she hadn't noticed bumping against the "5" button while swapping shoes in the elevator.

Jennifer hustled down the hall, past the water fountain. She glanced at her watch, smiled, and slowed her pace.

*It's really happening. I'm going to be on time!*

She turned the corner and tried to project a quiet confidence that had no basis in reality. As she approached the third door on the left, Jennifer took a deep breath and curled her lips into her most pleasant, professional smile. She turned the handle and pushed the door open.

At that precise instant, Jennifer Lane's life changed forever.

The door slammed back shut as a heavy-set, balding white man in his mid-fifties slammed against it, half turning toward her as he dropped to the floor. Blood mushroomed out of a hole in his chest. Behind him, less than six feet from Jennifer, stood another white man. He was large, muscular, menacing—and very much alive. A puff of smoke billowed out from the silencer on a massive handgun.

Jennifer noticed precisely three things in the instant before the door slammed back shut, blocked by the dead body now wedged up against it: The sound of the empty shell casing hitting something inside the room, the gun that was now pointed at her, and the steel-grey eyes of the man who clearly would have pulled the trigger had the door not shut first.

Jennifer was too scared to scream. She ran down the hall and around the corner. She hit the down button just as the elevator was coming back down from the sixth floor. The door opened, and Jennifer jumped inside. The door took forever to close, as if it didn't want to waste its effort on a single passenger. Jennifer considered running toward the stairs, but she was already short of breath. The door closed just as she heard the first heavy footsteps racing around the corner.

*Get off on the second floor, run to the exit furthest from the elevator. Go across the street and hide in a janitorial closet in the next building.*

She couldn't tell where the thoughts came from, but they made sense and she didn't have a better plan. The elevator door opened. She saw two exits, one in each direction. She half-jogged, half-ran toward the farthest one. Jennifer's heart raced and she struggled to suck in enough air. Years of indulgence and avoiding anything that resembled physical activity forced her to slow down even more as she passed a dozen suites. All the office doors were closed. She didn't bother to notice whether anyone opened up to see why someone was making such a racket this early in the morning.

+   +   +

Louis "Bull" Thatcher ran only a few yards, though his mind raced a mile. He couldn't leave the room open for someone to walk by and see the carnage. The young woman had too much of a head start during the several seconds he took to move the body away from the door. When he stepped out, he couldn't get off a quick shot. Plus, a long shot down the hall would significantly increase the risk of more witnesses while he brought her body back to his clean room. Carrying her back and leaving a trail of blood was also not an option. And if the shot only wounded her? Every option was a 'no.' Rather than drawing more attention from the two occupied suites down the hall, he quickly turned back to his room. Then he stopped. Just a few yards from the door to his room—a long-term rented suite for special occasions like today—there was a business card on the floor. It hadn't been there thirty minutes ago.

Bull picked it up, looked at both sides, and smiled. He stepped back inside the plastic-sheet-covered room, and then closed and locked the door. It was going to be a good day after all.

+   +   +

Panting hard, Jennifer collapsed on the floor in a closet. She wanted to scream. *Don't.* She wanted to cry. *Later.* She needed to call someone. *Mick.*

She pulled the analog flip-phone out of her tote and extended its antenna, hoping she could get a good signal.

"Pick up . . . pick up . . . come on. Answer your phone!" She trembled holding the phone to her ear.

After almost as long as it took for the elevator door to close, an exasperated voice boomed at her.

"Stop it! I'm tired of your games. Leave me alone."

"Mick . . . " she whimpered.

There was a pause at the other end. He hadn't hung up. Yet.

"Mick," she repeated, sobbing. "I just witnessed a murder. And he saw me. The murderer? He looked at me, through me, pointed his gun at me . . . ”

“Are you safe? Where are you?”

“I, uh, I’m in a janitor closet across, um, up in the third floor in a building across the street from, uh, I don’t even know what street . . .

“Jennifer! Slow down. You’re babbling. Was this the day of your appointment? Somewhere near your apartment?

“Yes,” she wheezed, barely above a whisper.

“Okay, I’m on my way. I’ll call when I get closer and you can figure out where you are and how I can get to you. And Jen?”

“Yes?” she sobbed.

“If this is another of your games . . . ”

“Just hurry!”

# 3. TIME CAPSULE?

## 2,300 B.C.

They all knew the stories. A perfect garden. No thorns or thistles. No work to produce food. Just eat what was there. Stories, from around fifteen centuries ago, about some place a dozen miles away. There were rumors of strange-looking creatures guarding the only entrance, and a terrifying, fiery sword that flashed every-which-way blocking the path. No one had dared go near there for hundreds of years.

*Whatever.* Noella smiled. She couldn't imagine anywhere being more beautiful than the rolling meadow where they enjoyed the lunch she had prepared, and where she gave the man every other delight he could desire.

Exotic birds whirled around overhead and landed in the nearby trees. A mild breeze made the typical year-round afternoon temperature of seventy-six degrees feel a little cool.

Then she proposed to him. She described everything she would do, and how she would be devoted to him and their children, and that she would bear many for him. She would cook, and clean, and meet his every need. She just wanted him to be her Protector.

Noella made a compelling argument, and Raim was thoughtful. She looked at his muscled torso under the sheer, white tunic. The young woman was drawn to his impossibly dark eyes, olive complexion, jet-black shoulder-length hair and beard, of course, his frame. He was, converting to 21st century measurements, six feet, two inches and near 200 pounds. Noella considered herself, a full-figured young woman with a slender waist, stood five feet, eight inches tall and weighed 145 pounds. She also had dark eyes and a dark olive complexion, but her long hair was more of a deep auburn color. *We'll have beautiful babies,* she thought. *And he'll be their Protector, too.*

"Noella . . . "

Just then, two older men, over twice Raim's age, emerged from a thick stand of trees on the side of the meadow, a few dozen yards from where they lay.

"Noella!" one said, mocking. He had a long scar on the right side of his face, from his temple to his chin.

"Well, boy, having some fun? Come on, boy, let's share!" said the second man. No wounds were visible, but he walked with a significant limp.

Raim jumped to his feet, glancing at them, then at Noella.

"Raim . . . " She cried, pleading.

He straightened up and faced the men. She had heard of them. They were tall, muscular, and had reputations as skilled fighters. Noella often wondered if these men killed her own father, who at the age of 480 had no longer been able to protect her mother and the family.

"I have agreed to be her Protector," Raim announced.

Noella's heart skipped a beat.

"Our ceremony is tomorrow."

"Well, boy, congratulations," Scar-face sneered.

"Yeah," said the second. "That's tomorrow. We'll help you celebrate today. Now join us, or step aside." He raised his hand and rested it on his sword. So did Scar-face.

They continued walking towards Raim and Noella and were now less than ten feet away.

Raim drew his sword. Noella jumped to her feet and stepped behind him, looking for anything close by that might be useful as a weapon.

Raim's defense was a sudden, unexpected offense. He jumped and kicked hard at Limping-man's weak leg. As the man hollered in pain and fell, Raim slammed the butt of his sword against the man's head. Then he jumped back ten feet to avoid the advance of Scar-face.

Raim and Scar-face danced around each other, trading blows, parrying thrusts, blocking sweeps, trying to hit or kick. Their jumps would carry them a full six feet or more in the air, and eight to twelve feet in distance.

Limping-man was on his hands and knees, groaning. Noella found a large rock and slammed it against the man's head in a single, fatal blow. She watched for a clean shot at Scar-face. The stone was probably a good sixty pounds, so she should be able to throw it at least fifteen or twenty feet.

Elegant swords crashed against one another, sparking and making strange noises with each blow. The material gleamed in the sunlight. It resembled a translucent, lightweight, hard ceramic. But it was stronger than steel. The fight took the men toward the trees. Scar-face swung his sword in a huge arc that Raim only barely ducked under, at the loss of several inches of his hair. The blade slammed into a tree resembling a yellow pine and the force of the blow sliced clean through the six-inch trunk.

Noella, still holding the large rock, jumped six feet to the side to avoid the falling tree.

Scar-face was off-balance and Raim had the perfect opportunity to run him through. Raim underestimated the older man's speed, however. The man jumped straight back before Raim could take advantage. Unexpectedly, Scar-face then immediately jumped back at Raim, sword straight forward in a muscular right arm. This time, Scar-face underestimated the young man's speed. Raim ducked low and swung his sword upward. Scar-face's sword made contact—with the same tree it sliced through seconds before—but the hand holding it fell to the ground, severed a few inches above the wrist.

Before Scar-face had time to scream in pain, the sixty-pound rock slammed into his head. Noella's aim was perfect. Another slice of Raim's sword removed the man's head.

Raim and Noella fell into each other's arms, and onto the soft ground.

"So, you'll be my Protector?" she asked between kisses.

"Yes. After what you did to those men, I want you on my side."

"Raim!" she screamed, looking over his shoulder into the sky.

He jumped up, expecting another fight. What he saw, what they saw, no man or woman had ever seen before.

The sheer fabric that made up their tunics, and the strange material of their swords were about to be lost to history. A swarm of massive meteors streaked through the clear sky. Some exploded above ground while others became meteorites as they cratered into the Earth.

In seconds, the bright sky that had always been cloudless since Creation became dark and foreboding. Oceans of transparent water vapor high above the earth condensed on dust particles from the celestial barrage. The droplets formed into clouds. And the clouds became a storm.

Deafening sonic booms were followed by actual explosions. As if to mock Noella's earlier sarcasm, water fell from the sky, first as a drizzle, and then as a hard, driving rain. As the Earth rumbled from the concussions of the meteorites, springs of water burst upward from the deep underground and formed streams which then became rivers. Comets slammed into the atmosphere and exploded, releasing even more water.

A supersonic shock wave from a meteorite that made impact a few miles away slammed against Raim and Noella, breaking their bodies against the trees. It stripped the trees bare as it blew them near-horizontal in one direction, then back in the other direction as the air rushed back to the point of impact.

Raim and Noella died instantly, as did many others in the region. Only a few survived long enough to drown in the prophesied flood.

A dozen miles away, a group of strange creatures recovered a massive flaming sword and ascended from the Earth. Centuries had passed, and now their mission was over. They returned home.

As they cleared the Earth's atmosphere, one of the largest comets exploded less than a mile above the Garden, and it was no more.

The supersonic shock wave of that explosion blew tons of debris outward. One small remnant, an unusual looking piece of fruit, was propelled a dozen miles away.

The fruit landed at the base of the pine-like tree that had been sheared by Scar-face's sword. The tree still had a tip of his sword in it, the rest having been broken off by blast debris. And at the foot of the tree, wedged up against it, Scar-face's severed wrist.

Sap ran down the tree trunk, coating the hand and the strange piece of fruit, a type of fruit that only two people had once seen but never tasted, 1,500 years before.

# 4. JACKSON LONGEVITY RESEARCH CENTER

*June 1990: One year earlier.*

"Really need some answers, Ed." Fred Jackson, the mid-fifties, balding founder and owner of Jackson Longevity Research Center—JLRC—plopped down into a chair beside Dr. Ed Richardson, looking like he'd lost his last friend. The casual short-sleeve, button-down shirt displayed a level of perspiration that didn't match with the coolness of the morning.

"Mornin', Fred," Ed Richardson replied. "Funding okay? Thought you found an 'angel' to keep us going."

Fred Jackson gulped his coffee, set the cup down, and opened a stick of gum. Ed was glad that his friend was finally trying to kick the smoking habit. The man stuck the gum in his mouth and stared at the floor.

"Maybe ten more months. No more than twelve. I know you can find work anywhere. Maybe double what you make here. Tanya? Same thing. No idea what I'll do."

"I just happen to believe in what we're doing. I think we can make a difference. Sorry to hear about the finances. How was the convention?"

Fred shifted nervously, and then slumped into a chair. "Probably shouldn't have gone. So, what do you have?"

They spent the next ten minutes in a terse, technical discussion of telomerase and extending the number of times cells can divide. Then they talked about the effects of those cells becoming more prone to cancer, with the soon-to-be published research on using something called $p16^{Ink4a}$ as a cancer inhibitor. But Ed's peer review of his friend's research raised more questions than it answered. Extend life? *Perhaps.* In good health? *Doubtful.*

"Just doesn't seem to be any way around it. At least, not from a pharmaceutical perspective," said Ed. "There's intriguing research being done on carotenoids, bioflavonoids, cruciferous compounds, and such. God provides all nutrients in balance, not in isolation. Tanya's seeing good results with our lab mice."

"But no patentable breakthrough."

"No, Fred. We could probably patent a proprietary combination and process. But you're right. No breakthrough."

"Your God needs to do more than package stuff along with vitamins and minerals, if we're going to make a go of this. Need a miracle. A real miracle."

The older man sighed, sipped his coffee from a shaking cup, pushed himself out the chair, and trudged to his office. *Fifty-five, and the guy doesn't look a day over seventy,* Ed thought, as he rolled his chair back to his new Windows 3.0 computer. *He'd probably have a different outlook on life if he'd drop forty pounds.*

Ed ran a hand through his thick hair while he waited for his hand-coded research spreadsheet to open. The jet-black hair, high cheek bones, and ruddy complexion all gave evidence of a strong American Indian heritage. The trim, fit physique on his thirty-five-year-old frame? That, he earned the hard way.

"Coffee? Fresh pot," Tanya offered, walking into the main lab from the kitchenette. She was petite, blonde, and the team's animal researcher. She coddled the men almost as much as she did her three young children. Four, she sometimes thought, when she added her husband's occasional quirks.

"Thanks," Ed responded as he held out his cup. "You heard?"

"Yeah. I know I can go back to a large research company, but I sure wanted this to work." She paused and lowered her voice. "Gambling again?"

"I have my suspicions. Yeah, I'm afraid so. He was so upbeat before he went to the convention in Vegas."

A ringing phone interrupted Ed's train of thought. He walked to his office to answer the call. Tanya returned the pot to the coffee maker and retreated to the company's largest room to check on her mice. Ed picked up his phone. "Ed Richardson."

"Ed? Good morning. It's Andy Stone."

"Dr. Stone! Good to hear from you. Ready for another debate?"

There was an uncharacteristic pause on the other end.

"Andy? You there?"

Ed was expecting a quick reply from the normally quick-witted, fast-talking professor of archeology. Instead, Andy answered slowly and quietly. "I think my debating days are over. Can we talk? In person? Privately? Maybe tomorrow?"

+  +  +

That night, forty-five minutes east of the lab depending on Atlanta traffic, three men were in a hot, stuffy warehouse office. Only one, or at the most two, would leave alive.

"Use this."

Skylar Brown watched as Louis "Bull" Thatcher pulled a clear, plastic sandwich bag from a coat pocket, and used a handkerchief to remove a snub-nose .38 caliber revolver. Bull handed the gun to his young protégé.

"Untraceable."

Bull's boss, JR, had seen a news story about Skylar and had Bull arrange to get the young, lean, muscular twenty-four-year-old black man released on bond. That was followed by high-level legal counsel, and then a job. Like Bull, Skylar was smart and resourceful. And like Bull, he could talk street-tough in back alleys or be articulate when the occasion required. Skylar was about to be initiated into a whole new level of service within JR's exclusive private organization.

"You got the guts for this, kid? If not, you and me have some problems."

Skylar trembled as he held the gun. The fact that Bull handed it to him without drawing a weapon of his own indicated that the older man was confident that Skylar wouldn't turn the gun against him. Or, if he did, that Bull would violently disarm him and wrap two corpses in the plastic sheeting lining the office.

Bull still had the brass knuckles in his right fist.

Skylar had been in fights. Serious gang fights, where people went to the emergency room—and sometimes to the morgue. He wasn't sure, but he suspected that he was responsible for at least one of those final body bag trips. He faced the man on the floor in front of him. The man was in his early forties. He was on his knees, swaying back and forth. Duct tape covered his mouth, and his hands were taped behind his back. Blood trickled down the side of his head.

Bull had been straight up with Skylar. "You want in? Today, you kill a man. Peter Jordan. JR's Number One, for years. Recruited me five years ago. The man got greedy. Sloppy. Almost allowed some bad stuff to get pinned on the Boss. JR? He don't like stuff coming back to him. An' nobody skims off the top."

The warehouse office, Bull explained, was their typical meeting place, at least once a week. What wasn't typical was that the shadow Peter had seen moving inside the dimly lit room wasn't Bull. as he had thought. It was Skylar. Bull, who had been hiding behind a crate, lunged out and knocked the older man unconscious with a crashing blow to the side of his head.

Now, Peter, barely conscious, moaned.

The dusty office was deep inside a large warehouse. It was nearly 20,000 square feet, one of several in a large, fenced-in area. The run-down complex was in the northeastern part of Atlanta, just barely in the city limits. No one currently lived within several blocks. Its air conditioning was failing to overcome the day's residual heat and humidity.

To the west, lightning from a distant storm flashed. A pack of stray dogs lingering in the parking lot barked. And inside an old warehouse, there was the subdued sound of what might have been a single gunshot from a .38 caliber revolver.

## 5.  FRED'S MIRACLE

The next day, Ed Richardson walked into the restaurant he had recommended to Andy. It was known to have good food, enough activity so they could talk without being easily overheard, and booths that offered additional privacy.

He saw Andy in a secluded corner booth, hard to miss with his reddish hair and light complexion. Andy stood and shook Ed's hand like they were long-separated best friends, with Ed only having taken a few more years around the calendar. They were similar in build and weight, but Andy appeared to have spent more time in research and archeological digs than the time Ed had spent at the gym.

"Andy, good to see you. What in creation is this all about?" Ed asked as they sat down.

"That's exactly what it's about. All hell's about to break loose."

Ed sat back and stared at the man he had debated on four separate occasions. In those debates, Ed maintained a firm stand on a literal six-day Biblical creation, while Andy would argue in favor of 13.7 billion years for the universe at large, with several of those billion years for life to originate and evolve on the Earth.

"Look," Andy confessed. "I haven't eaten all day. Missed supper yesterday as well. I'm starved. I'm going to order, then I'm going to lay something out for you, and I want you to give me your professional, even Christian, opinion. No sparring, no debate. Straight up."

The waiter came, took their orders, and brought them tea and bread. After he left, Ed leaned forward, concerned. Andy took a deep breath and exhaled slowly.

"Ed, you know there have been numerous instances of insects, plants, and even small animals that have been found preserved in amber."

"Right, the *Jurassic Park* movies at least got that part correct."

"Well, if archeologists were to find a human hand, along with large air bubbles, what would you expect based on your world view? The, well, the strata indicates Paleolithic."

Ed's mouth dropped open and he stared. He leaned back, started to speak, shook his head, and then looked at the ceiling. Andy nervously looked around the restaurant, as if he had just shared state secrets with a known enemy spy.

"Okay, Andy, here it is. I believe what you call the Paleolithic was sedimentation from the antediluvian world laid down by the flood."

"Yeah, I actually listened to you in our debates. Know thy enemy and all that. But what if the amber preserved the hand, air and some unknown fruit before that flood?"

Ed could hardly contain his excitement. He began listing specific points as he emphasized each one on his fingers.

"First, any air bubbles would be at a higher atmospheric pressure than today's, maybe up to twice as much due to a vapor canopy. Pterodactyls were too large and heavy to fly with our current air density at 14.7 psi.

"Second, much higher concentration of oxygen. Raptors couldn't suck in enough oxygen for their huge size through their small nasal passages, so figure, maybe, 30 or 40 percent concentration. Less nitrogen. No helium to speak of as there hadn't been enough time for radioactive decay to produce any."

Ed paused and stared at Andy, who nodded solemnly and motioned for him to continue. Ed slowed down, becoming more thoughtful.

"Third, the hand. No arthritis. No sun-related skin damage. The skin wouldn't indicate any known race since it was before the population dispersal many years after the flood. At the DNA level, no genetic defects. None. That's why family members could intermarry from the original Adam and Eve. Even well after the flood, from Noah and his wife along with their sons and their wives, cousins could still safely marry. God put an end to that in His law as the gene pool began to degrade. Now it's dangerous to marry first cousins. Too many cumulative defects."

Andy listened intently. "Fruit?"

"Good grief. Loaded with nutrients. Vitamins, minerals, flavonoids, carotenoids, and probably other stuff that we can't even identify. That's the only way animals and people could survive. With that atmospheric pressure and oxygen concentration? That high a partial pressure of oxygen today would quickly overwhelm us with free-radical damage. We'd be dead in months or a few years at best.

Ed paused, expecting Andy to argue, refute, scoff. Something.

Instead, Andy leaned forward and looked intently at the younger man. Ed couldn't read the archeologist; he'd never seen that strange expression on his friend before, either during debates or their less-formal meals and long discussions they had enjoyed on other occasions.

Andy glanced around the restaurant, back again at Ed, and whispered.

"Want some samples?"

+  +  +

One by one, the Six called in. They met in person every three months but held a conference call once a month. Getting all six together over multiple time zones and countries was always a challenge, and the fear of someone eavesdropping was ever present.

Each one of the four men and two women was highly intelligent. Most were members of Mensa, with IQs scoring in the 98th percentile or higher. All were multi-lingual. Still, the telephone connections and heavy accents required intense concentration, and a militaristic manner of cryptic communication to ensure clear understanding.

They never used their actual names, and they spoke around subjects in case their calls were wiretapped. Taken together, this made their strategy calls vague and confusing to any outsider who might be listening in.

"Brazen" spoke first, with a guttural accent that may have indicated a Slavic upbringing.

"The U.S. remains uncontrollable. Reagan set us back several decades. Everything seems in place according to our model, but it could be well into next century before key indicators are nominal."

He paused. Any of the other five would only speak if they didn't understand his point. Discussion would occur later, one person at a time.

"I propose we replace 'Stokes,' following his untimely death, with an American who specifically can tweak objectives there. I believe we need a new perspective. Not religious, or financial, or military. I propose a person with political potential, who also has clandestine points of contact."

Silence again.

"I have a person in mind and will bring his dossier at our next meeting. Upon approval, I would like to initiate contact. Discussion. 'Janie?'
"

A woman with a French accent answered. "Oui, the U.S., she refuses to submit. So small, so strong. Perhaps Iraq shall bring her down a bit financially. But we must return to our full number, and we must try a different approach with America. No?"

One by one they spoke, then back around in case there were any other points to be made or discussed. There were none, so in turn, they addressed other issues for the next two hours.

That afternoon, "Brazen" began preparing a detailed dossier on an American man in his early thirties who had just showed up on the political scene. The man had a well-manicured public persona. But Brazen had unique ways and means to go below—way below—what people wanted the public to see. And this man? He was hiding a lot. Even more than "Stokes," the previous American team member.

## 6.  MOSTLY SUNNY

### March 1991

W hat would an apartment look like, if the single occupant was lazy and spent more time at the pool and at parties than cleaning it up? What would be the stereotypical view of that apartment be after six months, if there was more beer in the refrigerator than food on the shelves? Add to that image, that he would appear to be a college freshman and probably from an upper-middle-class family—judging by the 1990 Honda Accord in his reserved parking space.

A few problems with that image: Meet Jennifer Karen Lane. In addition to not being a "he", Jennifer graduated six months earlier, and then moved up into the nicer, gated community. Of course, there's a pool, a party room, tennis courts, and a lot more.

But her apartment? Empty pizza boxes and beer cans, dirty clothes on the floor, clean clothes piled up on her couch, unmade bed, dirty dishes in the sink, trash cans overflowing . . . and Jennifer asleep in a chair beside her desk. The thirteen-inch monochrome monitor was the only light inside her apartment, while dark shades successfully fought off the morning sun. The Windows 3.0 operating system on her "386" computer had long since entered the screen saver mode, hiding her all-important WordPerfect document. The computer had been given to her by a previous boyfriend, who had also arranged a phone call with a literary agent. She now had less than two months to complete her promised manuscript that she had started two months earlier. The one that began just below her title page. The one that was still exactly two pages long.

Jennifer was startled awake by her cell phone, and knocked over a half-cup of cold coffee as she reached for it and pulled up its antenna

"Yeah?" she mumbled as she threw some napkins on the fresh coffee stain on her carpet. The napkins were still on her desk from last night's take-out meal. The stain? It would soon match several others.

"Are you on your way?" snapped Mick Thompson. From the tone of his voice, he probably realized that she wasn't, and wouldn't be. He was right.

"Aw, Mick, I'm swamped working on this novel." She stifled a yawn.

"Jen, you agreed to pick me up at the coffeehouse so I could get to my class. Remember? Car in shop, no wheels, I'll miss my class?"

"I can't. I'm right in the middle of this. Catch a cab." By now she had turned on her desk light, looked at the clock, awakened her computer out of "sleep" and looked at her blank third page. She slumped in her chair.

"You're joking? I thought we were getting close? Am I missing something here?"

Jennifer sighed, and scratched her head, fought off another yawn, and squinted. "Yeah. You're right. I guess you'll miss your class if you don't get a ride." She collapsed the antenna, set the phone back in its charger, and slowly got up and walked to the bathroom scratching her head.

+   +   +

Mick stared wide-eyed at his flip-phone, and then closed it and slid it into his pocket. At twenty-three, he was older than most college juniors. He had taken a few years after high school to "find himself" and had gotten some good technical training and on-the-job training. Now, he wanted to complete the academics for a four-year degree. Missing this class wouldn't help.

"Yeah, like I've got money to get the car fixed and get a cab," he muttered. He picked up his coffee cup from the outdoor table he was standing beside. Standing five feet nine and an exercise-occasionally 180, his hair was light brown, his eyes were hazel, and his normally light complexion was getting redder by the minute.

Around him, people from high school age and up were leaving the coffee shop. Some, on a budget like himself, or on a diet—or both—just had a single, black coffee. Others were loaded down with cups of designer coffee mixes and pastries. One young woman, just a few years older than Mick, had a medium coffee, a pastry, and her hands full. She had stopped to put her wallet back into her purse, get out her car keys, and balanced the coffee and pastry. She chuckled.

"Sounds like you got stood up. Need a ride to class?"

Mick nearly dropped his cup. His analytical mind jumped through the numbers:

Absolutely gorgeous. Long, brown hair, around five feet, nine inches tall, and a physique that shouted, "body builder." Oh, and killer eyes. Deep blue.

Close to his age.

Embarrassment—his. He indeed needed a ride, and he had no idea who his potential benefactor might be.

*Stop the analysis, you idiot, she's talking!*

"Civil Law, right? Come on, don't want to be late."

She walked away. He started to follow, remembered his coffee, and had to hustle to catch up. Her walk was feminine but authoritative . . . and fast.

She looked at him and smiled as he caught up. "Samantha Knowles. Call me Sam."

"Uh, Mick Thompson, and yes, and thanks."

"Yes?"

"Yes," he sighed. "Stood up."

She chuckled. "Been there a time or two. Glad to help, and I'm off after class if you need a ride to get your car."

They reached her car. Whatever Mick might have expected, this was not it.

"Let's go," she said, as she clicked the locks open on a black, 1990 Ford Mustang GT hard-top. As Mick slid into the leather passenger's seat and closed the door, he gawked at the interior.

"You're, uh, not just a college student. And you're off today from, exactly what?

Sam's pleasant, confident laugh was captivating, but it was quickly drowned out by the 5-liter, V-8 with modified exhaust. She shifted into first gear and pulled out into traffic.

"Let's say, I write good reports and follow up," she said above the exhaust noise, and shifted into second. "And my job requires Continuing Education classes."

Mick gazed at the scanner, Motorola transceiver, and several other mounted items he couldn't identify.

"Police."

"Was, until I wrote some of those very good reports, followed up, and helped bust a pretty good-sized drug ring. Car's confiscated. Now a detective." She glanced over at him and smiled. "Mags, turbo, and a sound system that rattles windows. Hey, girl's gotta have fun."

+   +   +

"Andy!"

"Ed, this will likely be our last contact."

"What in the world? Haven't been able to reach you for months."

"I'm on a pay phone now. Look, all this is going dark, fast. You may have the only samples that will ever see the light of day. But I'm holding you to your promise. My family and I have received death threats."

"No!"

"That's why I sold our home, changed my phone—and I've been on a sabbatical. There have been several questionable deaths, and I don't want to be next."

"But this is the greatest archeological find since, well, since, I mean, this is more important than the Dead Sea Scrolls!"

"Ed, you're thinking as a Christian. A Creationist. How many doctorates, professorships, and museums would this completely invalidate? Shut down? How many careers, very profitable careers, would this evidence wipe out?"

"Hmm. And how many people would have to re-evaluate everything they've ever believed, their entire world view, if they were confronted with proof that the Bible is true, all the way back to the days of Noah," Ed added.

"Exactly. Well, so much for intellectual honesty. What have you found?"

"Where do I start? We got the samples, what, almost ten months ago? I knew something was wrong when I couldn't trace the return address, and then when I couldn't contact you. But yes, like we agreed, I've sworn our team to secrecy until we are able to plan how to release this."

"Your lives may—probably do—depend on it," replied Andy.

"Point taken. Well, Fred Jackson's just barely been able to keep the lights on. He got a small business loan, but I think he's stretched his credit to the limit. We've made progress, though. We've cultured and preserved everything we can. As DNA tools get better and more affordable, I can't wait to compare this sample against the human genome that's being worked on. As I thought, the fruit has nutrient compounds we've never even heard of. And Andy?"

"Hmm?"

"My sample had seeds."

+  +  +

"Was that Andy?" Tanya asked. She was walking past Ed's door as the phone call ended.

"Sure was," Ed replied, and motioned her to come in and have a seat. "Tanya, you may lose some sleep over this."

Ten minutes later, the laboratory assistant hung her head and spoke, almost as if to herself. "Questionable circumstances?"

"An unusually violent single-car accident and fire . . . or, at least, it appeared to be a single car accident. Another drowned in his swimming pool, with a high blood-alcohol content. A third was ruled a suicide. But, the coroner commented that the gun had to have been fired from an awkward angle."

He gave her a moment to process all that and respond. She remained silent, looking at the floor.

"No one could blame you if you wanted to quit."

"Me quit? No way. Not till you or Fred run me off. Just having trouble processing this." She stood and walked to the door.

"The depravity of man?"

"Exactly," she responded and walked out.

Ed swiveled his chair around to a small side table and opened a thick research notebook.

"Ed!" Tanya's return and change of tone startled him. "I forgot why I wanted to see you. You know those seeds? One has sprouted!"

## 7. PARTLY CLOUDY

"Move. Go away. Scoot!" Tanya didn't want to hurt the feral cat, but she also didn't want him taking up residence inside the lab and gaining access to her mice.

"George?" asked Ed, from inside his office.

"Yeah, George. Maybe I can find a home for him somewhere. Just not around here."

She set her purse down at her desk in the room, and then walked to the kitchenette to put her lunch in the 'fridge. Ed met her there and picked up the coffee pot.

"Thank you. Yes!"

"Tough morning getting the kids ready?" he asked.

" 'Bout the same. I hope they're not passing a cold back and forth." He filled her cup and she added her flavored creamer and a single teaspoon of sugar, cutting back from her usual three as she tried to shed those final extra pounds from her last pregnancy.

"I need to show you something, Tanya."

She followed Ed to his office. The front section of *The Atlanta Journal-Constitution* was folded open, just a few pages in. Ed pointed at the heading:

"Renown Archeologist Found Dead; Suspicious Circumstances"

"No. Andy?"

"Body was found yesterday at Brasstown Bald, like he had fallen off the observation deck."

"That's like, two hours from here. And he fell? With people all around him? And no one saw, so he had to be 'found'?"

"Police are asking the same questions. Actually, I believe his family had a little cabin in Dahlonega, so that would have only been a short drive. The initial reports say he had a high blood alcohol level, and he somehow gained access after-hours."

"That could explain it . . . ?"

"Andy didn't drink." He let that sink in a moment. "As I told you and Fred, Andy said that we had the last samples anyone would ever see."

Tanya stood for a moment, then sat back down. Ed walked around his desk and did the same, facing her. She spoke first.

"I've got to believe that all this has happened for a purpose. Maybe we won't be able to go directly to the public with this, at least not yet. But maybe there's something here, something God wants us to find. Something that'll make a difference?"

"We may be a step closer," he said, as a slight smile crept across his face. "Our little plant has blossoms."

"What?" Tanya jumped to her feet, almost spilling her coffee, and raced to her lab, Ed close behind. She paused before opening the door and looked back at him.

"Bonus?" Now it was her turn to smile. "The leaves are edible. The mice love them!"

+   +   +

Another apartment. This time, a male occupant. Twenty-three years old, one year older than Jennifer almost to the day. Nice complex, but no gate and no activity center. It did have a small swimming pool, which the young man only enjoyed when he was caught up on his studies. Which coincided almost exactly with the end of each quarter.

If Mick normally presented himself as a seven on a scale of one to ten, today was a definite eight-and-a-half. Gone were the sneakers, jeans, and pullover shirt. In their place? Nicely coordinated leather loafers, collared golf shirt, and slacks. The pleasant grin was a positive addition, and he caught himself humming along to Diamond Rio's new hit playing on his modest sound system. As he took a last look in the mirror, his cell chirped. He flipped it open while he brushed his hair.

"Hello!"

His smile quickly faded.

"Oh. Hi, Jennifer." He pressed the phone's 'speaker' button and set it down while he took the top off his hair spray. The forecast called for high gusts in the afternoon.

"I'm about to go crazy cooped up in this apartment, and I'm starved. How 'bout taking me to dinner?"

Mick stared at the phone, incredulous.

"Uh, I haven't heard from you in two weeks, and now you want me to take you out to eat?"

"Yeah, like, I could really use a break."

He sprayed his hair, put the cap back on, scowled at the phone, and picked it up.

"Like, I could have really used a ride when my car was getting some new tires, and you promised!"

"Oh, come on, Mick. That was then. This is now," she teased.

"No. This is it! I'm tired of the constant up and down. You have a commitment problem and a lot of trouble seeing past whatever happens to be going on in your little head."

Mick's tirade was interrupted by his doorbell. He kept talking as he walked over, glanced out the peep hole, and unlocked his door.

"Figure out who you are, what you want, and whether you ever want to let anyone close to you. Whether you want to let anyone into your life, and more importantly, whether you'll ever be able to let yourself into someone else's."

Mick opened the door and smiled at Sam; black slacks, white button-up short-sleeve shirt, modest jewelry, hair down, and a smile as big as his.

"Gotta, go, Jennifer. I've got big plans for today."

He shut his phone, locked his door, and he and Sam walked to her car. He placed his hand around her waist. She placed hers around his.

"The girl who stood you up?"

"One and the same. Best thing that ever happened to me," he said, and smiled.

+  +  +

"Just give me the word, JR. What you want done, and when."

Skylar glanced at his boss and wondered what their next assignment might be. These phone calls normally took place in the early evening. They were always calls, not meetings. Bull Thatcher may have met with JR in the past but according to the new "Number One," such meetings were now rare. Bull also made it clear that Skylar would likely never meet the "big boss." This JR dude was even more secretive than "Bull." Meticulously so.

Skylar was a fast learner. So far, he had characterized Bull as a fascinating study in contrasts. By day, he went by "Louis." He and his secretary ran a small, respectable accounting service. Business shirt and tie. Intelligent and articulate. Evenings? Not so much. Black slacks, shoes, and shirt. Occasionally a black sport coat. Respectable? Not at all. Streetwise and able to role-play as needed to get the job done: Manage JR's "business." Actually, "businesses." Drugs, money laundering, and loan shark. His newest endeavor? JR seemed interested in the opportunities presented by human trafficking. Bull implied that the boss man's interest might be more than just financial.

Didn't matter. The work was done, the money came in, and Bull clearly knew his place. Follow orders, clean up any messes, and at all costs, make sure nothing could be traced back to JR. Ever. Oh, and when there was an assignment? Call JR with the results. Always.

The same rules would apply to Skylar. Peter had become greedy. JR gave the word, and Bull took care of the problem. That moved Bull to the top of JR's food chain, where he clearly intended to remain. Bringing Skylar on board? Having him pull the trigger? Skylar figured it out. Brilliant. Intimidating. Bull had him use an untraceable pistol and made sure that only Skylar's fingerprints would be on the gun. They dumped Peter's body in a high crime area, knowing it would be found and police would run ballistics on the bullet. If Skylar ever became a problem, the gun would mysteriously reappear, and with both Bull and the police looking for him, Skylar's life would become complicated, and likely, very short.

"Time for a last warning and ultimatum," Bull said as he returned his car phone to its cradle and started the engine. "We floated a large business loan for a long life and health research facility. The founder also had a gambling problem, so we raised the stakes. Boss is tired of all the promises over the years. Time for some results."

"One way or the other?"

"Yep."

## 8. *DRIZZLE BEGINS*

"It's been a long day. Get home to your kids. We'll go over every-thing again tomorrow," Ed told Tanya as he walked back to his office and slumped into his chair. "Lord, what have we missed?" he asked, leaning back and looking at the ceiling.

"Tomorrow will be a better day, Ed. 'Nite." Tanya said as she paused at his door.

" 'Nite, Tanya. Just wish we could pull in more researchers on this."

"Or at least Fred?"

"Yes, it would certainly help to add his brains and perspective on all this."

"Not to mention his hand at chemical analysis," Tanya added. "Gambling?"

Ed slowly nodded in the affirmative. Tanya sighed and walked out of the building.

Ed reached for his recorder.

"We've duplicated the expected hyperbaric pressure, oxygen con-centration, and all the nutrient factors we can imagine that should mitigate free radical damage. Initial rejuvenation and strength are off the charts. Unprecedented. Then a backlash of rapid degeneration. Not cancer, just everything shutting down. It's like there's a missing cata-lyst."

He turned off the recorder and, for the third time that afternoon, reviewed notes from the past week. A half hour later, he sighed, orga-nized the notes into a binder, and placed them along with a half-dozen notebooks. The notebooks, neatly organized and labeled, were the ef-forts of Aaron Sims, a particularly gifted graduate assistant

Ed turned out his office light. As he propped open the exit door with his briefcase and reached into his pocket for the key to lock the deadbolt, he was startled by a grey animal streaking past him into the dark building.

"George!" *Oh, great. Now I have to chase down a feral cat.* Ed picked up the keys he'd dropped, turned the lights back on, and walked to the lab.

"Not going to do you any good, old fella. They're all in cages."

He was not surprised when he heard the noise of an overturned cage. But the shriek of a terrified cat, and George bolting back out the door Ed had left open? Ed ran to the lab and turned on the light. He stood motionless, staring wide-eyed at the last thing he expected to see. The cage that had fallen to the floor had a large label, "Number 12." Two of its wires were spread apart far enough for a mouse to squeeze get out. The mouse, Number 12, had apparently spooked George, and then climbed onto the test table, navigated the maze, eaten all the food, and was now happily running on the exercise wheel. The mouse that was on the verge of death an hour earlier, after the initial short burst of extra strength and intelligence had worn off. The mouse was the oldest one in the lab but it was now acting like a spunky "teenager."

+   +   +

Jennifer Lane walked back through the federal disaster area known as her apartment, for the fifth time. Wringing her hands. Trembling.

"I'm losing it," she half-asked, half-exclaimed as she again checked the trash cans, counters, furniture, bathroom. She looked everywhere, anywhere that she and her unexpected guest may have set down their coffee cups or thrown away any empirical evidence of the unusual encounter.

Nothing.

*I need a drink.*

She opened her refrigerator and reached for a beer, then reconsidered and put two ice cubes into her one remaining clean glass. She opened her cabinet and took down a half-empty bottle of bourbon that she talked a previous boyfriend into buying for her.

*No! That may be why I'm fuddled . . .*

She really wanted that drink. She needed that drink.

"Is Sally shooting straight?" she muttered. Her club-hopping partner-in-crime, going all the way back to their freshmen year in college with their fake IDs, had warned Jennifer about her binge drinking, and her growing tolerance for alcohol. "Girlfriend, ya gotta come clean.

You becomin' a lush?"

Jennifer didn't see Sally much anymore.

She made a pot of coffee, for now, and sat back down in front of her monitor.

"I didn't just come up with all this on my own."

Weeks of false starts. Trash bags of crumpled papers, each with no more than a few paragraphs. A blank monochrome monitor staring back at her equally blank mind, day after day, week after week.

Now? Six thousand words and four chapters. The beginning of a novel that was almost writing itself. She had to force herself to stop long enough to eat a can of tuna. That's when she realized that there was no physical evidence of that day's strange visit or visitor.

Who was "Karen?" She looked so familiar, almost like a long-lost older sister.

*Yeah, someone with her act together, who thought about something more than her next party or boyfriend.*

The brutal shot of self-honesty made Jennifer uncomfortable. She almost poured that drink, but her coffee pot finished just in time.

Back at her computer, she pounded out three more pages—over 700 words—before she paused long enough to refill her coffee cup and use the bathroom. She washed her hands and took a sip of the delicious, hot beverage, and stared at the cup. Straight-up. Black. No creamer or sugar. She slowly looked over at her reflection in the full-length, "I love me" mirror she'd added to the wall beside her vanity. She gazed at the image looking back at her.

*Who are you?*

Another nagging thought weighed even more heavily on her: *I feel like I'm a character in my own story.*

+ + +

"Mama? Mama! Can you hear me? Yeah, it's Louis." Bull spoke loudly into the phone, hoping his mother could hear over the noise of all the intensive care unit equipment that had become a daily, painful backdrop to her failing life. Hoping that this time she would recognize him as he reverted back to the deep Mississippi drawl of his youth.

"Yeah, Mama, Louis. I'm gonna come see you again this weekend."

He listened intently, hoping he could understand her weak voice over the din.

"That's right, Mama. This weekend. I talked to the doctor. He says you be about the same. How ya feelin?"

Twenty minutes later, tough-guy Bull Thatcher had to wipe his eyes as he returned the car phone handset to its cradle. Twenty minutes of trying to talk to her, and trying to understand her as she tried to talk to him. Twenty minutes of the pain in her weak voice, and her struggle to breathe.

The doctor had, indeed, said that Myrtle was about the same. Which was bad. Maybe a few weeks, not much more.

Bull muttered as he drove up to his apartment and parked, "Mama, you hang in there. I may have something, uh, something that'll get you better. You just hang in there, Mama!"

# 9.  THUNDERSTORM WATCH

W hat in the world did I do now?" Detective Samantha Knowles asked herself as she walked to the Zone One commander's office. He didn't normally call her to come in individually. Unless there was a problem.

Major Garrett was on the phone, but he motioned for her to come in and have a seat. He ran a hand through his thick, dark brown hair, showing a touch of grey from his fifty-two years.

"Got it. Yeah, we're used to that here. We'll be out in force. Right. Goodbye," he said as he hung up with a loud sigh and look of exasperation.

"Why do we always get the crazies? Does Atlanta have some kind of, 'Stupid People Welcome Here' sign out for everyone?"

Sam wasn't sure if he expected an answer. Major Steve Garrett was tough but fair. She admired him as a man of integrity, a characteristic hard to come by when you're the police commander of Zone One in a city the size of Atlanta.

"Beg your pardon?" she asked.

"This Matthews guy, running for Congress? He's going to hold a rally here next Thursday morning."

"Right. Read about it on the wire. Nothing unusual . . . ?" Sam offered.

"Wrong," he snapped back, though not so much at her as at the stupidity at some level above both of them. "This guy's a nut job. A real piece of work. You read about his platform? 'Death with dignity for all,' he calls it. Slogan sounds great but then he talks about how it will save billions in healthcare, Medicare, everything else. More money in everyone's pocket. But try to pin him down on what it means?"

"Something about withholding heroic medical measures from the elderly, isn't it?"

The major stood to his full six-feet-one-inch stature and walked his 220-pound, fit frame over to his tenth-floor window. His dark brown eyes panned out over the city. "Now he's saying, anyone over seventy. Just a few years after retirement. You know what he means by "heroic measures?" he turned and asked her.

"No, he seems professionally vague."

"Professionally vague. Good term. Exactly right," Garrett said, stroking his conservative mustache, which extended just beyond the width of his lips. "So far, he's saying no resuscitations, no transplants, no heart surgeries. If you have a pacemaker before you're seventy, you can keep it. But anyone turning seventy after his bill passes? Make sure your will is up-to-date."

"I would have lost my grandmother last year . . . "

"Yeah, and it would bury both of my parents. No more drain on our economy, he says."

Sam wasn't sure what all this had to do with her, but she already didn't like this Matthews fellow. "He must not have any relatives he's worried about. And, who in the world would vote for such a jerk," she asked.

The commander returned to his desk, sat down, and looked hard at her. Almost through her. "Reports say he let his father die at seventy-one. Refused treatment. As for who would vote for him? Young people. Like you. You're an exception. A lot of young adults think they're immortal and can't imagine their parents needing healthcare. Short-term benefits, long-term consequences." He sighed. "Okay!"

His sudden change of tone startled Sam.

"So, the mayor expects protests. Large. Possibly ugly. He wants us out in force. All our Zones, all our top people."

Sam raised her eyebrows and cocked her head. *Where's this leading?*

"Need you to postpone your vacation, plan on several days of OT, and handle anything new that comes up here till we get the full team back."

"What about Wilson?" she asked, followed by a questioning look.

"Pat Jernigan, that reporter wanna-be that comes in here and looks through our police reports all the time? He found some stuff we have to check out. Wilson's on Admin Leave till we get him cleared back for duty."

Within a few minutes, Sam understood three things. First, the commander trusted her. A lot. He implied that while Dwayne Wilson was her senior, Garrett seemed grateful for the excuse to put her in charge. Second, she'd have to break the bad news to Mick while he still had time to sell the concert tickets. Or, she winced, to find someone else to go with him. Third, it was going to be a long week.

What she did not know, and couldn't even imagine, is that what Pat Jernigan had found on Dwayne was serious enough for an internal investigation. Nobody took Pat seriously there, or, to her knowledge, at any of the other precincts. Plus, Dwayne was by-the-book inflexible. If regs didn't say you could do it, it didn't get done. Sam followed the regs, too. But if a move made sense and wasn't clearly prohibited, and she felt she could justify her decision? She would take action.

Sam didn't keep a list, or figuratively carve notches in her service pistol. But she suspected that her successful conviction rate was at least thirty percent higher than Dwayne's. In retrospect, she also realized that over the past six months or so, she had been given some of the tougher, more important cases.

Sam stepped into a break room and poured a cup of ice water. She sipped it and stared hard at nothing in particular. She thought through all the harassment she had endured, and the pressure to be "one of the guys." *Not to mention the occasional pressure of older cops trying to hit on me.* It was tough being a young, athletic, attractive woman in a man's world. Women in administrative roles were professional but distant. But, was it possible she wasn't being dumped on like she supposed? If not Dwayne Wilson, there were still others—men—that Garrett could have put in charge.

As she passed Dwayne's desk, she realized she hadn't seen him in several days. She glanced past the usual clipboards, folders, note pads, and Georgia Tech coffee mug. No computer. He refused to learn how to use one, even with the easier graphical environment provided by Windows 3.0. "Badge, gun, notepad, and good memory," he would say as he brushed his hand through a premature, balding comb-over. The one picture on his desk was a picnic scene from the last Fourth of July celebration. Sam recognized the event. Dwayne and his wife posed with their son and daughter. Dwayne and his wife were both in their late forties, and both overweight. At around five feet ten, he stood at least four inches taller than her. The son took after his mother in stature and features, while the daughter appeared to favor her father. Both looked like they were in their late teens.

*What in the world has Dwayne done*, she wondered?

Another thought occurred as she returned to her desk and woke up her monitor. She really hoped Matthews would lose the election.

# 10. THUNDERSTORM WARNING

"Primate trials?" Ed asked as he brought Tanya some fresh coffee.

"Should be ready to start next week," she replied. Pointing to some capsules she had just finished filling with a green powder, she added: "Standardized for 120 to 240 pounds." She took the coffee cup, sipped, and smiled as she enjoyed her morning's second cup. "Thanks. And Ed?"

"Hmm?"

"So far, with what we're seeing with Number 12, I'm estimating for humans we could see full, robust health for something well over ninety years."

"Wow. And with the unimaginable strength and intelligence. Beyond anyone in known history." Ed sipped coffee from his own mug, then added, "Decades of drawing Social Security."

"That could bankrupt the country," Tanya exclaimed.

"It would crash pensions, insurance, hospitals, medical practices . . . "

"The pharmaceutical, plastic surgery, and nursing home industries," she added.

"Tanya," Ed's excitement changed to grave concern as he looked over at Number 12, continuing to show more strength and intelligence every day. "Here's the dark side. Imagine if world powers learned of this."

"Super-soldiers?"

"Exactly," he replied as he walked out of the lab.

"We could have a lot of enemies." Tanya shuddered as she turned back to her lab animals.

+ + +

Jennifer stared at her screen and shook her head.

"It's good," she muttered to herself. She'd finished a final read-through of her manuscript, plus a few last-minute tweaks, and was ready to start the hours of printing on her dot-matrix printer.

"Good. Really good." She stood, looking down at her desk, and the final page on her monitor. Eighty thousand words, three hundred and sixty pages, and a compelling plot that seemed to come from nowhere.

She wasn't into paranormal activity or metaphysics. But whoever Karen Richardson was, or wasn't, her story had gripped Jennifer. Taking that story and writing it down as a novel had met her deadline for a unique one-on-one opportunity with a potential publisher, possibly eliminating an agent. It had also begun to subtly change the young woman's life.

Jennifer looked around her apartment as she stretched. She had opened several blinds and curtains that morning, and the mid-day sun showed a layer of dust on her desk. She actually felt the need to clean it and vacuum. Maybe put another load through the dishwasher and take out the trash. If she finished her printing by late afternoon, she could walk down the street and get a chef's salad. It looked like a beautiful day.

+   +   +

"Please give me some good news, Ed." Fred Jackson plopped his large frame into the guest chair in Ed's office. He pulled out a handkerchief and wiped sweat off his face. Ed caught a faint whiff of tobacco smoke; the chewing gum wasn't working.

Ed smiled. "Actually, we have some. We've had solid success with mice. Appears very stable. We're ready to start tests with primates at the larger facility next week. Tanya has our first batch of product encapsulated, and we're processing the second batch now. Watch this." Ed turned away from his boss, pressed the power buttons on a seventeen-inch color TV and VCR, and inserted a VCR tape labeled "Number 12." Fred stood and walked the three steps to the front of Ed's desk to watch over his shoulder. As Ed rewound the tape, he didn't notice Fred reach into his shirt pocket and flip open a buzzing cell phone. Nor did he see the dark scowl on the older man's face or the additional drops of sweat beading on his brow. He didn't even see

Fred quietly step out of the room.

Ed reached a particular point in the tape and hit "Play." The little mouse was running through a maze with only a few wrong turns. It quickly got to the food and devoured it.

"Quickly learns and remembers mazes. We have to change them around several times a day. Incredible appetite. Plays longer and harder. And that was only the second day!" Ed fast-forwarded the tape a few seconds then continued narrating to his empty room.

"Here's the thing. Like I said before, God's got everything in balance. We thought we just needed the $p16^{Ink4a}$ inhibitor, or maybe a better way for telomerase to replace cellular telomeres shortened by mitosis. But as well as we can tell, it seems this antediluvian fruit actually resets the entire genome." Ed's excitement faded as he turned back to face his boss who was no longer there.

+  +  +

"Time's up. No more playin' around. You put up or we hang you up. An' I'm not talkin' broken fingers." Bull often dropped his "prim and proper" when he wanted to intimidate. And after the call that he just received from his mother's doctors—they were calling hospice—he felt like intimidating.

"Bull," Fred Jackson pleaded, "It's done! Look, here's the deal. Like I told JR, this is worth millions. Maybe billions! Completely legal, totally legit. How you use it is up to you. Sell it to the highest bidder. Armies would pay a king's ransom for what this stuff can do. Billionaires who want to live longer, stronger, and better. You listening to me?"

Hospice. Maybe only days left. His mother. Bull was listening. "What do you have in mind?"

"I bring you all the product we have. All the research. It'll all be yours. You and JR clear the books. We call it even. I never see you again. You two sell it, use it yourselves, do whatever. I don't care. Wipe my account clean. Deal?"

A few minutes later, Bull Thatcher had everything worked out. As usual, it was in meticulous detail. It would be perfect. If he was going to go behind JR's back, it had to be perfect. And quick. Peter Jordan had died for a whole lot less than what he was about to do.

But if that genetic enhancement product was really all that? He'd have the smarts and the strength to handle anything JR might bring his way. He'd be rich. And his mother would be well.

"Mama, you hang in there, just another coupla days. I'm comin'. Mama," he sniffed.

Next task? He called the secretary at his "legitimate" daytime job. He had a family emergency and would have to be out for a couple of days.

"Gotta keep Skylar out of the way. Dude's bright. Can't let him get in the way," He muttered as he turned into traffic. His late lunch break was over, and he wouldn't go back to the office until, actually? He would never go back there again. He chuckled at the possibilities. *Strongest linebacker. Fastest running back. World champion boxer. Smartest stockbroker. Yep. Kickin' JR to the curb.*

His thoughts returned to Skylar. "Send him to the boys down in Miami for a couple of weeks. Call it 'orientation.' "

## 11.   GUST FRONT

One regret. Just one. Well, of course, there was Sally. She was the reason that Fred Jackson had turned to cigarettes to calm his nerves. Alcohol, too, and Fred had to admit that he had become a social drunk. As far as he knew, even Ed didn't know about that. Ultimately, though, it was the gambling that really did him in. Sally's constant nagging, especially about money and "the finer things?" Well, that one trip to Las Vegas, and the one modest win at the table? It was all over. He couldn't stop.

The regret? That he had let Ed down. They had mutual, professional respect. The breakthrough, Biblical or otherwise, could have made them a fortune and helped mankind in ways unimaginable. And they—well, Ed and Tanya—deserved the recognition.

But Fred wanted to live. With all of his fingers and toes intact. He'd gone through the facility early that morning and collected notebooks, floppy disks, the bottle of capsules prepared for primate trials, and everything else he could lay his hands on. In an hour, it would all be over. Bull and JR would have the material and Fred would be on his way to Mexico. His car was loaded with clothes, personal items, and the remaining money he could lay his hands on. Sally? No more alimony. Good riddance.

*June, 1991. It's a good time for a new start*, Fred thought resolutely.

He didn't walk into the animal lab, where the mice, their cages and food, and the test and exercise equipment were located. Had he stepped in, even for a moment to take one last look around before abandoning six years of his life? He might have noticed a dead mouse in a cage. The cage was labeled, "Number 12." Even a non-expert would have concluded that the mouse appeared to have died an agonizing death.

+ + +

Jennifer double-checked that everything she needed was laid out on her couch, then put it all in her tote. A last look in the mirror, some mouthwash to tame the morning coffee breath, and she headed for the door. *Just ten minutes late. I'll walk fast . . .*

"Darn!" she was mildly shocked that her exclamation didn't include profanity, for once. She quickly unlocked her door and grabbed the pumps to match her pants suit. She was wearing comfortable sneakers for the few blocks she'd be walking to the bus stop, and then to the publisher's building. Once there, she'd put on the pumps.

"Now I'm ready," she said, smiling. The cloud cover and light breeze made the morning unusually cool for June. She lived in a safe neighborhood, and the building was in a respectable business complex. She felt the bus would get her there about the same time as driving and finding a place to park, and she'd be less stressed.

"It's going to be a great day."

+  +  +

"I sure hope these cages will be strong enough," Tanya said as she rattled the bars of one of two cages just delivered. She and Ed were at a larger facility, about thirty minutes from the main Jackson Longevity Research Center office. Fred Jackson desperately needed to break the lease but finally conceded that the location was more appropriate for large scale primate testing. He nervously agreed to hold onto it for at least another month.

"Ever seen an angry chimpanzee?" Tanya continued.

"Can't say I have, but I've heard stories," Ed said, examining the cage lock. "If these guys end up with twice the strength and twice the intelligence?"

"Scary," Tanya replied. "I think you're right keeping this test simple and small. We may only be able to handle one or two at a time. Think we'll be ready by Thursday?"

Ed checked his clipboard. "Video cameras and VCR tape system should be here later this morning. Lab animals by tomorrow afternoon. We've got all the supplies they'll need. Will our handlers be here to-morrow morning?"

"Yep, and I also have the names of a few others we can call in part-time, when they're not working at the zoo."

"Okay," Ed said. "I think we should be ready. We'll tell Fred this afternoon. We're ahead of schedule; ought to be done here by noon."

+ + +

Bull always knew how to play the part. This morning, his appearance screamed "mover." The tall trunk strapped to a heavy-duty, commercial grade dolly completed the look, as he rolled it off the elevator. Dozens of people saw him park the panel van, use its lift to lower the dolly and the trunk, lock up the van, and roll into the building and onto the elevator. There were several more who saw him on the elevator. Some got off at lower floors, and others continued to higher floors. No one took notice. Just another workman doing his job. Not a single person would be able to give a good description of what he looked like. Exactly as Bull intended.

He rolled the trunk down the hallway, past the water fountain, turned right, then went to the third door on the left. He unlocked it and rolled his trunk into a small office. Printed on the office placard was a number. Room 512.

Bull turned on the lights, unstrapped and opened the trunk, and began spreading out large sheets of clear plastic.

Bull found himself humming a tune Myrtle used to hum around the house when times were better. He pursed his lips, sniffed, and said quietly, "Hang in there, Mama. Just another day, Mama. You're gonna be all better."

He stepped back to double-check his work. Bull hated doing this alone, without a "safety man." But desperate times required desperate actions. And going against JR? Desperate secrecy. *Dude probably has at least one more team somewhere.* At most, Bull reasoned, he may have a two-day head start.

Convinced that he should be able to clean everything up within a few minutes, Bull waited, and reviewed.

Find out how much of the stuff I should take, and how much to give Mama.

Dispose of the body.

Drive north, rent a motel room for two days, leave the cell bag-phone plugged in and turned on, and leave the car at the motel. "Do not disturb" sign on the door.

Catch a bus to Macon, Georgia.

Get the medicine, or whatever it is, to Mama.

Start us a new life.

"Everything's about to change, Mama. Ya gonna have the life you've deserved," he said quietly.

He pondered, and then added one more task to finish before leaving Atlanta. It would significantly increase the value of the product, and he could use it to conveniently dispose of the body at the same time.

*Scarcity. Supply and demand.*

"Gonna be a good day."

## 12.   CURRENT DAY

*Discipline. Details. No loose ends.* Bull Thatcher repeated his mantra dozens of times as he carefully wrapped the body in plastic sheeting, stowed everything in a large trunk, and changed back into his moving company overalls. He retrieved his spent cartridge, policed the entire room once again, and wiped fingerprints off every surface he had touched.

*Discipline. Details.*

He loaded the trunk onto his heavy-duty dolly and casually rolled it to the elevator, then out to his moving van. Once his cargo was secure and the van doors were closed, he stepped up into the driver's seat and reached for his car phone.

*No loose ends.*

His otherwise "clean kill" had a witness. A young woman who dropped a business card as she fled.

He made the call. After several rings, a professional-sounding lady, likely middle age, answered the call.

"Tony Mendenhall Agency, Betty speaking. How may I help you?"

"Hello? Hi, Betty. I'm so sorry to bother you. Our computer is down, I think it ate a floppy, and I think we were supposed to have someone over there for an appointment. Did she show up? Should have been, I think, maybe half an hour or so ago?"

"Well, let me check our calendar. Uh, yes, we had an appointment with a Jennifer Lane, who was supposed to bring us a script. Never showed up."

Bull sighed loudly. "I knew we should have kept manual records. At least for backup. We always try to follow-up at least an hour before each appointment. I'm so embarrassed to ask you, but do you possibly have her phone number? I'll call her right away."

He listened intently and carefully wrote down the number in a pocket-sized notepad, reading it back to make certain he copied it correctly.

*Details.*

Betty continued, "Would you like to set up another appointment for Jennifer?"

"No. I don't believe she'll need to reschedule." He pressed 'End' and returned the handset to its cradle.

*No loose ends.*

+   +   +

"As serious as a bullet to the chest," Jennifer whimpered. Mick just stared. "I'll move out of state. No, maybe I could go to Mexico or something. Could you drive me there? If we left tonight, we could be there in a couple of days? No, wait, he might be a drug dealer with connections?"

"Jennifer!"

"I'll dye my hair. No, I'll cut it off. I'll . . . "

"Jen. Stop it!"

It was her turn to stare. After twenty minutes and several calls, Mick had found her, which was a miracle on a busy Monday morning in Atlanta. They were crammed into a small janitor's closet, sitting on the floor, talking quietly, leaning against the boxes of supplies. Jennifer looked at the young man just a year older than herself, as if for the first time. She had thought of Mick as a nerd. He had been one of the easier guys to manipulate during their three-month relationship. Hardly a challenge. But . . . was it because he was sincere, not weak? Some inner character was emerging now. With his black hair, dark complexion, black-rim glasses, and firm grip on her arm, he startled her.

"The only thing we're going to do is go straight to the police. There is no safety any other way, and you'll be hiding from shadows for the rest of your life."

"But, like, I'm scared. I don't know any police."

"I do. A detective."

"But, those guys. I mean, you know?"

"It's a woman. Just a few years older than me. "Come on, Jennifer." Mick grabbed her hand so hard she winced, but she rose to her feet as he cracked open the door of the janitor's closet.

The hallway was clear. "Let's go," he said. He opened the door wide, released her hand, and dropped his hand to her waist to pull her into the hallway. It was not a loving gesture.

"I'm coming!" she whined and followed him.

In three minutes, they were in his car. It had been just half an hour since she first called him.

"Mick!" exclaimed Jennifer, grabbing his arm.

"Ow! You trying to wreck us?" Mick hollered back, regaining control of the wheel.

Someone else noticed his car swerve in the downtown traffic. At that exact moment, she screamed, "It's him!" Bull was closing the van door. He looked right at her. Their eyes locked for a moment, and then Mick and Jennifer were safely past his parked van.

Mick glanced back in his rear-view mirror.

"Oh, no," he moaned.

"Is he coming after us? He'll kill me . . . " She turned around in her seat, looking behind them.

"No. And stop shouting. He just stood there. Stared at us. I think he got my tag number."

+ + +

Every fiber in his being screamed that he should chase after them. But Bull didn't trust feelings. He dealt in cold, hard facts. And the facts were clear. He wouldn't be able to catch them in the morning traffic. He would draw too much attention to himself if he tried, possibly causing a few wrecks along the way. Either would draw police attention. *That wouldn't be too good with a corpse in the back of my van.*

The remaining fact made up for all the others. He pulled out his notepad and wrote down the make, model, and tag number of the car the woman was in. The woman whose phone number he had already written down.

JR had connections. Since no one knew that Bull was going rogue, he still had access to those connections.

*No loose ends.*

Bull put the notepad back into his pocket, buckled his seatbelt, checked his mirrors, and smoothly pulled out into traffic. It was time for his next stop. According to the late Mr. Fred Jackson, no one would be there until the afternoon.

+ + +

"Mick? Wha . . . ?"

Detective Samantha Knowles stared from her desk, puzzled to see the man who for all practical purposes was her boyfriend, walking up to her along with an attractive blonde a few years younger than himself.

"Sam, this is Jennifer," Mick said. "We're in trouble."

"*We* . . . are in trouble?" Sam repeated.

"I just saw a murder," Jennifer blurted out.

"And, I think he got my tag number."

Without taking her eyes off them, Sam motioned to the two seats in front of her desk.

"What a day to be in charge. Okay," she looked at Jennifer. "You first."

Jennifer rambled, but she told Sam everything she saw, from the moment she opened the door to the moment Mick found her in the janitor's closet. Sam carefully questioned her again point-by-point, and she noted that her story remained consistent.

"And Mick, you know her, how?"

Mick blushed. "Uh, remember the ride I didn't get that morning?"

Sam looked back at Jennifer, who looked between the two of them and also blushed. "I'm sorry. I didn't know who else to call," she said quietly.

"Mmm. Mick, anything more you can add?"

"Just that she lost it as we drove by some guy loading a moving van. Jennifer said it was him. He just stared at us. I think he was memorizing my tag number."

"Not good. Okay . . . "

Sam picked up her phone, dialed an extension, and directed a dispatcher to send an officer to the building to take a quick look at the office. "The usual. If he finds anything, tell him to call it in, secure it, and stay there for the crime scene team."

He hung up and looked at Mick and Jennifer. "Normally I'd go myself. But as Mick knows, we're short-staffed today. I'm already running two hours behind. Why don't you get an early lunch and meet me back here around one?"

Jennifer stood to leave. Sam picked up some paperwork and looked at Mick. They exchanged a brief smile, and Sam noticed Jennifer hanging her head.

"Thank you," Mick mouthed silently to Sam.

"You're welcome," she mouthed back, then said aloud, "We'll work this out."

+   +   +

Road maintenance and traffic put Ed a few minutes behind Tanya on his way to their main FLRC facility.

"Ed!" he heard her shout from the lab as he stepped inside. "The place has been looted!"

A peculiar smell was even more disconcerting than the ransacked facility, or even the unexpected large trunk in the middle of the common area.

The odor . . . ? "Tanya!" he shouted. "Gas!"

His world exploded, and everything went black.

# 13.  SCORCHED EARTH POLICY

Activity at the far end of the room caused Sam to glance up from her paperwork. It was Pat Jernigan, the so-called reporter. He'd cornered Carlos, the new guy. No matter. She had personally briefed Carlos to watch out for Persnickety Pat, as they called him behind his back. Apparently, the thirty-something-still-single-and-living-at-home-loser had gotten one too many citations and lost his driver's license. Never mind that it was serious stuff, like DUI and reckless driving. Pat had a vendetta. He got his mother to pay his cab fare, or he rode the bus, and he started a weekly newspaper that trashed Atlanta's Finest. Every legitimate reporter in Fulton County and beyond had converged on the Atlanta appearance of House candidate Jason Mathews. But not Pat.

Sam's attention shifted again, to the attractive young man and woman approaching her desk.

"Good lunch?" Sam asked Mick and Jennifer.

"Yeah," Jennifer mumbled, looking down and ringing her hands.

"Yes, thanks. Brought you a sandwich." Mick handed her a bag.

"How thoughtful," Sam replied, taking the bag and opening the wrapper. "You remembered!" She took a large bite and enjoyed the taste of her favorite Philly cheesesteak.

"So, any news on the office?" Mick asked.

Sam looked back and forth between him and Jennifer as she chewed and swallowed. "Well, here's the deal. That room has been vacant for months. It's on a long-term lease, but no one ever moved in. We got a key, opened it up, and . . . nothing."

"Nothing?!" asked Jennifer.

"Nothing. Absolutely clean. No evidence that anyone's been in there for weeks. No smell of gunpowder. Nothing."

"Good cleanup? Air freshener?" asked Mick.

"Possible." Sam looked at Jennifer and spoke quietly. "Jennifer, I know you've been working very hard on some kind of project. Maybe staying up late. Possibly a lot of coffee, maybe some alcohol or, well, could you have imagined any of this?"

Jennifer stared at Sam, mouth agape, and slowly shook her head "no."

Mick commented, "How about the man I saw by the moving truck?"

"You said you swerved. Could he have just been a mover, seeing a car driving erratically, something like that?"

Mick looked at her thoughtfully, then at Jennifer.

He caught his breath. "Jennifer!"

His outburst startled both women. He looked hard at Sam.

"I know that Jennifer's kind of, well, not very tidy. And, you know, some issues. But she's crazy careful about her clothes."

Sam cocked her head, not knowing where this was going.

Mick looked back at Jennifer. Specifically, at the side of her blouse, now exposed because her jacket was partially open as she rubbed her forehead. The jacket could have also been open when she had opened the office door.

"Is that blood on your blouse?" he exclaimed.

Sam stood and leaned across the desk. Small red spots on a white blouse?

"It appears we have a murder to solve," she stated, and looked hard at Mick. "I don't think you should go to your apartment tonight."

Jennifer began sobbing softly.

"We'll take this by the numbers. First, I want you to read this statement I took from each of you. Make sure I didn't miss anything, then sign it. Next, this guy's obviously a pro. Clean room, well planned. Jennifer, you were at the wrong place at the wrong time. So . . . "

"Detective!" An officer walked up with a sense of urgency. "Bob?"

"Office blew up about ten blocks west of here. Some kind of lab. Natural gas leak. One dead, another hospitalized, unconscious."

"And?" Sam asked.

"Firefighters got the fire out pretty quick. They found a large trunk inside. And?" He looked at Sam. She nodded.

"And, a male body, probably in his fifties, bald, gunshot wound to the chest. Recent, maybe a few hours. They said RM hadn't set in yet."

Jennifer began sobbing.

+ + +

"What a rush," Bull exclaimed. "Stuff beats it all!"

He took the single dose of the product--Fred didn't have a name for it—and as promised, he already felt stronger. He seemed to be thinking more clearly. Faster. It had only been two hours. He'd had a couple of minor tremors, but nothing of any concern.

The clearer thinking brought better plans. No need to drive the van anywhere now that the body had been disposed of. Clean up things here in Atlanta then take his own car east to I-95, then north to Fayetteville, North Carolina. Motel plans would remain the same, and he'd leave the bag phone on and charging to help JR, or whoever, to waste time tracking it to a dead end. But if he still had the amphetamine-type rush he felt now? Don't sleep. Don't wait for a bus. Commandeer someone's transportation, follow I-95 back to Savannah, then head west on I-16 to Macon.

He could have the medicine to his mother by noon tomorrow.

"Man, I feel good!"

He parked the van in front of his apartment—no need to hide anything now—and climbed the stairs. Once inside, he unlocked a rifle case and pulled out an M-1 sniper rifle with a scope. The barrel was designed to accommodate a silencer, which he attached, and he inserted a loaded clip of cartridges that were not standard target rounds.

He hoped the young couple would be together. He hated being sloppy, but time was of the essence. He would have to drop them, then leave.

+ + +

It was getting late in the afternoon. Jennifer again wiped tears from her red eyes and answered with a shaky voice. "Yes. Yeah, that's him. And those eyes . . . "

"Alright," the artists said as he removed the sketch from his easel. "I'll fax it to other precincts and put it on our board as a BOLO, armed and dangerous, and a description of the van. Thank you, Jennifer."

Jennifer nodded and stood up, steadying herself with a hand on the edge of the desk.

Sam had walked up just as the artist finished the sketch. "BOLO means, 'be on the lookout.' You okay, Jennifer?"

"Headache. Exhausted. Can I go home now?" She looked between Sam and Mick. Mick looked at Sam and raised his eyebrows.

"You, probably. Mick? No. Do not stay at your apartment. If he made your license plate, he already has your address. Sorry, I checked, and it's in the database. I'm sure this guy could find it. Forensics said they'd never seen a crime scene so pristine. Absolutely clean. The guy's a pro. He may try to come after you. Any family or friends close by?"

Mick shrugged and nodded "no," then raised his eyebrows into a silent question. She ignored it.

Jennifer missed the exchange, as she was now staring at the floor. "I don't want to be alone. I'm scared," she whimpered.

"Same question I asked Mick. Do you have family or friends you could stay with?"

She also nodded "no" without looking up. Mick glanced at Sam, who gave a slight shrug of her shoulders as she raised an eyebrow. Mick sighed.

"Jen, want me to stay over? I'll sleep on the couch."

"Please?" she asked softly.

"I'll send a 'uniform' with you to pack some things at your apartment, and to make sure you're not followed over to her place. Jennifer, here's my card. If you think of anything else, please call. And I'll let you both know if we find out anything."

Jennifer noticed that the detective didn't also give Mick a card, but she kept quiet. She also noticed that Sam held on to Mick's hand a few beats longer when she shook their hands.

"Y'all be careful. I gotta go interview the guy at the hospital, see if we can put some pieces together."

"Pieces?" Asked Mick.

"Yep. After Jennifer identified the picture of the man inside the trunk as the one she saw shot, we also learned that he was the owner of that facility. Gotta see if we can figure out a motive."

## 14.    EF-5

"Three young kids," Ed moaned.

Sam looked around the ICU for tissues and handed Ed a box. He took one and dabbed tears from his eyes.

Sam noted that the man wasn't emotional over his own injuries—head bandaged from a concussion, badly dislocated left shoulder reset and taped, serious scrapes and cuts—but he was heartbroken over the loss of his co-worker.

"Dr. Richardson, there's more I have to tell you. You work with Fred Jackson?"

"Right. Jackson Longevity Research Center. He's the owner. I've known him for over a decade."

"I'm sorry, but he also died today." Sam carefully watched Ed's reaction. He seemed genuinely surprised.

"No . . . ! I didn't see his car there."

She shook her head. "Doctor, I have to ask you. Do you know if he had any enemies? Anyone who might have done this, for any reason whatsoever?"

Ed sighed and sadly shook his head. "He had a gambling problem. I thought he'd gotten beyond that. He's been missing a lot of work recently, though. It was his company, and we were really struggling. But he hasn't contributed much in, well, in several months. Yeah, probably gambling."

"Bad enough where someone would want him dead?"

Ed stared at her, like he was trying to connect the dots. "I don't follow. I know the facility was burgled. Maybe they knocked a gas line loose from a Bunsen burner . . . ?"

"Fred was already dead. Shot. Intentionally, at point blank range. Somewhere other than at the facility. His body was brought to the facility and left there, near a large trunk. I presume the hit man or team expected a much larger fire to hide the evidence."

Ed shook his head and winced. "Ouch."

"The blast blew you over thirty feet out of the building. You're pretty banged up. Actually, you're lucky to be alive."

Ed's eyes started to cross slightly, and he lay his head back against the pillow. "Can you ask them to turn the lights down? My head's killing me." He sobbed again and wiped his eyes using his good arm. "Poor choice of words. Has anyone contacted Tanya's husband? I really should give him a call . . . " His voice trailed off.

Sam could tell he was losing the fight to stay awake. She looked at the equipment surrounding him; the IV, the nasal oxygen tube, the monitors.

"Yes, sir. He's been notified."

"Both dead. We lost so much. Maybe everything. Irreplaceable." he said as he surrendered to sleep.

"We'll talk again soon. Get well." Sam said softly. She stood up and left his room.

+  +  +

"I'll catch a flight tonight. Be there tomorrow."

"See that you are. And Clayton?"

"Sir?"

"If I'm right about Bull, you do everything you can—whatever you have to—to get as much information as possible. This product they were working on, notes, samples, and everyone involved with it. I don't care if the entire operation in Arizona goes under. This is that important. Top priority. One other thing."

"Yes sir?"

"You better take at least one person with you. We didn't call him 'Bull' for nothing."

Clayton didn't know whether to be offended or grateful for that warning as the line went dead. On the one hand, Clayton Jennings specialized in intimidation. His 280 pounds helped, especially matched with his six-foot-four-inch frame. Exercise? Weights. Nothing else, no aerobics, no jump-rope or Pilates or any foo-foo fads. Not even exercise machines. Free weights. Six hours most weeks; eight to ten when he had the time. Near fifty, a lot of grey in his neatly trimmed black hair, dark eyes, and virtually no neck. Men half his age stepped out of his way.

He was not intimidated by someone nicknamed Bull. But he was intimidated by JR. He would take someone, probably Manuel, just in case.

+  +  +

Ten minutes at Mick's apartment resulted in a medium travel bag and a box of miscellaneous stuff. After five more minutes of driving through various neighborhoods, the police flashed his lights, waved, and pulled away, signaling that they had not been followed. Twenty more minutes, and Mick was pulling into a parking space at Jennifer's apartment complex.

Jennifer had been uncharacteristically quiet since her "déjà vu" comment when they left Mick's place. He just let her talk, and it frankly didn't make any sense. Something about, "This is my book. I'm my main character . . . " Then she started sobbing. Again. And became quiet.

Despite his many visits, Mick had never really "seen" the apartment complex. Maybe it was his relationship with the detective or the situation he was now in, but he studied it as they approached from the parking lot. Each building had sixteen apartments. Facing the road, there were two lower apartments, one on each side of the stairwell. One floor up there were two apartments above them, two more on the next level, and then a final two at the top of the stairwell. On the back side of the building, facing the courtyard and swimming pool, were eight more apartments, two at each level. Additional stairs at each landing allowed tenants to go to the front or back.

Mick trudged up the familiar stairs he had never wanted to see again. His bag was strapped over his shoulder, and he carried the heavy box. Jennifer followed behind carrying her tote and purse. Her apartment was on the second floor. Mick turned toward her apartment, which was on the left of the stairwell, then stepped toward the railing to give her room to pass by and open her door. She had apparently expected him to turn the other way, against the wall, so they had an awkward moment bumping into each other. Instead, he lowered his heavy box. It was the exact instant that Bull squeezed the trigger from inside his panel van. Where Mick's head should have been, the brick wall blew out and left a gaping hole in Jennifer's apartment wall.

Jennifer screamed.

"Run!" Mick exclaimed. "Back stairwell. Go!"

He dropped his box and travel bag and ran after her, and then slowed to keep from running into her as she tried to run in her pumps. Another hole blew open where his head would have been had he not slowed. They made it down the opposite stairs and ran as fast as they could across the empty courtyard. Mick noticed bathrooms near the pool.

"Those unlocked?"

"Maybe?" She replied, panting for air.

They were, and after he checked to make sure that whoever was after them had not come into view, they darted into the closest one, the ladies' restroom. The light was off. Mick locked the door. He turned around just in time to see Jennifer still continuing forward, her pumps sliding on the tile floor. Her momentum carried her under a sink where she slammed her head against the drainpipe. He darted to her side. She was out cold.

Mick grabbed his cell and speed-dialed Sam. After three rings, she answered.

"Sam! The guy found us. Shot at us. Help!"

"Where are you?"

"Jennifer's apartment complex. We were just about to open the door, and something blew a hole in the wall. Just missed me. I didn't hear a gun, so it must have had a silencer. We ran the other way and are hiding in a bathroom. She just slipped and fell, and she's out cold. Please . . . ?"

"Hold on. I'm adding 911."

Sam set up a two-way and identified her badge number to the 911 operator. Mick gave the name of Jennifer's apartment complex. The 911 operator patched in EMS, who explained to Mick how to check Jennifer's vitals.

## 15.  STORM TRACK

Bull was incredulous. "I never miss!" He felt a surge of strength, and he had every intent of chasing them down and killing them by hand, up close and personal. But an increased intellect had put that instinct to rest, and it also compelled him to violate one of his other cardinal rules. This would be one mess he would not clean up. First, it wouldn't matter. It was more a matter of pride than priority. And the priority? Get the medicine to his mother. Take the planned diversionary trip north in his own car. Be with his mother before evening tomorrow. Nothing, not even his pride, was more important.

"What a time for the jitters," he sighed.

He had strategically parked his van over a football field away, where he could see the woman's apartment out of a small port that he had installed on the side of his modified panel van. With the silencer and his location, no one would see or hear anything.

He climbed back into the driver's seat, and held out his hands. No shaking, no trembling.

"If they'd just waited another few minutes."

He sighed again, started the van, and drove out into traffic, just as he heard approaching sirens in the distance. Bull took in a long, deep breath and slowly released it, calming himself. He turned on his radio for local top-of-the hour news:

" . . . significant damage from a gas leak. Authorities stated that the damage could have been significantly greater had gas continued to accumulate. Even so, a woman was pronounced dead at the scene. A man was taken to a local hospital where he is listed in stable condition. And police are treating this as an intentional arson and murders after firefighters discovered a third body with an apparent gunshot wound."

Bull cursed and turned off the radio.

"Should'a been blown to pieces. Anything left? Charred to ashes. Musta' come back early and set it off accidentally before my timer. Of all the luck," he muttered.

It was 8:05 p.m.

+ + +

At that moment, it was 5:05 p.m. in Yuma, Arizona

Clayton slid his phone closed and put it in his shirt pocket. A summer dust storm was kicking up. It looked like a bad one. He needed to drive back to his apartment, get packed, and wait for the dust to clear . . . literally. On a normal day he could either drive west to San Diego, or east to Phoenix to catch a flight. Yuma even had a couple of outbound flights per day that would eventually get him to Atlanta. But the dust storm would soon make driving impossible, and all Yuma and Phoenix aircraft would be grounded. He would probably just end up catching a "red-eye" out of San Diego. It was going to be a long night.

There was a lot more than dust on his mind. He'd worked for JR, for what—going on seven years now? Yet he didn't know anything about an Atlanta operation, or some tough guy named Bull Thatcher, or a research facility working on a unique formula.

*Man plays his cards close-hold. Real close.*

What Clayton did know, is that this was important enough that JR was willing to sacrifice a complex, well-oiled $6 million annual drug operation without any hesitation. He also knew that this "Bull" fellow had crossed the wrong man. Clayton understood what JR meant, and though he disliked torture, he disliked even more being on the wrong end of the boss-man's wrath. Like the man he'd replaced three years ago. Like Bull was, now.

+ + +

"Here's the way it's going to be." An obviously tired Samantha Knowles stood at the foot of Jennifer's hospital bed. Jennifer was almost horizontal, the head of her bed raised just slightly and a small pillow behind her neck. She sported a large, dark blue bruise on the right side of her forehead. Mick was sitting to the side, listening intently.

"I arranged for you and Ed to have adjacent rooms. The hospital wants to keep both of you under observation overnight because of your concussions. Maybe longer. We'll have both a uniformed and a plainclothes here at all times. Mick, you're free to stay or go. But under no circumstances should you go near your apartment or Jennifer's."

"No argument there."

"I already have all of your statements, and since you two and Ed are now somewhat connected, I've told you about each other. The point I have to make is, and I've said it before . . . this guy's a pro."

"Any idea why? Why kill a man, blow up a lab, and try to get us?" Mick asked.

"Could have been Fred's gambling, but normally that kind of a hit is rough and fast. Intentionally so, to make a strong point to other 'customers.' Whoever did this, a person or a team, is methodical; thorough. So, my gut tells me there's more to it. We'll have our full team back at the precinct tomorrow and work out a path forward."

Jennifer didn't think she could shed another tear. She was wrong.

Sam gently touched her arm as the younger woman wept, and softly added, "If they offer you something to help you sleep, I'd take it."

After dabbing her eyes, Jennifer reached over and lowered the head of her bed all the way down, turned away from them and looked away toward the window. "Why?" she asked.

"Why?" Sam repeated the question. "Like I said, that's what we need to find out."

"Yeah. No. I mean, like, you. Why do you do this? You're maybe just a couple of years older than me, and you're going after criminals. Trying to help me. I mean, like . . . " Her voice trailed off.

Sam glanced at the ceiling, then at Mick. She hung her head. Then she looked up and took a deep breath.

Mick had known her for several months now, and he had been even more impressed by her professionalism over the past ten hours, and now by her compassion. But he didn't recognize this expression, or where it was leading.

"Lot of bad people in the world. That's just the way it is. Someone hurt me. And then? Someone helped me. I decided I wanted to be like the second person, not the first one."

"But, you could get killed," Jennifer pressed.

"Of course. This isn't Hollywood. The hero doesn't always ride off into the sunset. I just decided that I'd rather risk my life for something worth dying for, than waste it on stuff that doesn't matter." Sam paused again and shot an embarrassed glance at Mick, who smiled gently. "Try to get some rest, Jennifer," Sam continued. "I'll check on you tomorrow."

"Thank you," Jennifer responded quietly, still facing away.

Sam walked to the door, caught Mick's eye, and motioned for him to follow her out of the room. She closed the door behind them and stood a little closer than she usually would in her official capacity.

"Mick, I wish I could give you some good news, but this may take some time to sort out. I've gotta go talk to Ed again, then I have to go home and crash. It's been a long, exhausting day. Two things."

"Hm?" he cocked his head. She reached out and put her hand on his arm.

"I know this kind of stuff isn't your life. But you're really holding up well. You're doing a lot better than a lot of men I've seen at twice your age. Even some really tough guys."

His eyes met hers and he shuddered slightly. All he could say was, "Thanks."

"Second . . . " She dropped her hand. "Second, it may be against all kinds of protocol. But I'm concerned, and I care. If you want to crash at my place, you're welcome."

# 16.  FURY

In Yuma, Clayton reflected on a new lesson he had just learned about his boss. Bull had missed one scheduled call. Just one. So? JR called him, didn't get an answer, and then called the target, some guy named Fred. No answer from him either. Just two hours later, and JR had called in backup. Clayton glanced again at the approaching storm, now covering a large part of the horizon.

"No slack. Project must really be something important," he muttered.

His mind raced as he tried to wrap everything up and beat the dust storm. He would have to put Jeremy in charge of the operation and stay in touch with him by phone. He'd find his way to Atlanta, but he wasn't about to write off a comfortable across-the-border operation. Not yet. Maybe Jeremy could take over and he could eventually move back to the southeast? Take Bull's place? Now, there was a good thought. A very good one. He'd much rather be a few hours from the ocean than continue to change air filters and battle dust storms.

His first priority was to decide who would join him in Atlanta. Maybe two men?

*It wouldn't do to let JR down. Not now. Not ever.*

He made his decision, and then the call.

Next, he looked up Jeremy's number, and pressed Call.

*A multi-million-dollar operation. Took us years to set it up. What in the world could be so important that he'd put all this at risk?*

Jeremy picked up on the third ring, and the two talked for fifteen minutes. Outside, the sky outside turned a strange grey, and then darkened ominously. Street lights came on, yet they could only be seen from a few dozen yards away. Drivers turned on their headlights, long enough to find a safe spot to pull over. The sky eventually brightened into other-worldly shades as the setting sun filled the dust cloud with reddish light.

+ + +

Bull made his final cash withdrawal from an ATM as he pulled into Fayetteville. He had intentionally left a trail all the way up I-95, and he had now taken out all he was allowed to in a twenty-four-hour period. Next? He found an out-of-the-way biker bar that was hopping, and then drove his dark sedan to a cheap hotel several blocks away—the kind where he could park directly in front of his room. He secured a room using his credit card, for two days. He went inside long enough to use the bathroom, put his bag phone on charge—still turned on—and put the "Do Not Disturb" sign on the handle. Then he left the motel. And his car. When JR started tracking him from Atlanta, everything would point "north."

*Time to head south.*

Bull's evening attire was less intimidating and a little more functional than normal. While he stayed with his typical black, for once he wore a dark hoodie and sneakers. He intended to walk back to the biker bar. Feeling unusually energetic, he decided to jog while he contemplated his future after getting the medicine to his mother. Within a minute, he realized he wasn't jogging. Nor was he running. Without any conscious effort, he was sprinting.

*Elijah!*

Somehow, from centuries ago, the mental picture of an Old Testament prophet came to mind, outrunning a chariot. It was from one of the Bible stories his mother used to read to him as she tucked him in at night. He noticed several people along the evening street staring at him, and he quickly forced himself back to a moderate jog. Too much attention, and all his plans would be ruined.

"Man, I gotta get somewhere private and see what I can really do!"

He forced himself to slow to a walk as he approached the biker bar. As if on cue, a man stumbled out of the bar toward a bike that was off by itself, in the shadows.

None of it made sense. Bull could somehow visualize that the rider was exactly his size; the jacket and the "brain bucket" he picked up off the seat would fit perfectly. The boots and gloves? Probably. And the bike? Brand new 1991 Harley Davidson FXDB Dyna Glide Sturgis. Beautiful.

Before the large man could straddle the cycle, he was on the ground, unconscious.

Bull never had a day of martial arts training in his life. While he was fast with his fists, he preferred guns over close-quarters combat. Still, he had watched his share of Jackie Chan, Chuck Norris, and others. His jump carried him up to chest level, and while airborne he rolled into a crouch parallel with the ground, knees tucked in. As he passed in front of the man, he slammed both feet into the man's chest, propelling him straight back over fourteen feet. To his own amazement, Bull landed on his feet.

Bull approached the unconscious rider. The man might have been retired Airborne, a bouncer, a body builder, or all of the above. He was well over 220 pounds, mid-forties, and Bull's exact height. In seconds, Bull was wearing the man's jacket, helmet, boots, and gloves. And somehow, he was right. Everything fit. The man, still unconscious, struggled to breathe, likely from multiple fractured ribs and possibly a punctured lung. No matter. Bull picked him up as if he were a toddler, with every intention of slamming him head-first into the pavement. But . . . was that a flash of compassion?

*No loose ends,* he reminded himself.

*The man may have a wife. Children. He might be taking care of his own mother . . .*

Bull walked to the side of the parking lot and gently set the man down on the grass. He pulled out the key, got on the motorcycle, and rode into the warm late-June night. No one had seen him. Even if someone had, they would not have been able to recognize him in a line-up. He was on his way. North. Then in a couple of blocks, he would head south down different streets. Then down to Macon. To save his mother's life.

## 17.   BAD NEWS

"**D**r. Richardson?"

"Yes, come in."

Jennifer stepped into the hospital room just to the right of her own. She was wearing her outfit from the day before. Ed sported fresh bandages. He was still in bed with an IV. The oxygen tube had been removed.

"Hi. I'm Jennifer," she said softly.

"Hi, Jennifer. Please call me Ed. Looks like quite a knot."

"Yeah, they say it'll take a while to go down. No permanent damage, I guess. How are you?"

"Banged up, but it'll all heal. Just trying to make sense of everything, like I'm sure you are. I have two dead friends. You had an attempt on your life. Neither of us knows where to go when we leave here. Police here to watch over us . . . " He pushed away his rolling hospital tray with his half-eaten breakfast. "Not much of an appetite. Have a seat."

She pulled up a chair close to his bed and sat down. "I don't think I've ever felt so alone in my life."

"Wish I had some answers. The blast almost got me, too."

She stared at him in silence. He was older, maybe thirty-four to her twenty-two. She had to admit, even in his less-than-*GQ* hospital setting, the man looked like someone who took care of himself. Very good care. And no wedding ring. She felt her face get warm and looked away.

"I . . . I can't imagine what that must be like," she said.

"And I can't imagine what it was like to witness a murder. Then to have someone shoot at you. Are you alright?"

Jennifer again felt a twinge of embarrassment. She was uncomfortable, yet drawn to a man who seemed sincerely interested in her without any ulterior motives, or—for once—without her manipulating him.

"Uh, oh, I don't know. One day I was going to deliver a manuscript for a book . . . " She paused and looked at him, surprised. "You know, that was just yesterday, and I don't even remember what it was about. I worked really hard on it, and now it's a total blank. Is that weird, or what?"

"I've seen it a few times, doing my residency. Selective amnesia. Any other blanks or drop-outs?"

"Hmm. Don't think so. Doesn't matter now, everything's changed. Guess I can read it if I can ever get back to my apartment. Don't even know when I'll leave here, or where I'll go. You're a researcher?"

Ed stared at the ceiling and sighed. "We were close to a breakthrough. A medicine that could do more for the world than everything over the past fifty years. Maybe a hundred."

"Wow. Sounds impressive. Wish I could be part of something really important like that." Her statement surprised her. *I really wish I could be a part of something important, period . . .*

The man's eyes started misting over. "We lost it, Jennifer. We lost everything."

She wanted to encourage him, to say that he could rebuild, get another team, start again. He looked at Jennifer, who felt the full force of his hurt. There was a finality about what he said, and the way he said it. What had been lost, was gone forever.

+  +  +

Bull was already six hours behind schedule. The strength and clarity he'd felt since taking the drug remained. The euphoria and the stamina, however, had disappeared as quickly as they had appeared. At two in the morning he became physically exhausted. So much so that he had to exit I-95, find a deserted road, and park behind some trees. He rolled up the leather jacket as a pillow and slept on the ground until 8 a.m. Then he was back on the Harley heading down the Interstate. And he was hurting. It started with stiffness when he awoke, which he attributed to sleeping on the ground. But now, all his joints ached.

*Macon or Atlanta?*

His enhanced mind raced through the various alternatives, like a program manager running a cost-benefit analysis. He was rapidly approaching U.S. 78. Since he'd already passed I-20 an hour earlier, it was the quickest way to get back to Atlanta. If he could hunt down the doctor who Fred said developed the drug, Ed Richardson, maybe he could learn what was happening to him. He had to know before giving it to his ailing mother. But that would delay him getting to her in Macon until later in the evening, or even the next day. If he drove straight to Savannah and caught I-16, he'd be in Macon in what, just five more hours or so? But he was healthy when he took the stuff, and it was really bothering him. If these were typical side effects, they would kill her.

Bull was riding in the left lane, and he made his decision just as he was passing the U.S. 78 exit. He counter-steered hard left, throwing the motorcycle into a tight right lean. He cut between two tractor-trailers and onto the offramp. U.S. 78 would take him to Augusta, he'd catch I-20 to Atlanta, and then he'd get some answers from Dr. Richardson.

+ + +

Clayton had decided to bring just one man with him from the Arizona operation. Because of flight delays from the dust storm, though, Manuel had to catch a later flight. Clayton hadn't done much better. It was after 11 a.m. before he secured a rental car and drove to the address that JR had given him. He didn't like what he saw. The building was heavily damaged by the explosion, the fire that followed, and the water from the fire department's response. Even worse, it was taped off as a crime scene, with two patrol cars and a crime scene van parked in front as personnel processed the scene.

Clayton's next stop was at a convenience store for a newspaper, then to a 24-hour diner just down the street. Lunch, three cups of strong coffee, and thirty minutes of talking to locals, and he had a better idea of his next step. But it would have to wait. By now, JR should have faxed a couple of pictures of Bull to his motel. Clayton had to be sure he could correctly identify the man before he went any further. Then he'd need to go back to Hartsfield International to pick up Manuel.

+ + +

"This can't be right." Bull stared at himself in the mirror in the locked men's bathroom at a convenience store just outside of Atlanta. He'd filled up the Harley and gone inside to use the bathroom and grab some snacks. The image looking back at him looked . . . completely normal. But he felt terrible. Every joint ached. His head throbbed. His eyesight played strange tricks on him as he experienced his first-ever ocular migraine.

On the other hand, he felt even stronger than last night when he "borrowed" the motorcycle. His mind was not only clear, he started putting together things he must have read at some point or overheard in passing. He even knew the correct term: synthesis.

Bull's conclusion? He suspected that he was suffering from oxidative stress, like he was being overwhelmed with free radical damage. Or, a series of autoimmune diseases. Maybe cancer. Possibly, all the above.

"Gotta find Richardson," he mumbled as he washed his hands

As he started the Harley and pulled back into traffic, he had another thought.

*No. I've gotta go through the research myself.*

A nagging suspicion was becoming more of a conviction by the minute. Fred was wrong about the medicine. Whether he intentionally lied to save his butt or just didn't know, the man was now dead. So, Louis "Bull" Thatcher, who had never finished high school but whose IQ was increasing by the hour, had to get some answers while he still might be able help his mother. And himself.

## 18.  MORE BAD NEWS

"Hey. You up?"

"Good afternoon to you, too." Mick smiled. "Yep. Slept maybe another hour after you left, fixed breakfast, and got a shower." He muted the TV and the news story about Matthew's visit to Atlanta. As expected, his rally the day before had brought controversy and protests. No riots, though, thanks to heavy police presence, according to commentators. "Been watching the news on this Jason dude. How are you?"

"Tired," Sam answered. "Glad to have the full team back. So, are you going to get a bumper sticker?"

"If I do, it'll be for the bottom of a bird cage. The guy weirds me out."

"By the way? For the record, you have my full permission to give me backrubs like that any time you want. Thanks."

Mick smiled. "A lot more where that come from."

"We'll see."

"And, you're welcome." He leaned back against the pillows and the sheets and blankets he'd folded up on her couch, enjoying the pleasant country décor of her large one-bedroom apartment. "Anybody able to pick up my stuff that I dropped?"

"Yours, and Jennifer's. Let us know what else you need, and we'll go to your apartment for you."

"Good for now. Thanks. So, what's next?"

"Just left the commander's office. He really doesn't mince words about Matthews. Anyway, he agreed with my recommendation. We're putting all three of you into a safe house, at least for a few days. I'll stay there, too. Consider me your personal 24-hour security detail."

Mick's reaction was a strange combination of a frown and light grin. "Sam . . . will that be enough?" he asked quietly.

"We talked about that, too. I'm afraid for right now, it's the best we can offer."

"Thanks."

"Professionally? You're welcome. Personally? Consider it an investment in my future. Gotta go. I suggest you stay there for now. I'll get back to you soon."

+ + +

Bull closed the last notebook. He carefully, almost reverently, put all the materials back into boxes. For several hours he had read and studied the research documents, Ed's notes, spreadsheets, even handwritten logs. A day ago? They would have been as clear as hieroglyphics. Now? They made perfect sense. Perfect, fatal sense.

He'd left his main phone and his car in Fayetteville, hoping to delay any search JR might mount to find him. He had now abandoned the motorcycle at a busy twenty-four-hour K-Mart where he'd left his van. Now sitting in the back of that van parked at a mall, he stared at boxes.

*Maybe I'll let him find all this stuff. It would serve the man right.* He pulled out a pocket phone, a separate one he used for his "legitimate" day job and checked the signal. He climbed into the driver's seat, checked again, and entered a number. After several rings, a frail voice answered.

"Momma? Hey, Momma, it's Louis. Yeah, Louis." His eyes misted over. "Hey, Momma, I'm not going to get there today. I'm sorry. I hope to be with you tomorrow, though. Okay?" He listened intently for a few moments. "Yeah, Momma, it's Louis. Your son, Louis? I'm going to try to come see you tomorrow, okay?" He listened for a few more moments. "Louis! Momma . . . " And the line went dead.

"Oh, Momma," he moaned. "You did so much for me. Can't let you go alone. I'm comin', Momma." He looked sadly at the boxes of research and products. "We'll go together."

+ + +

It was mid-afternoon as Bull drove his van to the fire department closest to the offices and lab that had once been JLRC. The fire chief had left for the day, but Bull found a talkative assistant chief who was more than willing to help.

Bull smiled, chewed on a toothpick, and looked at a shipping document he had on a clipboard. He was again in his "moving man" attire.

"I was supposed to deliver some supplies to that Longevity Center a couple of blocks down from here. Some guy named Richardson? Looks like the place blew up or something."

Five minutes later and he knew everything he needed.

Since the doctor's injuries did not require Level 3 Trauma Unit care, the first responders had transported him to a smaller five-story hospital close by. Bull thanked the man and drove toward the hospital, making one stop along the way. He was at the hospital within half an hour, and drove around it to get his bearings. Then he parked, made sure no one was paying attention to him, and climbed into the back of his panel van. Within a few minutes he exited, dressed as a delivery man for a well-known florist.

Inside the hospital, an elderly Pink Lady volunteer at the Information Desk gushed over how beautiful the flower arrangement was. "Now, because of the investigation going on about his injuries, I'm not supposed to give his room number. But if you'll just take it to the nurses' station on the fourth floor, they'll be sure to see that he gets it." As Bull thanked her and walked away, she added, "I just love how you folks do such a good job!" He smiled.

Carrying the flowers, Bull casually walked around several floors, other than the one he wanted. He memorized the floor plans, how the rooms were numbered, where the nursing stations were located, and dozens of other details. The timing was good. It was dinner time and also shift change, so there was a lot of activity with no one concerned about a floral delivery.

The fourth floor looked about the same as the others. If anything, a little more turmoil. *Good.* A uniformed police officer sitting outside a particular room. *Not good.*

The young officer was reading a newspaper, so Bull took a moment to scan the rest of the floor in case there was a second uniformed or plain clothes officer. *Just him. Maybe short-staffed. I'll take him down and a dozen more if I have to. Gotta get in there.*

Bull adjusted the flowers to partially hide his face, and walked toward the room, his jaw clenched.

A food services employee rolled a large food cart up to Bull's side of the door, blocking the officer on the other side. The woman carried a tray into the room. As Bull approached, he saw the officer walking away toward a sign that read, "Vending."

*Really?*

Bull's jaw relaxed. He slowed down. In a moment, the woman came out of the room and rolled the cart to the next room, away from Bull, who quietly slipped into the room and closed the door.

"Hello, Dr. Richardson."

# 19.   TERMINAL

Bull set the flowers down and smiled. It wasn't pleasant. He then walked over to a heavy couch, the kind that folds out into a guest bed, and easily lifted and carried it across the room. He wedged it against the door.

Ed's eyes grew large. "Who're you?"

Bull faced Ed, who was sitting up in bed with his dinner tray in front of him. He casually rolled the tray cart out of the way and stood looking down at the man.

"Someone you don't want to mess with. I took your medicine."

Ed cocked his head and squinted a moment. Then he raised his eyebrows and his mouth dropped open. "No! No, it's not ready . . . "

"I know. I read your research. How long do I have?"

Sweat beaded on Ed's forehead. "What do you mean?"

"Don't jerk me around, Doc! Even before this stuff, I could kill you with my bare hands. Now I can pick you up and throw you through that window," he hissed.

"Yeah, and your strength and intelligence should double again within a few more days. What do you mean, how long?"

Now it was Bull's turn to look confused. "You didn't figure it out?"

"What are you talking about? My dad died of Alzheimer's. Mom had a heart attack. I've been researching . . . "

"Your research is squat, you moron! Whatever you came up with? Yeah, it beat the cancer issue. Even extended telomeres and reset the Hayflick limit. But it's increased free radical damage. I'm dying, man. Dying!" He grabbed Ed by his hospital gown and yanked him up like a stuffed teddy bear.

"The mouse. We were going to start primate trials."

Bull let go and Ed fell back into the bed, wincing at the pain.

"So. Fred lied."

"You killed him."

Bull looked hard at the man and drew back his fist. Ed tensed. Suddenly, Bull doubled over, grabbed his stomach, and moaned.

"I'm dying, doctor," he said again, his teeth gritted in pain. "This was supposed to help me and save my momma!" He looked up, while still bent over, wincing. "Your old man—had Alzheimer's?"

"That's when I left my medical practice and went into research. Your mother—how advanced?"

Bull slowly, painfully straightened back up. Softly, "Final stages. Other health issues, too. Maybe a couple of days. I gave up everything."

There was a noise at the door, then pounding, then more noise in the hallway.

Bull continued to stare at Ed. His features softened. He reached behind his FTD shirt, which was not tucked in, and pulled out a .357 revolver.

"I . . . I wasn't trying to hurt . . . "

"I know. Take this. You might need it." He set the pistol down on the food tray.

"Why?"

"There's a man I work for . . . worked for. Goes by 'JR.' Evil. He may have more people like, well, like me. He'll do anything to get hold of what you've got, if you can make it work."

The noise at the door grew louder as multiple bodies slammed into it in unison.

Bull reached into his wallet, pulled out a business card for his accounting firm, and set it with the gun.

"All your material is in a blue Ford E350 panel van. I'll leave it parked at this address." He walked over to the fourth story window, turned, and looked back at Ed.

"I was going to kill you. Not your fault. You're a good man, Dr. Richardson. I hope you can help others. I figure I've only got about 36 hours." He sighed. "You found a catalyst—adrenaline—to stabilize the change. But something's still missing. Maybe another hormone acting as a transcription factor, turning on a gene to better assimilate antioxidants. You're correct that we lack what was there before the Flood. If you get this right, we should have a solid hundred and ten years. Strength, intelligence, no disease."

"Five score and ten . . . "

"Make it happen, doctor."

He picked up a large chair, paused, and set it back down. He reached in his pocket and pulled out a vial containing a single capsule.

"In case I don't make it, here's the last one. I was going to give it to Momma. Save her life." He handed the vial to Ed, picked up the chair, and threw it through the window.

"Wait," Ed exclaimed. "Who do I watch out for?"

Bull glanced down a moment, then at the doctor. "Everyone," he answered. "Everyone." And jumped.

Ed hobbled to the door, hurting with every step. Between slams against the door he hollered, "Wait a minute! I'll try to un-wedge this couch. Hold on!"

He pulled up from the lower end with his good arm, while he stood to the side. "Don't hit the door; just push!"

Within moments the door was open.

The uniformed officer entered; weapon drawn.

After a quick glance to make sure Ed was okay, they ran to the gaping hole that had once been a window and stared.

+ + +

Manuel Alvarez ran one hand through his slicked-down shoulder-length black hair and used the other to point at a man striding purposefully toward a parking area. "There! Follow him!"

Clayton, who had driven them to the hospital after they chatted with the same assistant fire chief, saw the man Manuel was pointing at and carefully navigated through the parking lot.

"Good eyes, Manuel. Looks like him."

Manuel looked back at the hospital and saw the broken window. As shadows lengthened, he could make out the back-lit silhouettes of several people looking down. Was one man wearing a uniform?

"It's him."

Manuel turned back in time to see Bull's van pull out of his parking space, navigate through the parking area, and out into traffic. They followed from a discrete distance. Suddenly, the van lurched to the side of the road and stopped. Clayton had to drive past him to avoid being marked as a tail.

What they did not see was tough-guy Louis "Bull" Thatcher slowly closing his flip-phone and weeping uncontrollably. Nor did they hear him muttering again and again, "Momma . . . "

## 20.   DEAD END

Bull had to pull over. He could hardly see through his tears. He glanced one last time at the number on his flip phone before he shut it, never to call or hear from it again. The number to the facility in Macon, Georgia, where his mother is, was, being cared for.

"Oh, Momma . . . " the tough guy whimpered.

Nearly a minute passed. Bull wiped his eyes and evaluated his situation.

*Only one thing left to do.*

He shifted the van into Drive and glanced in his mirrors to pull back into traffic.

"You idiot," he shouted and slammed his hand against the metal dashboard, leaving a deep dent.

"Just one more block, then park. But no! I had to pull over in full view of the hospital!"

A police car, lights flashing but no siren, was weaving through traffic, approaching him. He didn't notice the rental sedan parked on a side street fifty yards away.

*One car. Probably more on the way.*

His mind raced. Rather, it tried to. Much of the enhanced clarity was gone. It would come back in flashes, surrounded by dark thoughts of his mother, and how he hadn't even been able to be with her before she passed. He tried not to dwell on that. He thought of JR, and all the work he had done for the man; all the people he had . . . well, he tried not to dwell on that either.

He thought of his brief encounter with Dr. Richardson. With a flash of his briefly enhanced intellect, he remembered his *de facto* acknowledgement of a global flood. The Genesis Flood. He quickly evaluated all the Bible stories he had heard growing up. Yes, he had even read the Bible through before he was twelve, at his mother's insistence. Didn't understand much. But now? He realized how it all fit together. It had to be true. He had to make sure Dr. Richardson could get all his material back, everything that was in the rear of his van.

Still mentally sharp, Bull felt like he was driving a muscle car with all the horsepower he could ever want, trying to drive on a road covered in ice. And he was starting to lose traction.

*Pull over, give myself up, they'll impound the van and maybe Richardson will get his stuff back. Nah, anyone with half a brain would figure out how important this is. Maybe foreign governments? JR! Definitely JR. With his connections? Not a crumb would get back to the doctor.*

*Or, try to evade, get the van where I told Richardson?*

Bull pulled into traffic. Not too fast; not yet. The cop car was catching up quickly as drivers saw the lights and moved out of the way.

"Come on, come on, come on . . . Yes!" He made it through a major intersection as the traffic signal turned yellow. The cars between him and the police car stopped at the red light and couldn't move out of the way. The police car turned on its siren and pulled into the oncoming traffic lane, navigated around several cars that had already come through the intersection, and made its way through the intersection itself.

Bull had already gone a block further and turned right, made a quick left, and then turned down an alley. He was about to turn onto another street when he saw a second police car, lights flashing, drive by from right to left. Bull waited until the car was well past, then turned right. He drove as calmly as his frayed nerves would allow, so he wouldn't draw attention in the evening Atlanta rush. He glanced a little longer than usual in the side mirrors of his large van, at what might have been a car pulling out of the same alley and also turning right, now several cars behind.

For the next ten minutes, Bull continued to drive a few blocks, make a turn, then several more blocks and turn again. Several times, he intentionally doubled back. But ultimately, he was moving farther away from the hospital, aided by the traffic and the deepening night.

Physical pain returned, now like some of the knife wounds he had acquired in his younger days. He also began shaking, as if his blood sugar was dropping. He continued to glance nervously at his side mirrors.

He took a sudden turn away from street traffic onto a ramp feeding into I-75. The long ramp only had light traffic, and the modified V-8 engine in Bull's large van produced forty more horsepower than the manufacturer's stock model. Bull was quickly past the ramp traffic and smoothly merging onto I-75.

He glanced again in his mirrors. Under different circumstances, he would have smiled. Instead, he grimaced as the pain intensified again. It was now to the level of a severe kidney stone. His blood sugar was definitely low. His thinking was dark, and his mental acuity was slipping again.

"Momma . . . "

He swerved through two lanes of traffic to take an exit, precipitating blaring horns, a station wagon pulling over to the shoulder, and an SUV that wasn't so lucky. It slammed into the retaining wall at sixty miles an hour.

Bull's fate was worse. He entered the exit too fast and hit his brakes to avoid slamming into slower traffic ahead. He was still in a tight turn. The van tipped, hit the retaining wall . . . and went over it.

In a final split second of mental clarity, "Jesus."

For the first time in decades, he was not blaspheming.

+  +  +

"That's it. We're leaving. Now."

Samantha Knowles's authoritative voice left no room for argument.

Ed had finished explaining the unexpected evening visit from the man responsible for the deaths of his friends. Sam put on a pair of hospital gloves, and placed Bull's revolver into an evidence bag she pulled out of her purse. There were two more things Ed wanted—desperately—to explain to her. He knew he needed to be careful about the when, where, and how. He got out of bed, grabbed his clothes, and went to the bathroom to change.

In half an hour, an officer was transporting Jennifer in the passenger seat of his cruiser. Ed was riding in another car, following the cruiser. It was a 1990 Ford Mustang GT hard-top. Sam was listening to the police radio, on a secondary band.

" . . . Correct. Appears to be the van. Landed on its roof. One body."

Sam keyed her mic. "Roger, that. Okay, call forensics. See if they can find anything."

"Detective?" asked Ed.

"Hmm?"

"Could you ask if there's anything in the back of the van? Boxes, crates, anything?"

She relayed the question.

"Negative, Detective. Firemen said that gasoline dripped down, then burned upward. The vehicle's completely gutted. Burned down to bare metal."

"Ten-four." She hooked the mic to the side of its radio and glanced at Ed. "Important?"

"You have no idea," he responded. As she drove on, he added, "Irreplaceable."

## 21.  SAFE HOUSE

"Hello?"

The young man had gazed at his phone several seconds before deciding to answer. He could count less than five people who should have known his number, and he didn't recognize this as one of them.

"Hello, Skylar. Are you being treated well?" Skylar didn't recognize the voice, which was firm, authoritative, and surprisingly pleasant, but he knew who it belonged to.

"Uh, yes. Hello, Mister . . . uh, sir. Thanks for all you've done for me. Yes, sir. They're, uh, they're treating me great."

"But? You sound like something's missing."

"Uh, well, sir, it's like they don't quite know what to do with me. I want to learn all I can, you know, try to be as valuable as possible."

The man chuckled. "I knew you were a winner. I like your attitude."

Skylar expected him to continue. After a brief, embarrassing pause, he responded with a quiet, "Thanks."

"Absolutely," JR said. "And everything's about to come together for you. Stop whatever you're doing and get to the airport. Your salary has been doubled, with an additional $10,000 added to your line of credit. You are needed back in Atlanta."

+ + +

"Ouch!"

"Too hard?" Sam asked.

Ed gingerly got up from the king-sized bed in the safe house's master bedroom. "That's an understatement. Like a rock. Hate to complain . . . " He hoped he could find a softer bed in the house, especially for his shoulder.

"House rules; he with most bandages, chooses best bed." She smiled.

Mick lay down on it. "Feels great to me."

Jennifer called out from the other two rooms, which shared a bathroom between them. "One of these queen beds is really soft, and the other is kind of firm. Not too much. I like the soft one."

"I'll play Goldilocks and see if the one in the middle is just right," Ed said as he walked over and tried the other one. "Yeah. Oh, yeah. Perfect!"

Sam smiled. "That was easy. Looks like we're all set."

The safe house was a three-bedroom, two-bath house that would soon be listed for sale. The police force tried to have a few of them available throughout the Atlanta area, but they couldn't hold onto them for long. No matter how careful they were, the locations always become known to the criminal class.

Sam had already made it clear that she would sleep on the couch in the centrally located living room, with her gun and radio close by.

After a few minutes, the group relaxed in the living room. Sam shot a concerned glance at the doctor.

"What's the matter, Doc? I know it's not a five-star, but it's clean."

"Detective . . . " Ed saw her stern glance and corrected himself. "Sam, the place is great. You're great. The force has been great."

"But?" Sam wouldn't let it go. "You've been pensive since we got here."

Ed sighed and looked from her, to Jennifer, to Mick, and back to Sam. He looked down at the floor and took a deep breath. They had started to watch TV. Mick shut it off.

"Okay. I'm going to tell you something that could put your lives in even more danger. But you need to know what all this is about."

For ten minutes, he had a captive audience. No questions, no argument, no distractions.

"So, the person who led us down this strange path, Dr. Stone, is dead, likely murdered. Separately, both Fred Jackson and Tanya Hastings are dead, thanks to my hospital visitor, who himself is now dead. That just leaves me and our part-time research assistant, Aaron Sims. And now you three. But there's nothing to show for any of it. Nothing. Unless there's anything at all left at the lab. Well, actually . . . ."

"What?" Sam asked.

Ed reached into his pocket and pulled out a vial. "Just this. One dose. Enough to make one of us into a brilliant superman," he glanced at Mick. "Or superwoman," he looked at Sam and Jennifer. "For a couple of days. Then a painful death."

Jennifer spoke up. "Isn't there anything we can do?

Ed considered a moment, then asked Sam, "Maybe two things. We're all tired. I know I'm exhausted. But now that this guy's dead, could you let me in the lab? Maybe I can find something—anything— that could keep this going."

"We still don't know if he worked alone. But yes, I think we can do that as soon as you feel up to it. What else?"

"The guy in the van. Blood samples?"

+ + +

"What are you going to do?"

Jennifer and Mick had each retired to their bedrooms. Ed and Sam were in his. He had sponged off around his many bandages as well as he could and was in his gym shorts so she could look over his bandages.

"What do you mean?" she asked, marveling at Ed's dexterity despite his obvious pain.

"The news will be all over this. Two homicides. Three deaths. The lab. Who knows who saw the man leap from a fourth story window and walk away? And all arguably linked to the archeological find of the ages, a severed hand and unknown fruit that, for all we know, could be from the Tree of Life? Something that turned a man into a modern-day Samson?"

"Yeah, then killed him. And no evidence, except maybe your last capsule and, less likely, some blood." She smiled and patted his leg, right above his knee. It was about the only part of his body that wasn't covered in bandages. "I'm not a med tech, but I'd say that these look good. And your key word was, 'arguably.' Remember, this is Atlanta. I know what you're asking. I think the approach you've already taken is the best one. Unless we're put under oath, we handle this as a gambling problem gone bad. We don't need a firestorm drawing the attention of foreign governments, tabloids, UFO chasers, and who knows who else. I'll talk to the others in the morning. Maybe drop a hint at the hospital. Suggest that maybe it's possible that a man could survive a 4-story jump, even with some minor broken bones, especially if he's hopped up on LSD or some other drug. I'd like you to have the time and freedom to change the world in a good way. Lord knows, we need it."

"Lord knows," Ed repeated. "And it's as if He only wanted a very small number of people to be aware of this."

"You're a good man, Ed." She realized that her hand was still resting on his leg, and she rose from the side of his bed where she had been sitting. If he noticed her faint blush, he didn't say anything. She added, "I really want you to make this happen."

"That's almost exactly what my hospital room visitor said, after he gave me his gun."

"Yeah, and then he torched himself. Well, you can't keep his gun, although if you don't have one, I suggest you get one and start carrying. And me? I have no intention of getting lit. Need anything?"

"Actually, hate to ask, but could you help me get on my shirt?"

"How bad is that shoulder?" She was glad he couldn't see her expression as she stood behind him and helped him pull on a clean cotton tee. Her pulse quickened and her face flushed. Despite the injuries, all of which would heal according to the medical staff, the man was really in good shape.

"Not quite as tender. Thanks."

"You bet. Call out if you need me." She smiled and closed his bedroom door.

Sam retrieved her overnight bag from the living room. She glanced at the hallway leading to Mick's bedroom, and then back at Ed's door. She sighed and went to make her bed on the couch.

## 22.   NOTHING

"Wow. It's a miracle it didn't kill you, too," exclaimed Aaron Sims, the young graduate student from Georgia Tech. Ed, Sam, and Aaron were scanning the wreckage of what had been JLRC.

"Just about did, Aaron. Did you keep any copies of your research?"

"Nope. With all the time and money it took to print those notebooks, I brought everything to you. Good news is, I've got a pretty good memory and I could probably retrieve and re-copy all that stuff in half the time."

"Well, so there's some good news to start us off," Sam said. "I'm told that the interior is stable. Ready to go in?" She handed them flashlights and stepped over the bright yellow "police crime scene" tape to what had been the entrance.

Within ten minutes they were back outside. Sam's optimism was gone. Ed appeared to be fighting back tears. Aaron, who was typically cheerful to the point of exuberance, was subdued as they walked back to their cars.

"Thanks for joining us. I appreciate the offer to re-do the research. Ed stopped for a moment and looked back at the building. "There's probably no need. And no funds."

The continued silently to the cars. Ed shook Aaron's hand and smiled the best he could. "Thanks for all your hard work, and best wishes on your academics. Stay in touch."

Several minutes later, Aaron was driving off in his '88 Ford Taurus. Sam was driving Ed in her Mustang GT in the opposite direction.

Neither Sam nor Ed noticed a plain white, 1990 Buick Regal pull out from a side street and follow them from a distance. It was the same one that had tracked down Aaron's address and had followed his Taurus to the JLRC facility not even an hour earlier.

+ + +

"This is, like, so good." Jennifer inhaled deeply, enjoying the aroma of the boxes of Chinese take-out Sam and Ed had picked up. She started eating from her piled-up plate, not waiting for the others to join her. Mick glanced at Sam and rolled his eyes. Within a few minutes, Sam, Mick, and Ed were also at the table. The others began eating. Sam noticed that Ed bowed his head briefly, and then also started eating . . . with chopsticks.

After their initial feeding frenzy slowed down, Sam shared what she and Ed had discussed the night before. Then she added, "It'll take a while to get more records. It does appear that Fred really did have a significant gambling problem. We never found Fred's cell phone, but his cell service provided a list of his recent calls. A lot were to a guy named Louis Thatcher. His phone has been traced to a location up in North Carolina, and we're trying to track it down.

"You think he was my hospital visitor?"

"At least a few of his calls were to known gambling addicts. We're checking on others. A lot of others. I'd say that's highly likely. I'll feel a lot better if we can link him to your visitor and the corpse in the van. Speaking of which," she glanced at her watch. "I'm having a sketch artist come here in about an hour. I don't want you and Jennifer talking about this guy's description. I want you to come up with your own sketch, and then we'll see if they match."

"I guess if they do, we're done," said Mick. "We're free to get back to our lives. Right?"

"Well, there's something else . . . " Ed was interrupted by his cell phone. He glanced at the number, shrugged his one good shoulder, and took a quick sip of hot tea.

"Hello?"

The others could only hear his side of the conversation. But they each noticed a deep furrowing of his brow. After listening for several moments, Ed spoke to the unknown caller.

"Well, yes, Fred mentioned an "angel" who was funding our work. He never mentioned a name."

Pause.

"Everything's lost. I just went there today. No notes, no computers or floppy disks, none of the genetic material we were working with . . . " Sam noted that he was speaking slowly and very carefully. "I'd say we're back to where we were over a year ago."

Pause.

"Good Lord knows, I thought we might be able to do something that could help a lot of people. I'll probably just have to go back into private practice."

What the caller said next was almost loud for the others to hear, and Ed winced and moved the phone a few inches back from his ear. Then the call ended.

All eyes were on the doctor as he closed his phone and set it down.

He looked up, directly at Sam.

"As I started to say, there's something else. I told you about the gun, and the man warning me that there may be others out there like himself. He said that the man he worked for goes by the initials, 'JR.' He said the man was evil, and that's saying a lot from a man who'd already killed several people." He paused and took another sip of the hot Jasmine tea. "He told me that this guy would do anything to get hold of what I had, if I could make it work." He stared at his teacup.

"Who was that on the phone?" Sam asked.

"JR."

+  +  +

"My professional opinion? Perfect match. This would hold up in court."

A sketch artist from a different precinct compared the sketch he just completed from Ed's description to the one Sam pulled out of a folder.

An hour later, after the artist had left and Sam had made a few phone calls, the four of them were together in the living room. Sam and Ed were on the couch, Mick was in a rocker, and Jennifer was stretched out in a recliner.

"So, here's the latest," Sam said. The commander believes the case is solved and we should all go back to our own lives. Since he only knows about Louis and the gambling issues, he sees no further threat. For the two of you," she nodded at Mick and Jennifer, "I'd agree. And you're probably safer apart from Ed and me. Because, Ed," she softened her voice, "I'm really concerned about this JR fellow. But to continue providing protection, I'd have to tell Major Garrett about everything else."

"I understand," Ed replied.

"We're okay here through the night without any questions, so I believe we should stay put and have supper delivered. Jennifer, in the morning I'll drive you back to your apartment and thoroughly check it out with you. When you feel everything's okay there, I'll come back and do the same for you," she added, nodding to Mick. "Ed, it's up to you. I do I have a recommendation." She said it as more of a question that a statement.

"Please," he said.

"Okay. I've put in a lot of OT, and the commander suggested that I should take some time off."

Sam noticed some negative body language from Mick, and ignored it. Facing Ed on the couch, she wasn't in a position to notice an equal but opposite response from Jennifer.

After Ed humbly but reluctantly accepted her offer, she took a lighter tone. "So, that should be the last of my official business for today. Anyone for a board game? Hall closet."

## 23.  ENGAGE

Sam tried to fit in as one of the group. But she had a deeper purpose for her last suggestion. The commander had agreed when she brought it up, and even seemed to respect her all the more for having thought of it.

She wanted to evaluate how each of them was doing . . . emotionally. Jennifer had witnessed a murder. Two of them had been targeted by the killer. Ed had not only lost his co-workers and friends, he had come face-to-face with the murderer. All of their lives had changed, significantly.

She watched how they interacted over the next few hours over two games of Yahtzee and four cut-throat hands of Uno.

She was pleased to see Mick begin to relax. He smiled more, and even started laughing. All good signs. Jennifer? She seemed moody. When she did smile, and the few times she laughed, it came across as forced; fake. Of course, in the short time she had known her, Sam struggled to evaluate whether or not that was typical.

Sam watched each of them, and especially Ed. The weight of the world was still on his shoulders, and it showed. Probably not to the others, but Sam had some experience with PTSD both personally and professionally. They had dinner delivered—pizza, by a unanimous vote—and she noticed that he bowed his head even longer before he began eating. He had been through so much; he had every reason to be a basket case. She felt his tension. She hurt with him, and for him. But there was something else. Even in the midst of it all, he projected a level of inner peace that made absolutely no sense.

Sam set aside her quiet evaluation for the time being. She would have at least a few more days with the doctor, to make sure he was alright. She took a big bite of pizza and smiled.

*This is really, really good!*

+ + +

Skylar paced in his small apartment. Then he walked around the apartment complex. Twice. He changed clothes and went to the gym. Ate supper. Played Nintendo. Paced some more.

*Why doesn't he call?*

He checked for the thirtieth time that he hadn't missed a call, that his cell phone was turned up all the way and showed a good connection. He noticed that his battery was down to fifty percent, so he plugged his phone in.

And he paced some more, waiting for JR to call him back.

He had called him as soon as he was cleared to turn on his cell phone back at the airport. Well, that is, as soon as he could get a good signal. He spoke briefly to the man, who said he would call back shortly. That was hours ago.

*Why the big raise? Why haven't I heard from Bull?*

He wanted a drink—or something stronger—so bad he could taste it. But he knew he'd better be at 110 percent when JR called. It wouldn't do to let this boss-man catch him muddle-headed.

He put the Pac-Man cartridge into his Nintendo and sat in front of his new twenty-seven-inch RCA color TV.

+ + +

Jennifer excused herself and enjoyed a long shower. The hot water washed away some of the tension. She didn't like feeling so alone. She also didn't like being the "odd man out," feeling like she was the only child among adults. Back in the bedroom, she took a hard look at herself in the mirror. She pinched some fat around her waist. Or rather, she grabbed a handful.

She selected a casual, soft pair of cotton pants, suitable for lounging around with the others, and pulled on a matching colored V-neck T-shirt. She smiled at the hint of nipples, and walked to the door. Before she reached it, she stopped, hand outstretched. She slowly returned to her suitcase, took off the T-shirt and pulled out a flesh-colored, thin, cotton bra.

*No nips, unless I get cold or excited. Same effect, but it'll appear I'm modest.*

She paused again, and deliberately put that bra back. She took out one of the newer ones, one of the few she had that was padded, the popular new design. Expensive, nice form, but nothing would show through, no matter what.

"Hey, guys, got a question for you," she said light-heartedly as she walked back into the living room.

"Go for it," Mick said, smiling.

"Well, all this has been kind of life changing, if you know what I mean. So, like, where do we . . . what do you plan to do from here? Sam, I guess this is your calling, right?"

Sam slowly nodded and looked toward the ceiling. "I'd like to work my way up to the GBI or FBI. Something at the state or federal level. Guess I'd like to lead a team of investigators, eventually."

Jennifer looked over at Mick.

"Wow. You know, I've been thinking since all this came down. I want to do something I enjoy. I . . . well, I guess college isn't it. I went to tech school and worked in a machine shop, if you can believe it. I really got a kick out of making stuff. I miss that. I've been reading up on how computers can control machines. Pretty cool, you know?"

They all looked at Ed, who lowered his gaze and stared at the floor.

"Ed . . . I'm so sorry. That was pretty insensitive after all you've been through," Jennifer stammered.

*I really am heartless . . . have I always been such a jerk?*

He looked up at the others with a faint smile. His voice was soft and gentle.

"Friends—and after all that we've been through together, that's how I see you—I've been struggling with this, so cut me some slack and help me sort this out."

He sat up straight and spoke the same way. "I'll try not to ramble too much. Like I told Louis, I lost my father to Alzheimer's, and shortly after that, my Mom died of a heart attack in her fifties. They both should have lived many more good years. I finished med school, started a private practice, even got engaged. That didn't last long. Neither did the practice. I had little patience for narcissistic men and women coming to my practice, more concerned about their appearance than their health. Smoking, drinking, terrible diet, lazy; wanting me to prescribe dangerous drugs to make them look like movie stars."

Jennifer blushed and tried not to squirm

Ed continued. I just didn't have much of a bedside manner. Besides, I was too focused on research. I finally left my practice a few years ago and went into research full time with Fred. You all know how that ended."

They nodded and seemed to be listening, so he continued. "I have an overarching purpose for whatever I do, so that hasn't changed. First, I became a Christian back in high school. I stopped trying to be good enough to get to heaven. I couldn't—can't—and I realized that Christ came here, paid for my sins, and offers eternal life to me by receiving him as my Savior.

"Second, and a lot of folks never get this right: He's Lord. I'm not. So, well, my purpose is to follow Him. Like I said, that hasn't changed.

"Third, I would like to continue the research. Absolutely. But there's no more money and nothing to work with. Just one little capsule that can't be duplicated. Would I like to be married? Maybe have a family? Yeah. Should I go start a medical practice again? I just don't know. But the foundation is Christ, and He's all about caring for people, so it'll be something along those lines."

They all sat thoughtfully for a few moments.

Sam spoke up, not even trying to hide her admiration. "Ed, you've got more together than about anybody I know. I can't believe that after all you've been through."

Ed answered. "I appreciate that, coming from you. I for one am really grateful to have you as our guardian angel."

"So, don't I remember something in the Bible about acknowledging God, and He'll direct your path?" she asked.

He smiled. "Yep. Good reminder."

Mick spoke up. "Doc, I want you to know you've been a rock around here. Kinda like a mentor?"

It was quiet for a few moments, and the attention shifted to Jennifer, who started fidgeting uncomfortably.

"Jennifer," Ed asked quietly, "How about you? Where do you plan to go from here?"

## 24.  PURPOSE?

Jennifer had begun the conversation, asking what changes the recent events had made on their lives. The responses were not at all what she expected. Now, they were waiting for her response.

Her lips quivered. She stroked her hair and her eyes glanced around the room, eventually focusing on Mick. "You're quitting college? Couldn't you make a lot more money getting your degree?"

"Life's not all about money. I'm sure I'll do okay. I can get a solid technical foundation and go back for a degree later if I choose. I want to make stuff."

She looked at Ed. "So, having your life threatened . . . ?"

He smiled and answered. "Not the first time. During my medical residency, I spent a lot of time at a major ER in a pretty rough city. Weekends, we often saw the results of what we called the 'knife and gun club.' Those nights were very, shall we say, challenging. We tried to keep people alive, sometimes while they were still trying to kill each other. Occasionally one of us got in the way."

"Wow." She stroked her hair again and looked at Sam, only a few years older than hers. "We're trying to get out of danger. You? You go toward it. To protect us."

Sam took a deep breath. "Like Ed, I made up my mind. I want my life to make a difference. If I go young, I'd rather be remembered for doing something good than die old and be forgotten for not doing anything."

Jennifer looked down at the laminate wood flooring. Her face flushed, and her eyes filled with tears. After several moments she stood up. Without making eye contact, she walked to her bedroom. "Thanks, guys. Got a lot to think about. Good night."

She suspected that for her, it would be anything but.

+  +  +

"Ready . . . set . . . go!"

Clayton slid his phone shut, dropped it in his pocket, and slammed against the side door. Manuel likewise closed and secured his phone and kicked in the back door. Two seconds and they were inside, guns drawn.

"You move, you die," Clayton said, his .357 revolver aimed at no one in particular but everyone in general. "I've got two men and a woman," he barked at Manuel. "Search everything."

Manuel started with the master bedroom, Mick's, still unmade. Bedroom, large walk-in closet, and empty bathroom. He went across the living room to the next bedroom; Jennifer's. Bed made, no indication that anyone had slept there. Closet and bathroom empty. Before he could step through to the adjoining room . . .

"Don't even think about it," Clayton barked. Now his .357 was directed at one person; Sam. She had just come out of the master bath when they burst into the house. In all the hours they'd been in the house, she had only been unarmed for twenty minutes. Ten of those minutes were right then. She had tried to slowly move over to her gun.

"Everything okay?" Manuel stuck his head out the bedroom door.

"Yeah, just a young lady moving too much like a cop for my liking. Might have to take her down first. Keep looking."

Manuel went to the last bedroom; Ed's. A mess. No one there. He opened the bathroom door from that side. Empty. He walked quickly through the kitchen and dining area. "All clear, boss."

"Alright, folks. Here's what's going to happen. Each of you are going to die. One at a time. Any questions?"

He gave that a moment to sink in, and for them to nervously glance at each other.

"Now there's a chance . . . a very slight chance . . . that if you give us what we're looking for, we'll let one, two, or? Well, probably not all three of you, live. But? We'll see."

"Whatever you want, look through everything! We don't have anything," Mick blurted out.

"Well," Clayton continued, "you see, that's a problem. You've got to have something, or tell me where it is, or give me some information, or you're all going to die. Do you understand me, Doc?"

Ed stared at him, confused. "I have absolutely no idea what you're talking about."

"Cover the others, Manuel. All the neighbors already went to work, so if you don't like what they're doing, blow a foot off or something. So. Doc, seems you've been working on something really important. I want product, material, research, whatever you've got. Or people start dying. Starting with her." He pointed the gun back at Sam.

Sam stared directly at him, pale but defiant.

"Do you have any idea what's happened the last couple of days?" Ed asked. "Somebody broke into our research facility and took everything. Or maybe it was already cleaned out by our owner and given to some guy to pay off a gambling debt. But the place was cleaned out. Then he killed my boss, put his body in our building, and blew it up. Killed our assistant and almost got me. Day before yesterday, he gets into my hospital room and threatens me. Then he says he's going to leave everything in his van and tells me where to get it."

"An hour later," added Sam, "we hear that a van matching that description, with one body, was wrecked and completely burned. He's right. There's nothing here."

"Not my problem," Clayton responded. "Start over."

Ed hung his head. "You don't know how much I wish I could. What we had? What we were working with? It was from a plant, a fruit, actually, dating back all the way to . . . " He looked up at Sam.

She nodded. "Go ahead and tell him. Doesn't matter now," she said.

"Yeah. Okay, an archeologist friend of mine sent me some samples. I believe it's from the Garden of Eden."

"From the Bible? Oh, that's rich!" He walked over and knocked Ed to the floor with a blow to the jaw.

Ed moaned in agony, both at the blow and the hard landing on his injured shoulder.

"Not one word. Not a sound," Clayton said as he shifted his aim between Sam and Mick.

"My name is Clayton. This is Manuel. I'm telling you this because, like I said, I doubt that any of you will be alive by tonight. You," he pointed at Sam, "over in that chair."

Sam walked over to the dining room chair Clayton had pointed to and sat down. "Lamp cord, Manuel, Tie her up. Young lady, you move, you die."

Manuel holstered his 9 mm pistol, ran a hand through his black hair, and pulled out a large pocketknife. In seconds he had it locked open and sliced through a lamp cord. He threw the lamp against a wall. He tied Sam's hands behind her back, weaving the cord through the back of the chair. Sam noted his expensive cologne as well as the popular logo of his casual clothes and shoes. The man was in his early thirties, with a dark Hispanic complexion. He stood about five foot six inches and weighed around 180. Stocky. Very little body fat.

"He told you, we don't have anything," said Sam.

"Go ahead, Manuel."

Manuel hit her and knocked her and the chair to the floor. Then he set her back upright, pulled a small roll of duct tape out of his back pocket, and put a wide strip over her bloodied mouth.

"Now you. Over there." He motioned to Mick, who walked over to the other dining room chair. Another table lamp was sacrificed, and in a few moments, Mick was tied and taped, too.

"Doc," Clayton said as he walked over to Ed and squatted down. Ed looked up, wide-eyed. "I've got all day." Clayton grabbed him roughly and jerked him to his feet, and then shoved him over toward the others. Ed just barely stayed on his feet. "Grab a chair and have a seat."

Another minute, and he was tied and taped as well.

"So, here's how this is going to go. Like I said, we're not in a hurry. But we do report to someone who's very interested in what you have, Doc. We sit here for, oh, three or maybe four hours. Manuel and I decide how we want the pretty cop to die. Probably a couple of strategically placed cuts, so you can watch her bleed out. Anyway, before we do the first one, we'll take your tape off and see if you've got anything for us. If not? She dies. A few hours later, he dies," said Clayton, motioning to Mick.

## 25.  *NO GREATER LOVE*

The worst night of her life was now followed by a waking nightmare. As soon as Jennifer heard the others stirring, she had packed everything up, including toiletries, and made her bed. Looking over the room, she surprised herself. It was as if she had never been there. Completely uncharacteristic.

Also unusual were the thoughts that had kept her awake most of the night. Thoughts about needing a life purpose, something—anything—that could give meaning and a reason to get up each morning. Frankly? She was sick of her miserable self, being just as manipulative as her own mother. Sure, she hadn't gotten into the drugs, at least not yet. But the alcohol had her close to the same level. Would she also have a Jennifer Junior who would end up in foster care while she served time in prison? *Or?* That was the big question. *Or, what?*

She put all her stuff by the front door, ready for Sam to take her back to, well, her apartment; the trash pit that she had called her home.

Sam just finished a shower and Jennifer stepped into the other bathroom one last time. That's when she heard the doors being knocked in. Only by the strangest coincidence did the one man not come through the bathroom into Ed's room, where she had tiptoed. By the time he checked out that room, she had quietly hidden back in Ed's room which he had already been through.

Jennifer's eyes flooded with silent tears at what she heard; the man's threats, and Ed being knocked to the floor and groaning. She almost whimpered out loud when she heard Manuel hit Sam.

"These are good people. Leave them alone!" she wanted to shout.

She looked longingly at a large window in Ed's bedroom, and tiptoed over to it, grateful for the plush carpet on a concrete floor. But she still glanced at the open bedroom door.

*Move the curtains out of the way, unlatch the window, raise it, jump through, and run?*

She went through the scenario a dozen times, thinking about each motion and the exact sequence and precise timing. If anything went wrong, if she couldn't get the window open, if she got stuck?

*I'm a klutz. No way. If I don't, they'll die. If I try, they'll know I'm here and I'll die. I'll be the first one . . .*

The tears ran down her face. She wiped them with a shaking hand, fighting against every instinct to sniff and blow her nose.

*There's nothing I can do. We're all going to die.* Her thoughts returned to the conversation from the previous evening, as it had all through the night. Her gnawing emptiness added to her fear.

*Mick said life was about more than money. Sam doesn't want to live unless there is something worth dying for. Ed just wants to help people, to honor God.*

Jennifer bowed her head. *Oh, God. I don't know You. But I want to. Please help.*

A clear image came to her. So fast, it startled her.

*No!* She clamped a hand over her mouth to keep from shouting the word. She closed her eyes hard against the tears.

Jennifer seriously considered running into the living room and turning herself in to the thugs. It might have been easier.

*No, no, no . . . !*

Purpose. Meaning. Trust. *Do you trust Me?*

The sound of laughter returned her attention to the conversation in the living room. The laughter was dark, sinister. She heard the word, rape. And more laughter.

Jennifer was beside Ed's bed, next to the nightstand and in front of the window. She looked at it again, assessing whether there was any way possible . . .

As in a dream, or like a character in a story that she was now living out in person, she eased open the nightstand drawer. There it was. How did she know it would be there?

She opened the vial, closed her eyes, and swallowed the capsule.

+   +   +

"Well, folks, this has been fun. But, it's like I said. We work for someone who really wants your stuff." Clayton yanked the tape off Ed's mouth and leaned close to his terrified face. "Am I going to have something to tell him? Or do I turn Manuel loose on the pretty cop?"

"There's just one thing," Ed stammered. He was trying to figure out how to buy them some time. "The stuff is fatal. Believe me, I wish there was more. I can't duplicate it. I don't even know how to study it. We never got that far. Honest,"

"Manuel, see what kind of knives they have in the kitchen."

Ed was shaking, sweating. "Okay, fine. There's a capsule. It's in the nightstand by my bed. Just please don't take it or let anyone else. It'll kill you, and it isn't pretty."

"All this for a little capsule?" Clayton said, condescendingly. "No Doc, you've gotta do better than that. Manuel, you find anything?"

"Just steak knives. Nothing fancy."

"The capsule," urged Ed. "It's in my nightstand, that first door over there."

*God, I don't know where Jennifer's hiding; please keep her safe.*

"Alright, Doc, let's see about this magical capsule . . . " He was interrupted by his cell phone. Glancing at the number, he swore, stepped into the master bedroom, and closed the door. Several minutes elapsed. The door swung open and he stomped across the room to Ed, placed his hands on the chair arms and his face less than two feet away.

"As I started to say, let's see about this capsule." Clayton straightened up. "And if there's nothing to it? I kill both that guy and the cop, any way I choose. Got it?"

"Please," stammered Ed, "I've told you all there is. It's one capsule. There's nothing more!"

"We'll see," and Clayton walked to the bedroom door.

As he stepped into the doorway, a large chest of drawers slammed against him with the force of a pair of NFL linebackers but at twice the speed. It knocked his 280-pound muscle-builder frame twenty feet against the opposite wall and broke into pieces against him. A split second before the furniture hit him, he caught one quick glance of a young blonde woman in her early twenties. It was the last thing he saw. Ever.

Manuel stared in shock, then fumbled for his gun. He pulled out his 9 mm pistol and aimed it at the impossibly-fast woman. Did he manage to squeeze off a round before she smashed him against the wall, crushing him into the sheetrock? Was that the explosion he heard, or was it

104 Five Score and Ten

her fist shattering his jaw and breaking his neck? Whatever it was, it was the last sound he ever heard. Except, maybe, a final, soft whimper. His own.

"Jennifer!" Ed screamed, choked with emotion. She was on her knees, left hand just above her right breast, blood pouring through her fingers. "Jen, can you untie me? Let me try to help you," he begged.

Sam and Mick scooted their chair-backs against each other, trying to untie each other's knots.

Jennifer crawled over to Ed, ripped the power cord loose, and collapsed.

## 26.  *NEW BEGINNINGS*

Flashes piercing the darkness. Bits and pieces. Pain. Voices.

Ed: "Exit wound . . . good."

Sam: "Lot of blood."

Ed: "I'd expect more."

Mick's face, concerned. Touching her cheek.

Mick, over by Clayton's broken body: "Wow!"

Sam: "Yep. They're dead."

Ed, checking her pulse. "Where's EMS?"

Sam: "Can she make it to the hospital?"

Ed: "I need their supplies. I *am* her hospital . . ."

Sam, holding her hand.

"Sam . . . guess . . . I guess I don't get to ride into the sunset," Jennifer said, just above a whisper.

Sam squeezed her hand and stroked her hair, tears streaming. "Jen. You've got to. You're our hero."

Darkness. Pain.

+  +  +

Time passed. Perhaps it was only a few minutes. It could have been several hours. Possibly a lifetime.

"Welcome back." It was Sam, holding and stroking Jennifer's hand, the one without the IV.

Jennifer tried to raise herself up off the gurney, for about half a second.

"Ohhh . . ."

"Let's not try that again for a while," Sam said softly.

"She's awake?" Ed asked, surprised, as he came back into the living room.

An EMT stepped aside. "Yes, doctor. Vitals are weak but stable."

"Good," Ed replied as he stood over her and shone a flashlight into her eyes. "Incredible. Okay, go ahead and pack up. Let's transport."

The two EMTs carried equipment to their ambulance. Jennifer looked up at her friends standing around her gurney.

"We owe you our lives," Mick said solemnly. The others nodded.

"How . . . how long do I have, Ed?"

Ed stroked her forehead and pursed his lips. "You're in uncharted waters. We now have exactly two humans. The first one? Well, he was a *he*. Significant chromosomal differences in every cell of your body. Several organs are different, significantly different hormones and hormonal balances. Over 300 differences, just based on XX verses XY. You also had a huge rush of adrenalin within a few hours. Shortly after that, we got you on pure oxygen. Already, I've seen something totally unexpected."

"What?"

"You're alive. Jennifer, that shot, at that range, and where it hit you? I've never seen or heard of any survivors. Ever. Your right lung closed on its own; no pneumothorax. Same with blood vessels . . . "

"I'd say the good doctor had a lot to do with that, too," interrupted Sam.

"Thanks. But the truth is, I really don't know. But three things. First, you're absolutely unique in the world today. Second, you're responding differently than the lab animals or Louis." He paused, tears welling up in his eyes.

"Third?"

"Third, we had to . . . I had to try to bring you back long enough to say thank you."

The techs came back in and picked up a second load of equipment to return to the ambulance. After they left, Jennifer looked at each of her friends. Sam held her hand. Mick had his arm on her good shoulder. Ed continued to gently stroke her face. Now they all had tears.

A gentle smile slowly replaced the painful grimace that had taken residency on Jennifer's face. "Ed. You don't need to worry. I know where I'm going."

Sam and Mick looked at Ed, who shrugged.

"Where I'm going. If I don't make it. It's okay."

"What in the world are you saying?" Mick said.

She smiled. "I took the capsule an hour or so before the guy came to the room. I didn't know what would happen, or how long it would take. My mind started to clear within thirty minutes. I started remembering. Things started coming together. One of the foster homes I was at? Where I wish I could have stayed? They used to take me to church. I remember. And Ed?"

"Hmm?"

"It's true. It's all true. If I get through this, I'm reading it all, cover to cover. But I remembered enough. And now I know Him. And . . . I have a special request for you."

+ + +

"Yes, sir. The house was quiet for hours. I'm sure they were in control. Then one gunshot. I assumed they were wasting one hostage to raise the stakes. It's what I'd do."

Skylar drove into his apartment complex, parked his car, and shut off the engine.

"Thanks," he responded to a comment on the other end of his cell call. "So, I kept watching. Then ten minutes later an ambulance, then two police cars. Two hours later? The ambulance carried off a woman. Looking through my scope—I was over fifty yards away—it was a young woman, maybe in her twenties. Blonde. An hour later, they pull out two body bags. I was afraid they might see me, so I left."

Pause. This time, Skylar's hands began to shake.

"Yes, sir. I'll send you the address. And I'll try to find what hospital they took her to."

"Understand. See you soon, sir."

The call was over. Skylar stayed in his car, shaking, swearing, and sweating in the cool, evening air.

"Coming here, with all his teams. Who is this guy? Who else is on his payroll?" He wrapped his arms around the steering wheel and rested his head on his forearms. "Oh, man. What have I gotten into?"

+ + +

The man looked quizzically at his cell phone as he stepped into the back of his limo and slid closed the small window that sealed off his world from the front seat.

"Yes?"

"Hello, JR," a deep male voice with a slight Slavic accent said through his phone.

"I believe you have the wrong number. Goodbye."

"Not so fast, Jason." The man froze. Not only did he not recognize the caller's number or voice. More significantly, no one who referred to him by his initials also knew his first name. Or, so he thought.

"Jason Robert Matthews. Going by JR for, shall we say, your less-public activities? Surprised you don't go by RJ, or RJB from your previous name; Robert Jerome Buonel. Do I have your attention?"

Jason smiled ever-so-slightly. "Illuminati?"

"Oh, heavens no." The voice chuckled. "Sorry, I toss in words like that occasionally, so I can trample them under foot, if you know what I mean."

"Yes, actually I do. So, do we continue this game while I go to my next rally, or will you tell me who you are and why we're talking?"

"Very good!" the voice responded. "Not asking how I know all this . . . the details . . . but asking the more important questions of purpose and motive."

"I'm listening."

"Alright, Jason Matthews. First, we're on the same team. Illuminati? They're a diversion. If anything, a proving ground for the real shakers and movers. Me? The organization I'm a part of? We're the ones who make things happen."

"Second?"

"Oh, I do like your style. Alright, Jason. Second: There are some things you need to know about the, shall we say, 'longevity formula' and why it's so important for our overall plan. That fits directly into the third point, which is that we expect you to drop out of the Congressional race. It's frankly just a waste of your time. We have more important matters to address."

In ten minutes, Jason knew, understood, and completely agreed with a whole new course of action. His smile was no longer slight.

"So . . . we really do have a living link to the formula," he muttered as he put away that phone, and took another out of his coat pocket.

## 27.  GONE

"What'll we tell everyone?"

Dr. Ed Richardson looked down at Jennifer, lying flat on a hospital bed except for a small pillow under her head. After only one night in ICU, she was now in a regular room. Her color was returning.

Ed smiled. "Well, let's see. I guess we can tell them that you're the only link to a piece of fruit dating back to sometime before the Flood. You not only survived taking it, you also single-handedly killed two seasoned thugs half again your size. Oh, and you're recovering from a gunshot through your right lung at close range. You should be going home less than two days later. How's that?"

"My enhanced cognitive capacity and broadening understanding lead me to conclude that somehow, in this case, the truth would be counterproductive."

Ed stared at her. She blushed. "Good grief. Did I just say that?"

He smiled again. "Yep. And you're right on both counts. Yes, I expect your IQ will continue to increase, according to Bull. And yes, I was being sarcastic. I think we'd best let Sam navigate that mine field."

"Speaking of whom . . . "

"What?" he asked, just as the hospital room door opened. It was Sam. Ed shot a questioning look at Jennifer.

"She has a unique walk, and stylish but functional shoes," Jennifer said, and smiled.

"How's our hero, Doc?" Sam asked.

Ed slowly shook his head. "Amazing. Far more questions than answers. Don't know if the world has ever seen anything like this. Ever.

Now Jennifer was confused. "You're saying that this isn't how everyone was before the Flood?"

Ed looked between the two women. His smile was gone. He winced and rubbed his injured shoulder, walked over to a chair, and sat down. He took a deep breath. "Jennifer, no. I suspect they were stronger and healthier than anyone we can imagine. There was a sub-set called Nephilim that was even more so, and then later there were the giants of

Gath, like Goliath. But . . . "

Jennifer motioned for him to pause.

"Hi, Mick," she said as the door started to swing open. Mick entered with a confused, "Uh, hi."

"That's going to take some time to get used to," Ed said. "You'll likely want to keep that capability on the down-low."

"Yep. Already thought of that. Same with the IQ and strength. Sam, we were just talking about that. Where do we go from here? What do we tell everyone?"

+   +   +

Pat Jernigan was living the high life. At least, his version of it after finally paying his DUI fines, reinstating his car insurance, and getting a new driver's license. He had filled his car's gas tank, driven to a Cracker Barrel, and was splurging on a meatloaf dinner. Maybe even apple pie and ice cream.

At 6 p.m., the restaurant was crowded and noisy. Perhaps that's why the EMTs sitting at the booth behind Pat spoke a little louder than they intended. In only a few moments, Pat's attention was on full alert.

"Nothing like that in the medical books," exclaimed the younger man. "She ain't human!"

"Human, yes. Normal? Nowhere near. And the corpses!" replied the older.

"Glad I'm not on that cleanup detail. Looked like they got slammed around by a gorilla with a bad hair day."

"Look, I've done this for ten years. ER several years before that. Nobody takes a chest shot like that and even makes it to the hospital."

"She should've bled out before we got there. Maybe that doctor?"

"Guy's a miracle worker, yeah. Impressive. But her? No way. I'd like to go back to the Medical Center tomorrow and peek in on her. She's something else. Oh, thanks." He concluded, as the waitress brought their meals.

Pat lingered over his meal until the men left. Unfortunately, that was all they said about their very unusual shift. It left more questions than answers. Pat's imagination ran from an alien to a DARPA project gone bad to some new fitness steroid product. But in the end, he knew two things. Where she was, and that he had to go check it out.

He smiled. He had bounced around from job to job since his parents threatened to kick him out, for all the good that did. The one he stayed at the longest? A janitor at the Atlanta Medical Center. Always someone there to hang around and share interesting stories with. Especially during the graveyard shift. Which would begin in . . . he glanced at his watch and smiled. He still had the work clothes, and while he didn't have the actual badge, he could make something that would look similar if he kept it flipped toward his shirt. No one ever checked.

"Yeah, maybe I'm in for a good story here," he muttered as he picked up his check and headed for the cashier, grabbing some snacks for the road. "Could be a long night."

This was a chance to make something of himself. Maybe even earn respect as a legitimate news source. Time for some investigative journalism.

Whatever that meant.

+   +   +

"You . . . what?!"

The head nurse fidgeted at the police badge Detective Samantha Knowles held in front of her face. This was not a polite, "How was your night shift?" question.

"Uh, Ma'am," the heavy-set woman stammered. She was twice Sam's age, becoming even paler than her normal "needs more Vitamin D" pallor. "Best we can figure, we lost her when they took her to X-ray."

"Who took her?"

"Well, we had an order, and two technicians came to get her around 2 a.m."

"Bed or wheelchair?"

"I'm sure it would have been in a wheelchair."

"I want to know who saw her, how they took her, whether she was awake or not, everything! No one leaves here this morning until I have answers. You lost a gunshot victim, and I've lost my patience. Got it?"

"Yes, ma'am."

Sam stepped back into the now-vacant room for another look around, and called Ed. After three rings, he answered.

"Good morning. I agree with Mick. Very comfortable couch," he said.

"Ed. Our patient is gone."

"She, she died? Oh, no . . . " he blurted out.

"No," Sam snapped. "She's gone. Vanished. The staff says she was taken for an X-ray at 2 a.m. She never arrived there. No one knows where she is."

"I didn't order an X-ray—and certainly not one at 2 a.m. I'm her attending physician, so no one else should have either. She could have easily fought off anyone trying to abduct her. Unless . . . "

"What? I'm scared for her, Ed. Unless what?"

"Sam, no one could have overpowered her. They'd have to sedate her, either through an IV bag or a direct injection into the IV port. Is the bag still there?"

Sam glanced at the stand.

"It's still here, almost empty. Ed, what's left isn't clear like what they gave her yesterday. It's amber."

## 28.  *FULL DISCLOSURE*

It had been a long night. Pat had never been more excited in his life. He didn't just learn about a certain dead-to-rights young woman the EMTs had picked up the day before, who was somehow already out of ICU and in a regular hospital room. He had found that specific room and even walked past it. While staff members were distracted by a "code blue" down the hall, he even had time to read her chart.

Pat found an area that could use some cleaning, returned later with a mop bucket, and then engaged a nurse in conversation while he cleaned the floor. He saw two orderlies wheel the young blonde out of her room and down the hallway, ostensibly to take her to X-ray. But something didn't seem right. Why at 2 a.m.? And why would they send two orderlies? One was a heavyset black woman in her early fifties. The other, a white man in his late forties, average height, maybe 220 pounds and balding. He had gripped the patient's gown in each hand along with the chair's handles, as if he had to keep her from slumping forward. Her head hung down to one side. Unconscious.

Pat had turned down a different hallway, and peeked to see which elevator they entered, and which floor it went to. The basement. He ran down the stairway, nudged open the door, and saw the man and woman lift her out of the chair and into the back of a van. After studying the van, he closed the door and ran to the other side of the hospital where his car was parked.

He was able to drive back to the basement parking exit just as the van pulled out. And somehow, in the most stressful driving of his life, he had been able to tail the van to a building in a Buckhead business district. He'd parked a few blocks away, walked back close enough to see them carry the woman into a building, and got the address. Now back in his car, he realized that he was the sole witness of a kidnapping. Possibly, the kidnapping of a very remarkable young woman.

Pat knew he should tell the story to his parents, or to the police. Or maybe even better, to one of the local TV reporters he had befriended. He might even make the national news! But he needed to know more, and his life was likely in danger if he got sloppy. He calmed down, ate some of his Cracker Barrel snacks, watched the business from a safe distance, and considered his next actions.

+ + +

"I've had moral dilemmas before, Sam." Major Steve Garrett stood up from his desk and walked to his second-story window, turning his back on his unexpected visitors. An early afternoon thunderstorm limited visibility to just a few blocks.

He turned around and looked hard at his youngest detective; almost through her. He ignored Ed and Mick.

"Young lady."

"Sir?"

"I don't know whether to fire you or promote you."

Sam didn't flinch. "Honestly, after what's happened the past week? I just want her back and safe. She went from a brat—well—not someone I had any respect for. She went from that, to saving our lives. She fully believed that taking that stuff would kill her. Let's get her back, then you can do whatever you want."

Now Steve looked at the others. "Mick, tell me. If you were put under oath tomorrow to tell the whole truth and nothing but the truth, what would your story be?"

Mick didn't hesitate. "No-brainer, sir. We've already agreed that if it comes to that, we'll lay it all out. The only thing I'd add to what Sam said? Sam's also a hero. She made some good calls. I don't think we'd be having this discussion if she hadn't."

"Absolutely," Ed added. "And thank you for supporting her."

"Full disclosure," the commander asked. "Something going on between you two?" He nodded toward Mick.

"Full disclosure?" replied Sam. "Yes. We've dated." Mick frowned at the past tense reference.

"Alright. I'll come up with a cover so you can pursue this. But if we're put under oath, our best protection is the truth. That's how I roll."

"Thanks, commander," Sam said. They stood and walked to the

door.

"Sam?"

Sam turned back, hand on the doorknob.

"Keep it legal. And gentlemen, if you haven't already, I encourage you to start carrying."

The men followed Sam as she walked to her desk, each lost in their own thoughts. She hadn't been to the office in a few days, and, with the new urgencies, likely wouldn't be there for several more. She picked up some folders and a notebook and they started to leave. Then she stopped and turned around. That desk—Dwayne Wilson's—was cleaned out. The man was gone.

+  +  +

A loud moan. Jennifer tried to force her eyes open against the blinding light. After a few moments she gave up. She heard the moaning again, only louder. Then she realized it was her.

"More," someone commanded.

"We've given her enough for a Silverback gorilla," another voice argued.

"I didn't ask your opinion," First Voice snapped, a male. "You think a Silverback's dangerous? Did you see the picture of that house, with a man hanging through a wall?"

The pain in her right hip started to ease.

"I just need one more vial of marrow," said First Voice.

"Another minute or two on the blood draw. Bag's almost full," said Second Voice, a woman. "Look, we can't anesthetize at this level forever. If this is going to continue, we'd better get someone who can induce and monitor a coma."

"Already on his way. Some dude named Dr. Winfred. He'll meet us at the facility."

"We going there tomorrow? Gotta be something better than this if we're going 24/7," responded Second Voice.

The pain was almost gone. Jennifer didn't hear herself moaning any more. She felt suspended in the air, weightless.

"That's my understanding. By tomorrow evening."

Fade to black.

+ + +

Skylar was pacing in his apartment again. Not because he was waiting for JR to call. Because he had.

"I'm so proud to have you on my team. I knew I could count on you. I'm bumping your pay another hundred a week. I'll need you to check on a few things for me. Not get involved, I just need to make sure other people are doing their jobs. My eyes and ears on target, so-to-speak."

They talked for another few minutes, but that was basically it. All earlier instructions were replaced with this one: "Memorize names and faces from the pictures I'll fax to you. But have no contact whatsoever until and unless instructed." He was to watch over that same old warehouse outside of town where he and Bull had offed Andy last year.

Skylar kept pacing, mumbling to himself.

"Set up CCD cameras, run coax, video monitoring. There's an old shed I can sneak into from the back. Set up some observation blinds . . . gotta see and not be seen . . . better binoculars. Man, I'm gonna need some serious hardware."

He made a list, paced some more, scratched off a few items, and then added others. An hour later he grabbed his keys and made sure he had the credit card JR had sent to him a few days earlier. "Twenty-thousand line-of-credit. Man!" he exclaimed as he walked out his apartment door. An afternoon thunderstorm had just ended, and he'd have a few hours before dark to get everything he needed and start setting up. He understood that the warehouse would be occupied continually starting the next afternoon. "Gonna be a long night," he muttered, as he drove to a drive-through for a tall cup of coffee.

## 29.  *HUMAN SUBJECT*

By 7 a.m., Skylar had three cameras mounted unobtrusively on light poles. He had strung cables for remotely monitoring and powering them. The cables ran down to a small shack at the edge of the fenced property. He already mapped out where he could hide his vehicle, the short walk through woods, and the section of fence he loosened where he could slip through and sneak into the shack. He set up his VCR and monitors, wired everything up, and checked it all out. Pan, tilt, zoom, and good video feeds from each camera.

He finished just in time, as a caravan of rental vans and trucks drove in and unloaded.

"Man, if the dude had given me one more day, I could scope out the inside of that place," Skylar muttered as he put in a VHS tape and hit 'Record.'

Within an hour the vehicles left. Two hours later they returned. The activity continued all afternoon. Four vehicles, four trips, six people. As they were unloading their last delivery, a different van also drove up, followed at a discreet distance by an Oldsmobile Cutlass Ciera

+  +  +

After he turned into the industrial park, Pat drove the Cutlass a block farther. He was exhausted after only a few hours of sleep over the past few days. Other than quick trips every few hours to use the bathroom, grab fast food and more coffee, he had remained on point near the building where the van had parked. Finally, some men loaded up what appeared to be a rolled-up carpet . . . likely disguising the young woman . . . got into the van and drove away. Pat followed them for half an hour to what appeared to be an abandoned industrial facility. He found an unobtrusive side road, pulled in, and parked. As Pat got out and walked around for a better look into the complex, he noticed another car.

+ + +

"A human being did this?" Dr. Julian Winfred asked incredulously, adjusting his reading glasses to get the full impact of the pictures taken from inside the safe house. He looked up and tried to take in as much of the room as possible. It was dirty, and strewn with lights, tables, medical equipment, supplies, cameras, and a few chairs. Then he glanced at the two people standing next to him. The balding man in his late forties, Edgar Foley, had been a senior EMT for years—until he was caught with a drug habit. Julian didn't know much about the other, Lanora Wellston, a heavyset black woman in her fifties. Except that she didn't look happy.

"Not just a human," replied Edgar. "This human. Her. You got me, doctor?"

"Why, yes, certainly I do, Edgar. I got you," the smallish, bald physician in his early seventies responded. "Yes, yes, I understand. My, my. She can't be more than one-fifty-five, soaking wet."

Julian stared at Jennifer. She was lying unconscious on a gurney, clothed only in a disposable diaper and bra, and had an IV in her arm that was connected to mixed bags of glucose and an amber liquid.

"I'm getting tired of cleaning her up, if you know what I mean," said Lanora.

"Yes, well, certainly. No, we can't have that. Certainly not. And the poor woman needs some real food. And we have to have some interaction for the tests."

"Doctor!"

"Yes, yes, Edgar, I'm thinking. Say, that much anesthesia . . . we need to keep her between Stage 2 and 3 on the Glasgow Coma Scale . . . A minimally conscious state we call it. She'll be able to do some things, you see, like go to the bathroom with some help, but can't—oh, dear—can't try to attack us. My, my, my."

"Doc. What they got on you, anyway? How'd they get you here?" asked Lanora, as he scribbled down weights, medications, and doses.

"Me? Oh, my. Well, uh, I suppose that I made an error one time.

Just once, mind you. Yes, a few errors. Bit of alcohol, you know? Like to drink some, made some errors." His voice trailed off as he finished writing. "Okay," he looked up. "Yes, well, where are the pharmaceuticals I ordered? And, well, Mr. Foley? I, uh . . . ugh," he glanced at the pictures now on a table, face up, "I'll do the best I can. I sure will. But you know?"

"What is it, doctor?" Edgar snapped.

"Well, I just, I mean, I think we should consider restraints. And, well, maybe someone, oh, maybe in a chair over there, in that corner? Someone with a tranquilizer gun."

+ + +

"Medical supply houses. Pharmaceutical suppliers. Not corner drug stores, I'm talking the facilities that supply hospitals and nursing homes. I've made lists of what they may be looking for. Uhm, labs. Yes, medical labs. We'll be looking for unusual, specific tests."

Ed was tired. They all were. It was late in the evening, and just under forty-eight hours since Jennifer had been abducted.

"How in the world do we cover all this, Sam?"

Sam leaned back, finished chewing her bite of Philly Cheesesteak, and wiped her mouth. "Ever hear of the term, 'gumshoe?' "

Ed looked at her blankly and stuffed down a couple of French fries drenched in ketchup. Mick shrugged. "Before my time."

"Before all of our times. Somewhere around the turn of the century. Bottom line is, we'll have to do this the old-fashioned way. A lot of driving, walking, and talking. Set up some contacts, then follow up by phone. And it's pretty much all on the three of us. Can't pull in more help without raising questions we don't want to answer. Major said he may call in some favors if needed. Have to be careful there, too."

"Got that right," said Mick.

Ed looked thoughtful. "I've got the largest net to spread. Sam, I need the computer from my place."

"I thought all your records were lost at the lab?"

"All the lab's records, yes. I've developed years of contacts around the country. A few in other countries. I need them watching for any unusual lab requests. Tests, research, that kind of stuff."

"Hold it . . . let me watch this," Sam said, staring at the deli's television. A video of Jason Matthews at a news conference had gotten her attention, with the caption underneath, "Jason Matthews suspends campaign." The picture went to split-screen, showing a news anchor:

"That was the announcement earlier today, as controversial candidate Jason Matthews confirmed suspicions that he was suspending his campaign for U.S. Congress, effective immediately. Jason commented that the country was not quite ready yet for his compassionate, end-of-life-with-honor ideas. He stated that he would be taking a sabbatical, and refused to answer any questions. In more news . . . "

"Wow. Major Garrett will sure be glad to hear this," Sam commented.

"I'll sleep better," added Ed. "The guy commented to the CDC that if critical vaccines were scarce, he'd want them withheld from children and the elderly, and give them to working adults only."

"Aren't children and the elderly usually the ones most at risk?" asked Mick.

"Exactly."

The waiter refilled their water glasses and left to run their checks.

"Do you really think she's still in the area?" Sam asked.

Ed washed down his food with a swallow of water and answered, "All we can do is pray, and work. All the supplies, facilities, labs and anything else they may need is available around Atlanta. But it would be easy to transport her somewhere else. What do you think?"

Sam paused a beat. "Yes. Yes, I think they're here. Look, whoever is behind all this, this JR person or whoever else? I think Atlanta is his base of operations. Yeah, they might prefer New York—where it's easier to get lost. But they'll want faster results. Long drive, more chance of getting caught. And . . . " she paused.

"Overconfident?" Mick offered.

"Overconfident."

"Let's certainly pray that's the case," Ed added.

## 30.  MINIMUALLY CONCIOUS STATE

Jennifer heard voices in the distance, fading in and out. She tried to listen intently. It was hard.

"Yes, yes, well, see that? That indicates that she's waking up. Activity increasing in both cerebral hemispheres."

Her eyes flickered open. She saw three people, an elderly, short white man, a younger muscular white man, and a large black woman.

"Isn't that bad, Doc?" asked the black woman.

"Oh, my, yes. We want these readings to calm down. Kind of a twilight sleep, in and out, and easy to control." He started adjusting the IV drips of two new bags feeding into a machine that mixed the meds into a line feeding into the back of her hand.

Jennifer watched the monitor and struggled to calm her thinking, to intentionally lower the indications of wakefulness that the "Doc" was pointing out. It was unnatural, a struggle. Slowly, she began to make progress.

"Yes, yes, very good. See how that's calming down? So, we know the right dose, at least for now. We can't leave her hooked up all the time, of course. I'll check her EEG several times a day and adjust accordingly."

He shifted his attention back to Jennifer, who closed her eyes just in time.

"Yes, well, okay. Hello?" He gently shook her. "Hello?" he repeated, a little louder, lightly tapping her face. "You see, when we get this just right, she should be able to respond groggily to basic commands and answer simple questions— mostly by nodding 'yes' or 'no.' Hello?" He slapped harder.

Jennifer controlled her initial response to slap him into next week, and instead fluttered her eyes open. Not knowing how to properly respond, she chose to act out what she had seen and far too often been; a drunk.

"Uh . . . hello . . . " she muttered, and again closed her eyes.

"Perfect! Oh, yes. Are you hungry?" He shook her.

Actually, she felt starved. Without opening her eyes, she nodded.

"Good. Okay, let's raise you up, and get you something to eat. Edgar, you got anything here?"

"Cafeteria staff hasn't made it in today, doctor. Gotta sandwich in the fridge," a gruff male voice said.

*Edgar. Voice One.*

"And something to drink? Preferably with a straw? Lanora, you might have to help her."

"'K, Doc, long as I don't have to continue diaper duty."

*Lanora. Voice Two. Diapers!?*

"Yes, yes. Well, I imagine she'll be okay in a little while. You might need to help her in the shower, you know? Especially with those restraints?

"Don' know if they even gots a shower around here. We'll come up with somptin."

*Restraints. Just what I was afraid of. Okay, stay calm.*

+ + +

Ed yawned, sat up on Sam's couch, and stretched.

"Oh, that smells good."

Sam smiled from the kitchen. "Extra strong. We call it, 'graveyard shift blend.' "

"I'll have a double." He walked over to her kitchen counter and sat down. She poured a large cup and set it in front of him, walked behind him, and gently massaged his shoulder.

"How is it this morning?" she asked.

"Gotta admit. A lot better with the massages. Thanks. I'm running out of excuses to stay off the weights, though. Got it all stretched out, now I need to work on getting my strength back."

"You're welcome. You didn't even budge this morning. What were you doing so late?"

Ed sipped the coffee, closed his eyes, and inhaled the aroma. "Wearing out your phone book writing down business names, addresses, and phone numbers. Then dividing everything up by zip code. Thanks for letting me set up shop." He nodded over to his computer, dot matrix printer, and three stacks of paper.

"Wow." She stopped massaging his shoulder, brought over her coffee, and sat beside him. "An organizer as well."

"MD and researcher. Guess it's in my DNA."

"DNA. I wonder how Jennifer's is doing," Sam commented.

Ed stared at his coffee and didn't respond.

+  +  +

Three days. Four additional personnel. No opportunity for Jennifer to escape. Not yet.

Jennifer reviewed what she knew up to this point. She was amazed how different a person she was from the embarrassingly ditzy, shallow child in an adult's body she had been less than a week ago.

A small table clock sounded. It electronically mimicked a grandfather clock, chiming every half-hour. Everyone hated it, except the eccentric Julian Winfred. And Jennifer Lane. Dr. Winfred was adamant that he would have the clock, or he was out of there. Even threats of violence were met with surprising resistance: "Take me out, and she'll take you out. The clock stays, yes it does." For Jennifer? She knew how many days she had been there, the time of day, and the schedule of various trains that sounded their horns every time they approached some far-off intersection from either direction.

Lanora? At least the older woman insisted that Jennifer would be dressed in bra and panties. The next day, she went and bought somewhat more modest workout clothes for her attire, at least when the researchers couldn't come up with excuses to strip her again.

The researchers. Three lecherous men, with ages that would qualify the youngest to be her father, and the oldest her grandfather. Apparently, JR had something on each one of them, and they were not happy about being there, other than their delight in making her miserable.

Jake was the youngest. Early forties, wiry, dark complexion that might be East Indian. He specialized in musculoskeletal anatomy.

Rodney was mid-fifties, white, and always smelled of cigarettes and cheap cologne. He came across as a true medical researcher, much like Ed; but only if Ed had an evil twin.

Greg? The oldest. Good shape for a man in his late sixties. Some indeterminate mixed-race background, and brilliant. He had apparently been a leading-edge genetic researcher until he fell from grace and into JR's grip. He was even now working on a blood transfusion to try on some other subject. The thought of another super-person brought countless science fiction heroes and villains to mind. And it terrified her.

There was one other man. Early to mid-thirties. Jennifer could tell that he always wore a disguise. A very good disguise, and it's likely the others didn't even recognize it as such. The man only came by once a day, typically for just a few minutes. When he did, it was clear that everyone there knew exactly who he was, as if he owned them.

JR. He had just left.

Jennifer played her "drunken" role well, acting out the expected behavior of the drug-induced minimally conscious state. When the EEG was attached several times a day, she consciously suppressed her brain activity to a level that pleased Dr. Winfred. As she was able to metabolize the meds more readily, she let her response rate increase, just a little, so he would give her more. Just what he expected; but not too much.

They continued drawing blood, amazed at how quickly she regenerated blood plasma and components, including red and white corpuscles. She would moan, as expected. She didn't have to act when they took marrow. That hurt. It also gave her permission to stretch against the restraints as they would expect. Not too hard; she didn't want to give them a reason to use stronger restraints. Just enough to make them think they were adequate. Which they were. For now.

Jennifer's train of thought was interrupted by footsteps.

"Well, yes, well young lady. Time to check things out. Going to give you a little more now, okay?" Dr. Winfred re-attached electrodes to the EEG machine, watched the monitor, and adjusted the IV drips.

"Big day coming up. Seems we're going to start tests on you. Um, hm. Yes. Let's see what you've got. Yes, indeed."

## 31.  TESTING

"Nothing?"

Ed shook his head. "Not a single lead." He opened up a box of Chinese take-out and put a serving of Sweet and Sour Chicken over his rice.

"Me neither," said Mick, as he loaded a stir fry onto his plate of rice.

They were in Ed's apartment this evening. Tomorrow they would meet at Sam's, then Mick's, then back to Ed's. Ed and Mick worked full-time on finding Jennifer; Sam had to maintain her position and contacts with the police force, so she met with them every night after a full day at work. In reality, part of her eight-to-five qualified as working on Jennifer's case as well, and she gave confidential status updates to the commander at least once a week.

"More of the same," Sam added, as she poured a cup of hot, black tea. "Good news is, still nothing with hospitals, morgues, or funeral homes."

"Bad news? Nothing from medical and pharmaceutical supply houses," said Mick.

"And nothing from researchers," Ed added, not looking up from his dinner.

They ate in silence for several minutes. Then Mick leaned back, looked at his friends, and spoke. "Isn't this the point where someone says, 'Maybe we've been going about this all wrong,' and comes up with a fantastic idea?"

"Garrett and I talk about this regularly," Sam offered. "He can't come up with anything either. He stays in touch with other zone commanders, looking for anything out of the ordinary. Missing persons, deaths, robberies? Nothing out of the ordinary. No more than usual. He did say he had a long-shot idea he'd try. He didn't go into any detail."

Ed spoke up, choosing his words carefully. "I'm not about forcing anything on anyone, and I'm not sharing this to brag, believe me. But I've been setting aside time every day to pray for Jennifer. Yes, certainly, for us to find her and for her safety and all that. But I believe there's more. She's become a Christian. She's unique in the world, and I believe that God has some specific purpose for her. If that's true, Satan will do anything and everything to stand against that. I believe she's that important."

"Spiritual warfare. Like in Ephesians, the full armor of God," Sam added.

"Exactly," Ed stated.

+  +  +

Phase Two began. That's what they called it. Jennifer had far more eloquent words to describe it.

She screamed in earnest as an electrical shock convulsed her body. She squirmed and pulled against the restraints, which were connected to calibrated sensors. Part of her scream was the sheer concentration of intentionally limiting how hard she pulled against the bonds. Even so, she could hear them excitedly calling out the readings. Two hundred pounds; two hundred and fifty; three hundred, from each of the four restraints. They had no idea! She fought with everything she had to keep from doubling those readings. Just before passing out, she gave thanks that because of the electric shock, Dr. Winfred couldn't monitor her EEG. It would have been off the chart, and he would have immediately doubled or tripled her meds.

They disconnected the leads, reconnected the EEG, and Dr. Winfred monitored for several minutes while balancing her IV. Jennifer's body continued twitching involuntarily, even with the meds. Finally satisfied, he disconnected the EEG, patted her shoulder, turned down the lights, and left the room.

She groggily regained consciousness in time to hear some more bad news. As the door closed behind Dr. Winfred, she counted what sounded like six new voices—men—introducing themselves to Dr. Winfred, Edgar, and Lanora. They were all security. What little she heard? Very serious security.

+  +  +

Major Steve Garrett didn't get out on the street much anymore. Most of his days were overwhelmed with executive and administrative duties, occasional press conferences, and any number of other "duties as assigned."

Tonight? This was an exception.

Steve drove around a 1940s-era elementary school, long since boarded up. It was in one of the older, lower income parts of Atlanta. He drove behind what had once been the school cafeteria, pulled up beside a late '80s Ford pickup, and rolled down his window. The driver in the pickup cranked down his.

"Steve, gotta tell ya, man. Things? Ya know, they're heatin' up," the older man said. He was likely in his early sixties, and looked every year of it, plus a dozen more.

"What's the word, Lenny?"

"Man, you already know about the dudes what got wasted at your safe house. Like, they were some heavy-duty dealers in Arizona. Cross-the-border stuff an' all that. Left it. Left it all to come here on some errand. Now? Guys comin' up from Miami. Down from New York. Just a few, but they're top dudes, heavy duty heat, leavin' big-time operations. Ya know? Like, somethin' goin' down here that's more important than all that?"

"Drugs? Organized crime?"

"You'd think. But no, man. Nothin' like that. Don't know what's playin' out."

"Any idea where?"

"Where? Hmm. Try to find where. I'll be back atcha."

+ + +

"Second and third order effects, Jason." JR listened intently to the deep male voice at the other end of the conversation, known to him only as Brazen. "Like ignoring a drug's primary purpose, and specifically prescribing it for its side effects."

JR loved the intrigue. "Like LBJ's 'Great Society' initiatives, and the food stamps, Medicare, Medicaid . . . "

"Absolutely. Promise things that sound good, which help a little initially. That's the appearance. But the greater purpose, the ultimate reality, is to make people more dependent. In a constitutional republic, especially one with considerable wealth and firearms, you can't just declare martial law and take over."

"So," JR pondered, "Increase dependency, grow government . . . it's like . . . "

"Feeding an addiction," Brazen finished for him. "Let crime increase? They'll be willing to give up guns for more police protection. Increase financial instability? They'll pay more taxes to make sure what they have is kept secure. Whatever you can do that also makes them feel good about supposedly helping others? Bonus."

"The problem is not the problem. It's an opportunity," JR commented.

"Always an opportunity. And if there isn't a problem? Create one. Especially when we need to draw attention away from another major initiative, or when we need to distract from some undesirable issue that doesn't benefit our cause."

"I'm tracking. Misinformation, distraction, retreat in one direction to advance your cause in several others. Very good."

"We'll talk again soon, and I'll recommend some material for you to study. For now, you might enjoy Orwell's *1984* as a good read. Lot of wisdom hidden in fiction. I'd like to get you on a steering committee to help move things forward. We've got a good candidate that should make Bush a one-termer. This man and his wife could do a lot to advance our agenda."

"Reagan just about ruined everything, didn't he?" JR asked.

"He came out of nowhere. There's so much in the U.S. that we still don't control. We had to work overtime to cut our losses. He set us back several decades, at least. Fortunately, Bush is pretty much on board, appearing to be conservative but downplaying everything. Giving us a chance to regroup."

"Steering group, you say?" asked JR.

"The U.S. is our hold-out. You know that. Came up from nothing in World War II and has been a thorn in our side ever since. Can't bring it into submission externally. We've got to collapse it from within."

"Rome," JR commented.

"Rome and every other once-great nation," Brazen agreed.

The conversation ended, and JR smiled as he walked to his home's master bathroom. He carefully removed his expensive disguise. He would bathe later. For now he combed his short, natural hair. Then he scrubbed his face and put soothing lotion on his face and neck. He liked the way things were going. Very much according to his own plans.

JR walked to the kitchen, opened his elaborate bar, took out his most expensive bottle of Scotch, and poured his first drink for the night. He never drank more than two.

## 32.   *NUMBER TWO*

Jennifer had cleaned up with Lanora's assistance. She had also enjoyed a large Italian dinner that was actually quite good: Linguini, Veal Parmigiana, and a salad. She had to suppress her emotions and actions, as always, to avoid suspicion.

She tried not to think about what might be next. Instead, her thoughts shifted to her friends. Her entire life, she had talked about all her friends, only to now realize that they had been acquaintances at best. Mostly just other narcissists like herself. Like what she had been. She vaguely remembered some kind of Scripture about old things passing away and all things becoming new. How she longed to read and memorize key verses.

*Her friends.* Mick wouldn't play her games, and he didn't play her. Ed? What a class act. A man of integrity. And Sam? She could certainly understand why Mick was interested in her, and she couldn't blame him. Strange, she wasn't jealous. She really wished them both the best. How desperately she wanted to spend time with all three of them, as soon as she could break out.

Not unexpectedly, as his clock chimed nine times, Dr. Winfred came back in for his final check for the evening.

He checked and chattered for several minutes, seemed satisfied, and started to turn the lights out. "Oh," he exclaimed. "And you're going to have some company. Yes. Yes indeed. They just brought someone else in. Next door. Greg's working on him now. Let's see how that works out, shall we? Good night."

Phase Two continued in the morning. Bathroom break and breakfast at eight, then by nine, Dr. Winfred significantly increased her meds. To "take the edge off," as he explained. The team brought in cameras, notepads, and timers. They began. Dr. Winfred showed Jake, the musculoskeletal specialist, how to make consistent one-inch incisions approximately one quarter inch deep. Rodney and Edgar acted as test recorders and took pictures, noted the time, and wrote down the locations. Jake had never finished med school, but he had enough lab experience that he quickly met Winfred's approval. He worked down Jennifer's left side, with Edgar as his recorder. He placed cuts on her shoulder, upper arm, lower arm, abdomen, thigh, and lower leg.

Dr. Winfred had allowed Rodney to light up, and he would take his cigarette and create second- and third-degree burns, side-by-side, in roughly the same locations on Jennifer's right side. Rodney took pictures and notes.

Throughout the process, Jake talked excitedly about the possibility of breaking some bones. First, to see how much stronger her bones were than normal, and what exact force would be required to break a humerus or tibia. Then, to see how quickly it would heal.

Finally, Edgar had enough. "Nobody breaks nothin' unless JR approves. Anybody does anything to get on that man's wrong side, there's a group of enforcers out there getting real bored. Got it?"

Nobody said a word. Once they finished down both sides of Jennifer's scantily clothed body, Dr. Winfred stood up and looked at Jake's incisions.

"My, my would you look at that? Have you ever? Why . . . Edgar, please take another set of pictures. Hardly any bleeding at all! Already coagulating! Hmm. Let's monitor her every three hours, not six. My, my my . . . " he stammered as he walked out of the room.

No one noticed the tears trickling down Jennifer's cheeks. Their "subject" had to play her role, and not let them know she felt every excruciating cut and burn. She couldn't reveal that the increased meds were only like two beers instead of one.

When the last person walked out, she wept quietly and prayed silently.

The pain subsided. Jennifer looked at the wounds and burns that she could see without being too obvious to the video cameras. Dr. Winfred was right; they were healing remarkably fast. While she didn't have the luxury of any real exercise, she did carefully do some isometrics, tugging against the restraints.

For the past two days, there were times they had left her alone, usually after Dr. Winfred convinced them that his extra meds were making the "safety man" with a tranquilizer gun unnecessary. Apparently, her ruse of concealing her true capabilities was paying off. Maybe just a few more days . . .

She thought about his comment the night before. *Another person? A man?* She winced. That could ruin everything. If he didn't exercise the same self-control, he would quickly show the true power of Five Score and Ten, or FSAT as Ed had named it. She ran the numbers. If he were average build of, say, five feet nine, 190 pounds, and around forty-five? He would exceed the strength she had demonstrated within . . .

Jennifer sighed. Her cover could be blown within three to five days. Worse, within about two days they would realize how quickly he was metabolizing the coma-inducing meds, and they would figure out that she had been playing them. Unless he also learned to trick the EEG, which was highly unlikely. Consequence if he didn't? One way or another, Jennifer might have three days to break loose and escape, at the most. Or she never would.

Her thoughts were ripped to shreds by the sound of a man screaming in agony. Then loud thuds. A rifle shot. Running footsteps. A door slamming shut. More footsteps, shouts, and what sounded like a very large, very angry beast trying to break out of a solid room with reinforced walls.

Jennifer listened intently and was grateful for Dr. Winfred's clock chiming "eleven" to give her a time hack.

The man's screams continued. So did the pounding, as he slammed heavy equipment against the walls. He was in the next room! She could occasionally understand some of the heated conversations in the hallway. While she couldn't make out the voices, their raw fear was unmistakable.

" . . . Thought he was drugged!" (Slam.)

"Yeah, and I thought (Wham!) . . . restraints. "

"Broke them!"

Another loud concussion shook Jennifer's wall. Was he going to break through and put her at risk?

"Didn't miss! Right in the stomach!"

"Next shot will be a real bullet . . . a full clip!"

Her wall shuddered again.

"Boss will be upset!"

"Not his life on the line. This guy's three times what that woman . . . " (Slam!)

The man screamed again. And again. There was a lighter blow against the wall. Silence for the better part of twenty seconds. A very light blow against the door. A soft thud. Then nothing.

Jennifer's mind raced. This was completely different from her experience, or what she had learned about Bull. This man's strength seemed to have increased much faster than either of theirs. What about intelligence? She knew that if he had continued hitting the same spot again and again, he likely would have broken through their adjacent wall, even with what sounded like plywood reinforcement. He should have thought of that with even normal intelligence.

Two points came to mind. She and Bull had both taken a capsule, based on the original antediluvian fruit. Absorbed through the stomach and intestines. This man was one-off; he was either given something by mouth, or more likely was injected. Second, if it were based on blood serum? As careful as Greg may have been, there could have been an issue with incompatible blood types. A third thought crossed her mind. Even if everything was perfect, a sudden direct-to-bloodstream injection could have simply overwhelmed the man's system. Far too much, far too quickly.

Ultimately, though, the outcome was likely merciful. Whatever the differences that allowed her to survive FSAT, it had slowly and painfully killed Bull—or it would have if he hadn't died in the wreck.

For Jennifer? *Maybe I'll have a reprieve; maybe a few more days to prepare an escape.*

Her hopes were short-lived.

JR arrived just before noon. She heard him order everyone to the hallway outside her door. A minute later, he addressed them all with a slow, commanding voice that implied unimaginable threats.

"There's a unique, higher calling on my life. You'll be a part of making that happen. I won't let anything get in the way of my destiny,"

Jennifer couldn't know all that happened next. She could tell that JR wasn't making them comfortable. She calculated that each interview, if that's what it was, lasted about ten minutes. Greg, the genetic researcher, was the last person called in. After that, JR left.

Lanora came in to help her to the bathroom, and the shackles she now used were far more substantial, and tighter than normal.

The team didn't make it back to her room until two. They were noticeably somber. Edgar Foley doubled her bed restraints. Dr. Winfred increased her IV. Once they were through taking notes and pictures, they left. A security guard with a tranquilizer gun stayed. He also had a large caliber handgun clearly visible, within reach.

Jennifer's late lunch was okay; not great. She didn't have much of an appetite.

## 33.  DILEMMAS

The merciless testing of the "left and right limits" of Jennifer's enhanced physiology continued. For the next week—she could tell, thanks to Dr. Winfred's clock—they tested how her body responded to fasting. They withheld food for two days and again hit her with electric shocks to see how much the fasting reduced her strength. She made sure to appear that it did, significantly. Next, they gave her food, and withheld water for a day, while repeating the shock test. She made sure it showed even less strength. The last thing she needed was for them to suspect that her strength was continuing to increase.

Jennifer remembered Ed sharing that, at least notionally, it seemed that strength and intelligence would continue to increase at a certain rate upon every doubling of time since taking the capsule. A certain increase in strength in one hour; more after two hours, then four, then sixteen, then 256 or ten-and-a-half days. The next increment would be gradual over seven-and-a-half years. But simultaneously, there would be less of an increase with each doubling. She experienced an incredible surge of strength in the first few hours; less after sixteen, even less after the ten-and-a-half days.

Same for intelligence. There would likely be an upper limit regardless of how long she lived. But already, she suspected her intelligence had nearly doubled.

It all made sense. She had thought it through dozens of times. But it wasn't happening. She was holding back, yes. Yet based on her strength just two hours after taking FSAT, she should now easily be stronger than the poor soul who had just died next door. If he broke those bonds, she should be able to break hers . . . even the new, stronger ones . . . without even trying. The few times she felt she could try without drawing too much attention? The older, lighter restraints?

*Maybe Dr. Winfred's drugs are having an impact after all,* she thought.

The rest of the week's tests were fearsome, and only Rodney, Lanora, and the ever-present Dr. Winfred came into her room for days.

They wore HazMat suits.

Outside her room, at least ten hours each day, there was the sound of construction. She thought at first that they were making repairs to the room next to hers. Then, it sounded like they were building some kind of a chamber in an adjacent area. The construction was as ominous as the injections Rodney was giving her.

+  +  +

Pat looked through the binoculars again. As usual, he had parked in his clandestine spot a full quarter-mile from the industrial complex. He then verified that the other car was not where he had seen it before. Finally, he followed a path off to the side so he could approach the facility's fence without leaving tracks.

Pat spent nearly an hour looking at the facility, mostly at the one building where several vehicles were parked. But something about a shack, maybe 150 yards from there, around sixty yards from him, kept drawing him back as it had several times before.

*What is it?*

He wished he had some serious binoculars, or a camera with a quality telephoto lens. He found a tree he could lean against to hold the lenses steady, and he could just barely make out some small, black cables coming out from the top of the shack. That was it. They were not part of the neat power, telephone, and other wiring around the plant. No, this was thrown up quickly, not a union job. He traced the sloppy wiring up and over. Were those cameras? He counted three cameras in different locations. They all appeared to be pointing at one location. The building.

Pat walked along the fence line closer to the shack and realized that he was also approaching the place he had spotted the other car. The sun was starting to set and he would soon need to get back to his own car; he didn't even have a flashlight. But there was something peculiar. He approached within ten yards, so he wouldn't add his tracks to those that he saw leading up to the fence. The tracks continued toward the shack, through a section of fence that had been cut, and could be pulled away and put back without being obvious unless you were within ten yards.

"So . . . " Pat struggled, trying to connect the dots.

"So, someone is aware of what's going on, and is secretly watching. More likely, recording. Maybe sneaking in late at night to swap out tapes," he muttered.

+ + +

"Guys, I'd be proud to have either of you on my team. Well, we've actually been a team," Sam said, as Ed and Mick sat in her apartment after dinner. "But, look, we've done all we can. I'm not going to stop, and I know neither of you will. I just don't know any more we can do right now."

She looked at the two men, emotions welling up within her. Ditsy Jennifer had saved her life. All of theirs. She was now completely unique, alone, and in extreme danger if not already dead. They would not give up on her, but the men had to get back to paying jobs or they would both have to move in with her.

That was the other quandary. She and Mick hadn't dated since they went to the safe house. The three had met every night for almost a month after Jennifer was kidnapped. That was a mixed blessing, because during those few days that Ed Richardson stayed on her couch, she had developed very strong feelings for the doctor. Mature, focused, humble, ripped . . .

Her thoughts were interrupted, just as she had started to blush.

"I've checked with every potential supplier on Ed's list, every single week. They know me by name. Nothing," Mick said. "I found a machine shop looking for an apprentice, and I can make calls before they open each morning."

Ed sighed. "I should be able to sign on at an urgent care facility, twenty or so hours a week."

Sam's heart skipped a beat. Maybe . . . ?

Again, Mick interrupted her thoughts. She also admired his spontaneity, his spunk. "Can we still meet two or three times a week? And call each other if anything breaks loose?"

"Of course," Sam said.

Ed looked off in the distance, hung his head slightly, and whispered:

"Jennifer."

Sam's heart sank.

+  +  +

Jennifer never traveled much while growing up. She hardly ever saw her father. Her mother made sure of that. When she wasn't in prison, her mother had to work two jobs to support them. Then, she was overcome by cancer and died just before her only child entered puberty. After that, years of foster care. No, Jennifer hadn't traveled much. And never to the far north. She hadn't really known what extreme, bitter cold was like. Until now.

The construction noise she had heard for several days was an environmental chamber being assembled. She was now shackled inside. Despite complaints and threats by Lanora, Jennifer had been stripped down to just an adult diaper. Her only other covering was strong adhesive tape, tightly securing dozens of electrodes and sensors. She was laid on a table, on a thin mattress . . . her only isolation from the cold. The shackles on her arms and legs drew them down to the bed, preventing her from yanking the electrodes loose.

Even the IV tube had been removed. The fluids would have frozen in minutes at minus forty degrees Fahrenheit. Or, more scientifically, minus forty degrees Celsius. It didn't matter, as that was the one magic temperature where both scales read identically. It also didn't matter, because regardless of the scale, that extreme cold was life-threatening. Exposed flesh could begin to freeze in a few minutes. With most people.

Jennifer had been exposed for nearly four hours, when the soft hiss of the cooling equipment stopped. Just about the time she lost consciousness.

## 34.   PAT ON OFFENSE

Pat had struggled long enough. Days. Several weeks. This was life-and-death real, and it blazed a soul-searching spotlight deep into his miserable life. His personal crisis included realizing that he had treated his parents horribly for years.

Recently, it had all been about his "newspaper," his constant barrage against corrupt police. Yeah, a few bad cops. Mostly, they just held him accountable when he screwed up, to keep him from hurting himself and others.

Now? Along with constant checks on activity at the industrial complex while being careful not to run into the other "observer," Pat had lost a lot of sleep worrying about what he should do. He was likely the only "good guy" who knew where the strange woman was being held, for whatever sinister purpose. Was he committing a crime by not going to the police? Probably.

Time to man-up.

But what if something happened to him? Maybe he'd at least be remembered as a good person, maybe even a hero, if he made sure the right information got to the right people.

He printed all the information he had collected and made copies of the pictures he had taken of the complex and its activities. He sealed it all in a large manila envelope. Pat thought long and hard, and finally decided to address it to the police precinct where Dwayne worked, and wrote "To Be Opened by Dwayne Wilson Only" boldly across the bottom. Yes, Dwayne had issues and made some mistakes. But if Pat had gone to the commander with his information, gleaned from looking at records from neighboring counties, rather than blasting it in his "paper?" Pat hoped Dwayne could recover, and maybe breaking this case could help.

He hand-wrote a note that he taped to the outside, asking his mother and father for their forgiveness for his years of irresponsibility. He didn't go into any detail about his plans—he just told them to mail the package first thing Monday morning if he hadn't returned. That was the one day of the week his mother would come into his basement "apartment" unannounced, to collect his dirty laundry.

To make sure his mother would see the package in his cluttered room, he made his bed for the first time in years. He set the package right in the middle of the bedspread.

It was Thursday, 9 p.m.; five hours before the other observer typically went to his shack to swap out videotapes. Pat had figured that the cameras were not "live," but recorded to videotapes, which were retrieved and swapped out with fresh tapes daily. Two consecutive nights, he drove by where he had seen the other car, ten minutes after every hour. Each night, the car was there by 2:10 a.m. and was gone by 3:10 a.m.

Dressed in black, Pat drove to his own secluded parking spot, grabbed his camera, and locked the car. He walked down his own quarter mile path to the fence, then along the fence to the loose section. He was grateful that recent dry weather would hide any tracks. He quietly slipped into the dark industrial park.

Pat had studied up on the confusing world of video surveillance cameras, but he had no idea how good these were. Since there was no outside lighting—most likely to make anyone passing by think the warehouse was still abandoned—he hoped the men inside couldn't see far outside in the dark. Still, he walked a long distance before approaching the warehouse where all the activity was, constantly watching out for any guards. They typically emerged every several hours, and only for a few minutes. Maybe they were overconfident? He certainly hoped so.

Pat had never been so afraid. He tiptoed around the back of the building, hoping to find a window or an open door. He took several pictures with his point-and-shoot, which was all he could afford. He hoped the high-speed film would help. Fortunately, the camera was quiet. So far, though, there was nothing he could put in his planned "exposé" and report to authorities.

Decision time. Either go back the way he came, get a good night's sleep, and go to the authorities in the morning. *Or?* Walk across the front of the complex. Pat struggled for five minutes. He even walked halfway back around the building to relieve himself, and then came back to the corner. Finally, he stepped around in front, and made his way to behind the five vehicles parked there. He pulled out a notepad and a small keychain flashlight and wrote down vehicle descriptions and license tag information for each one.

Before he finished his notes, several things happened in rapid succession. None were good. An overhead light, a good ten feet above the large awning that covered the main warehouse doorway, flooded the area with light. Pat squatted behind the last car, as the warehouse door opened and a man stepped out. The man lit a cigarette and walked toward the cars. Only then did Pat realize that a vehicle had pulled through the gate and was driving toward the warehouse. He barely had time to cower around the far corner of the car, trying to quiet his pounding heart and wheezing breath.

The car pulled up and the sole occupant stepped out. The man with the cigarette tossed his smoke to the ground, snuffed it out under foot, and joined the driver. Without exchanging a word, the two walked toward the warehouse.

That's when Pat dropped his camera.

+ + +

JR spoke quietly into his phone. "Go ahead."

"Sorry to call so early. Thought you'd want to know something," said Skylar.

"Quite alright. That's what I need and expect."

"Well, I finished reviewing yesterday's tapes. And last night? Time hack of, uh, just after 10 p.m. A light came on at the warehouse—like often happens when they're expecting someone?"

"Go on."

"Yes. Well, so, here's the thing. As soon as the cameras adjusted, I saw some dude huddled behind one of the cars. Somebody came outside, couldn't tell who, and the intruder ducked behind a car. About that time a sedan drove up. Same one, a green Cadillac, I see for an hour or so just about every day. Anyway, the guy scoots around the car and the two men start toward the building. Guess the intruder makes a noise or something. They run around the car, get the guy, and pull him into the building."

"An intruder. Last night."

"Right," Skylar said, excitedly. "And, he never left. Neither did the

144 Five Score and Ten

Cadillac. At least not by the time I got the tape. You better believe, I'll be watching for that tonight."

"Good work, young man. Very good. Be sure you do that. Anything else?"

"Uh, no sir. Just thought this would be the kind of unusual activity you'd want me to report."

"You're absolutely correct. Goodbye."

JR smiled and slid his phone into his blazer pocket. He stepped back into the side room near the warehouse entrance—the room where a man was tied to a chair, his bloodied head bobbing slowly.

"What would you like me to do, JR?" asked Edgar. His expression made it clear that he could clean the guy up, feed him, and let him go. Or, just as easily, strangle him and toss him in a dumpster.

"Some lone-wolf wannabe. Nothing more he can tell us, and nobody important will miss him. Tell Rodney and Greg that we've got our next volunteer."

Without another word, JR walked out into the early morning dawn, stepped into his green Cadillac, drove to the security gate, entered his passcode, and drove out of the industrial park.

## 35.  NOW THREE

"**W**ell, yes, alright now. Um-hmm. Good, you're coming around. More interesting data you gave us there, young lady. World records. No frostbite. Yes, very interesting indeed."

*Dr. Winfred. Just shut up!* Jennifer wanted to scream. But again, she had to play the game.

"Uhh . . . where . . . when . . . ?" she mumbled in her best drunk impersonation. She allowed her sleepy eyes to open and look around. She was out of the chamber, on a cot, and restrained. Thankfully, she was again dressed in modest exercise attire, likely Lanora's doing. Jennifer also noticed that she was in a different room than before. Dr. Winfred continued chatting as he adjusted her drips in the reattached IV.

"Yes, well, you're back, you're fine. Never seen, actually never heard of anything like it. Nope, never. And you've got some more company. Yes, indeed. Got here late last night. Greg's trying again. Coming along quite nice, now. You know?"

Satisfied, he patted her shoulder, turned, and walked out of the room.

Jennifer's eyes grew heavy. Her breathing slowed. Was it the ordeal in the temperature chamber? More meds? She was so tired . . .

+  +  +

*Where did all this come from?*

Pat wasn't thinking about his condition. Not directly. That would come in a few beats. His current amazement was the logical, almost scientific approach he was taking to analyze his circumstances. What was in that stuff they gave him this morning?

*High school? Sci-fi I've read or watched? TV?*

Regardless, his mind functioned at a level he'd never experienced, and in a manner that baffled him:

These people have already kidnapped and held an extraordinary woman against her will for weeks.

They've likely been testing her; possibly to duplicate her abilities for military, criminal, or other financial purposes.

They captured me, beat me, questioned me, and injected me with something that they are monitoring.

They want to see if it works on me.

Whether it does or doesn't, they do not intend for me to walk out of here alive.

It'll be days before my package gets to Dwayne and he brings a SWAT team.

Either I escape, or I die.

His conclusion was problematic. Other than a few faces he saw last night when he was captured, he'd only seen a couple of them since they injected him with whatever that stuff was, around 9 a.m. One man, Edgar, would dim the lights, tightly shackle him, unfasten the restraints, take off his blindfold, and walk him to the bathroom every four hours or so. Bring him back, and then reverse the procedure. Even with the room darkened, Pat's improving eyesight could make out a dim figure sitting in a chair off in a corner, with what appeared to be a rifle aimed at him.

The other man, Julian, had taped electrodes to his head and would hook up a machine to them every two hours. He also drew blood every hour, and did other things with and around him that Pat didn't understand.

At least two men, plus the guy in the corner. He had no idea how many others he might have to contend with.

Edgar and Julian wouldn't let him talk beyond basics. When he tried to ask questions or start a conversation, they taped his mouth.

It was like they were waiting for something. But what? He had no idea.

*Either I escape or I die.*

Escape? Pat's hearing continued to improve. Also, his eyesight, at least as much as he could tell during his few bathroom trips. His strength? Oh, yeah. He would slowly pull against the restraints and hear the bed creak. He didn't want them to know what he was thinking. What if he exerted all his growing strength, maybe just using his left arm, which was stronger, with his legs and right arm holding firm for good grip? If he could break that one strap, yank off the blindfold, free his right arm, and then his legs? Pat suspected that he could move much faster now as well.

How much stronger might he get? How much faster? How soon? *Where's the woman?*

If he could break free and locate her, the two of them might have a chance. Sure, either or both of them might get wounded. She seemed to heal quickly. Would he?

What was the alternative? He kept analyzing, speculating, planning. Trying to think things through.

His improved hearing could just barely make out the sound of a clock, the old-fashioned kind that chimed. He counted eight bells; Friday night, eight o'clock. Almost twelve hours since his injection.

+ + +

Dwayne Wilson was also trying to think things through. At ten on that same Friday night, in the bar he used to frequent, he stared at the single cube of ice he allowed in his double Scotch. He thought about those many times when he told his nagging wife that he had to work late. Now he was trapped, and he was trying to find a way out of a snare of his own creation.

The pieces were coming together. How many times had Debbie tried to tell him? But now, during divorce depositions, he couldn't just storm out. He had to listen. He had to respond. In the sterile, legal environment he was so familiar with as a long-time police officer? He was laid bare.

Dwayne glanced at his too-familiar surroundings. He didn't just come here on occasional Friday nights. He was usually here at least one other night each week. Sometimes twice. Often till well past midnight, watching football, playing pool, shooting the breeze with other cops, lawyers, doctors. All the "in" crowd, who were likely dumping all the home and family responsibilities on their wives, too.

Dumping. That hurt. Brandon Wells, his wife's attorney, had asked him how police partners operated. Dwayne went into his lecture mode, and explained the balance of responsibilities, how they would back each other up and split the workload. How they would risk their own lives to ensure their partner's safety and well-being. Why? Because they were a team. Their jobs, their mission, their very lives depended on it.

Wells had just looked at Dwayne and let the silence linger. Even the stenographer looked up. Then? The Question.

"Mr. Wilson. Would you say that you have consistently afforded Mrs. Wilson the same degree of partnership during these years of your marriage?"

Dwayne replayed the moment and hung his head. No pool tonight. No football. He was at a table by himself in a dark corner. Judy, a waitress he had known for years, brought him another drink, briefly touched his shoulder, and went to her next table.

Years of lies. Years of Debbie taking the kids to daycare. Picking up the kids from daycare. Making the beds each morning, cooking dinner each night—which he often missed. Picking up clothes which he rarely put in the hamper, which he never hung back up even if they were still clean. Washing. Folding. Putting away. Cleaning. Something needing repair? She handled it. Why? He was always "too busy." Same with her car. Her car? The one she used to drive the kids to daycare, later to school, and then to all their many other activities. *Our kids.* He rarely participated unless it was something he wanted to be a part of, or be seen at. *Her car. Always several years older than mine.*

Intimacy. Emotional intimacy for her sake? Forget it. Physical intimacy, primarily for his sake? He expected it, and he couldn't understand why after taking care of the home, the car, the children, and him . . . plus her own stressful full-time job . . . she was often "too tired."

He had a pretty good physique during the early years of their marriage, and he would maintain it by going to the gym on a regular basis. "Have to stay fit for police work," he'd tell Debbie. She never had time to take care of herself. She didn't lose weight after the first one before getting pregnant again. She was still twenty pounds overweight. And tired.

She nagged. He isolated himself even more. And especially in his younger days? There were nights when he was out late, that he wasn't with the guys.

Dwayne finished his drink, paid his tab, and walked to his car. He'd have at least one more nightcap once he made it back to the apartment he had recently moved into.

Had he consistently afforded Debbie the same degree of partnership during their marriage as he did on the force?

He drove to his empty apartment. Lonely and more ashamed than he'd ever been, he drank himself to sleep.

## 36.  SHALL WE CONTINUE

Saturday morning, and for Jennifer it was *déjà vu* all over again. This time, it was heat. Dr. Winfred wasn't concerned that the heat would bother the meds themselves, but he didn't trust the electronic IV dispensing equipment to operate correctly at the temperatures they were dialing into the chamber. He disconnected the IV tube.

Jennifer was stripped down as before, electrodes in place and held firmly by a bath cap against the expected heat and sweat. The wires snaked through a port in the chamber, where Dr. Winfred could monitor the EEG in comfort. Jennifer did sweat. They increased chamber conditions to mimic the heat of mid-afternoon in Death Valley, in the dead of summer.

She was miserable. Yet still, knowing the electrodes were monitoring her brain activity, she had to manage her EEG readings. She had to allow them to slowly increase to near normal as the meds wore off, then get erratic due to the heat. The latter would be easy. The former? Not so much.

+ + +

Not far away, Pat was also miserable. He could not have cared less what his EEG or any other readings may have shown. His head hurt, his body ached as if he had a bad case of the flu, and his major muscles had begun twitching. He felt a wave of anxiety welling up and had to control his breathing to keep from hyperventilating. They, whoever "they" were, had covered his mouth hours before and had just left the duct tape in place, forcing him to breathe through his nose.

Pat wasn't angry. He was glad he had written the letter to his parents, and he hoped they would understand and forgive him. But he was determined. Whatever was going on with him, he likely wouldn't be around when Dwayne got permission to assemble a SWAT team and storm the place, or when they turned Pat's package over to the GBI or

FBI. So . . .

He took several long, slow breaths. He increased tension against all the straps, and with all his might he pulled his left hand toward his chest.

The bed frame moaned and bent.

"He's trying to break free!" A man shouted from the corner of the room, where Pat knew an armed guard had been posted. "Lay down or I'll shoot to kill! Do it now!" He knocked his chair over as he jumped to his feet.

Pat redoubled his efforts. He couldn't tell if the straps or the bedframe were about to give. Suddenly, a metal clasp holding the arm restraint to the strap attached to the bed bent and broke.

"He's getting loose!" the man bellowed.

Pat carried through with the momentum toward his right side, causing the entire bed to fall over. The tranquilizer dart fired harmlessly into the bottom of the bed. At the same time, he grabbed his right restraint. Now that he knew where the weak link was, he was free of that in moments.

More gunshots, clearly not from a tranquilizer rifle. But the 9 mm bullets were high, as the bed was being pushed toward the gunman at a full sprint; right edge sliding across the floor, left edge facing up, and the back of the bed straight at the man. Pat, as un-athletic as he had been his entire almost-thirty-years? He was hunched over low like a linebacker, the broken restraints flapping from his wrists and feet.

The gunshots ceased as the heavy bedframe slammed the man against the wall.

Pat yanked the tape off his mouth and gulped in huge breaths as he ran for the only door he could find in the room. *Best defense is a good offense,* he thought as he yanked it open and ran directly into two men almost twice his size. Their guns were drawn, yet before they could squeeze off rounds he pushed between them, shoving them apart and throwing off their aim. Their shots went wild. A third man was running toward him. He stopped, faced Pat directly, and put three .38 Special rounds into his chest in two seconds. Pat was dead before he hit the floor.

+ + +

"Yes, yes indeed. Let's get you hooked back up. Goodness. Glad something is working around here," Dr. Winfred muttered as he nervously reattached the IV lines from the two bags and the machine into Jennifer's line. She was sweating profusely and heard that her core temperature was up to 104 when they brought her out.

"My, my. Okay, no more. No one. Don't care what they say. I run things, we're all safe. They run things? People die."

*Someone died? The guy from yesterday?* she wondered.

Lanora entered, with a light sheet to cover Jennifer for modesty, and a small fan to blow cool air to help bring Jennifer's temperature back down.

Jennifer reveled in the delightful, cool breeze. She even welcomed the IV meds, which seemed a little stronger than before.

She continued to relax, re-evaluating her current status.

They didn't know about her intelligence. They didn't know how successfully she'd deceived the EEG. What Dr. Winfred believed was a Stage 3 coma state was actually more of a light buzz, like drinking a single beer during her college days. While he'd increased the IVs several times, it was more like a dirty martini strong, at the most.

She was less encouraged about her physical strength. It should have fully doubled from the time she confronted the men at the safe house. Something was suppressing it.

To her advantage, though, everyone except Lanora continued to think of her more as a "subject," not a person. Jennifer remembered a *Reader's Digest* joke about a young doctor treating an elderly lady. When he needed to ask questions or discuss her condition, he would ignore her and talk to her daughter. During one such encounter, the elderly woman spoke up. "Sonny," she asked sweetly. "Do you do crossword puzzles?" Baffled, he responded, "Well, yes Ma'am. Sometimes I do when I'm traveling." "Good for you," she smiled. "Do you use a pencil or a pen?" "Well, uh, I guess I use a pencil." The lady's smile grew wider. "I use a pen."

Like that doctor, JR's team didn't take Jennifer seriously. They talked openly around her, and she learned all their strengths, their weaknesses, and just as importantly, information about the facility. She learned about tests they had considered, tests they were planning, and

Greg's progress on his serum. Greg didn't brag. He didn't need to. Jennifer was convinced that the man knew what he was doing, which added to her conviction that she had to break loose and bring the law down on the team. Or take care of matters herself.

Greg planned to cut the dose in half, and that the next "subject" would be a woman with the same blood type as Jennifer's. It all made sense; eliminate as many variables as possible and reduce the sudden impact on the body. Jennifer assumed that they would still fail without the person also being under significant stress and, within a few hours, an exceptionally high level of adrenalin. In her case, she had also been exposed to pure oxygen, if that made any difference. She suspected that there was still some missing ingredient; a "secret sauce" that allowed her to live yet killed Bull. And now, two more.

She heard Lanora humming to herself as she walked past the door. Lanora was the "odd person out." She was not as gruff when she exchanged the shackles for manacles to walk the compliant, Stage 3 Jennifer to the bathroom, or to the shower every other day or so, or to help her with other personal needs. But even Lanora was careful not to underestimate Jennifer's strength. Very careful. So far.

Jennifer stopped her analysis and began silently praying. Maybe because she was dehydrated, or hungry, or just tired . . .

After several more minutes she was in a deep sleep.

## 37.   DRAKE AND ANGELO

Jennifer enjoyed a long night of rest recovering from the heat stress. She had a large breakfast, and Lanora helped her bathe.

Once secured back to her bed, Lanora rolled her back into the chamber. She had thought the chamber was built for more than just temperature testing, and she was right.

The chamber was also built to test her response to altitude. Denver, Colorado. Then Pike's Peak. They simulated the air pressure as if she were climbing up Everest. Would she suffer from altitude sickness? Would her lungs fill with fluid, High Altitude Pulmonary Edema? They didn't take her all the way to that altitude, just to the "dead zone" level of 26,000 feet above sea level. But they did it at a perilous rate of 2,000 feet every six hours. That was much faster than an actual climber would ascend. It provided far less time to acclimate.

+  +  +

Sunday night, Skylar noticed that the Oldsmobile he had discovered about a quarter of a mile from the complex, was gone. He had walked around the complex after spotting the intruder on his videotapes, found the old car, and reported it to JR along with the tag number. And now it was gone. JR seemed pleased when Skylar called him Monday morning and reported that the car was no longer there, and he agreed with Skylar's assessment that it had likely just broken down and been towed.

What Skylar didn't know was that on Monday afternoon, the car and its owner were found in a different county, partially submerged in a shallow lake. The official report was that Pat Jernigan was drunk and lost control. The report conveniently omitted the part about the bullet holes.

What neither Skylar nor JR knew, was that earlier Monday, Pat's mother had followed his instructions and mailed the package.

+ + +


At 6 a.m. Wednesday morning, Dr. Winfred terminated the altitude test because the IVs were running low. They took the next hour to bring Jennifer "back down" to sea level pressure.

As best they had been able to tell from visual observations, along with Jennifer's carefully-suppressed EEG readings and other telemetry, she hadn't experienced any ill effects.

From her perspective, Jennifer had plenty of food and water she could reach from her bed. The worst part was being in the adult diaper again. Her most difficult challenge? Continuing to spoof the EEG all three days of the test.

Once she was back to sea level, they opened the chamber. They changed her manacles back to shackles and Lanora took her to the bathroom to clean her up.

Other than securing her back to her bed, removing the EEG tabs, and refilling the IV stand, Jennifer was again "the invisible woman." They talked; she listened.

Dr. Winfred and Greg discussed the progress of their new subject. She seemed to be doing remarkably well. All evidence from her years of severe drug abuse were already gone. She was articulate, her strength was increasing, and she seemed to be in good spirits. Apparently, they had convinced her that her trial was federally funded and she had been specifically chosen. Further, that she would receive a large financial pay-out and an ongoing stipend for the duration of the follow-up.

Good scam, Jennifer mused. Wonder how they explain the shackles?

After they left, she overheard another conversation outside her door. She recognized the voices as two of JR's "security" team, the apparent leaders; Drake Cavanaugh and Angelo. "Just, Angelo," he would say as he introduced himself, the only time Jennifer actually saw the man. All she had learned about him, is that his parents had escaped from Cuba as it was falling to Castro. Angelo had quickly made a name for himself in south Florida gangs, and was now near the top of the food chain of JR's Miami operation. He stood only about five-feet-six, and he was stocky; maybe around 230 pounds. Dark, short hair, slightly receding, squarish face, dimpled chin. He looked to be around forty-six.

She had seen Drake more often. He frequently took the "tranquilizer gun" detail and would sit quietly in the corner of her room for hours. But he would, occasionally, chat with the medical team, as JR called them. Drake was from Chicago and made his way up through a different type of gang; the back-room illegal activities and occasional violence of Big Unions. He even boasted of the early-90s statistics of crimes in Chicago. In a single year, "the Windy City" recorded almost 3,000 violent crimes, leading Oakland, Los Angeles, New York City, and New Orleans. It's like he played a personal part in the notoriety and was proud of it.

Drake looked a few years younger than Angelo. Maybe forty-three or forty-four. He was taller and not as heavyset; maybe five-feet-ten and 190. His dark hair was curly, and he kept his beard closely trimmed like a three- or four-day growth. Where Angelo might have to carefully dress to avoid looking like a thug, Drake looked out of place unless he was wearing a sport jacket. Regardless, neither looked pleasant.

Jennifer shuddered. JR had surrounded himself with people completely devoid of conscience. Jennifer hadn't paid much attention to her classes in high school and college. They interfered with her higher priorities of boys, partying, and booze. But FSAT allowed her to "replay the tapes" as it were, in fast-forward, and learn all that she had been exposed to. Even as she intently listened to the men in the hallway, she thought back to stories about World War II.

Hitler had intentionally surrounded himself with young men without conscience. If they didn't like someone, they would summarily execute him. They were a law unto themselves. He had even stated that as his goal. He wanted to raise a generation of young people devoid of conscience—imperious, relentless, and cruel.

She remembered other stories. The "medical experiments." Horrible tests to determine the limits of what a human being could endure. Extreme heat, cold, transplants, high altitudes, deprivation, and more. *Just like me*, Jennifer realized. Then, there was the direct war-related experimentation; wounds, head injuries, disease and chemical warfare experiments, effects of incendiary bombs, poison, and much more.

Didn't matter if the subject was a man, woman, or child. Or, how much it hurt. They were simply test subjects.

"Bored stiff," said Angelo.

"Not my kinda action either," agreed Drake.

"So, she's it? She's all he's got? That why the man spendin' all the green on this op?"

"Well," Drake mused, "he's got a lotta blood and other stuff from her. They did that before doing the dangerous stuff. Day before you got here, I learned that she took out a couple of guys JR brought in from Yuma. Unarmed. Single-handedly. Nasty. They were checking out the doctor in charge of research, but JR's convinced he's lost everything. They tried real hard to break him; got nothing. Yeah, she's it."

"His research?" Angelo asked.

"That, along with whatever stuff the research was based on. Some kind of archeological find. Jurassic Park kinda stuff," Drake said.

"Come on, man. Somethin' that important? Like, you know, world changin'? Had to be more than just one doc involved," Angelo muttered.

"Hmm. Good point. The lab's owner was killed . . . long story . . . and the research assistant died when the place got bombed. But you know . . . "

Drake's line of thinking was interrupted by Lanora bringing dinner.

" 'Scuse me, guys. One of you get the door?"

The door opened and Lanora entered with a tray, and Jennifer could hear the departing footsteps of Angelo and Drake. She hadn't realized just how hungry she was. Yet as good as Lanora's cooking was, Jennifer couldn't help being distracted by Drake's line of reasoning. Could there be anyone else they might put in danger? Would they go back after Ed?

## 38.  MERCILESS

*N*ot again.

Thursday morning, Jennifer was startled by a woman's screams in the room next to hers. Subject #4 was in severe distress. No words, just screams of pain. Apparently, the shackles were holding, as there was just the sound of the gurney bouncing around.

The screams increased. Jennifer had trouble making out the conversations in the hall, far less fearful this time. She caught Lanora asking Dr. Winfred to show some mercy. Several minutes later, the screams ended. Jennifer heard mumbling in the adjacent room for several minutes, and the squeak of the gurney's wheels as it was rolled down the hall.

Greg's adjustments had slowed the transformation and allowed it to progress farther. But it still killed her, Jennifer thought. And still more quickly than with Bull. She shuddered.

An hour later, she heard voices outside her door. Actually, just one. JR. And it was not a pep talk.

"Not pleased. Not at all. No screw-ups. Medical, I expect results. Security, stay tight. And everyone, I mean every single one of you, I expect you to fight to the death to keep this woman alive. You come under attack? Fight. Get her out of here to our reconstitution location and call in. But she lives. Got it?"

The silent response was deafening. Jennifer rightly assumed that heads were solemnly nodding up and down.

"She's our only link to the success of this stuff. Security, make sure Medical has handguns and they know how to use them. Get more test subjects if they need them. Greg . . . "

A few moments later, Jennifer's room lights came on. Greg and JR walked in and stood over her.

Jennifer moaned and fluttered her eyes. Even with her act, she could discern two things. Greg was nervous, and JR was struggling to maintain self-control. The man's clenched jaw, glaring eyes, ruddy complexion, tightening neck muscles? He was clearly furious.

"Tell me you're going to be able to find a way, Greg." His words were soft and slow. They sounded like a threat.

"Uh, JR, we, uh, we're dealing with something beyond human here. I mean, this stuff could have come here from a UFO, or, uh, I don't know, maybe God Almighty . . . "

JR snapped his head at Greg, glaring.

"I mean," the nervous geneticist continued, "no one has ever seen anything like this. Never. Uh . . . "

He stared at the floor, stuck his hands in his lab coat pockets, and began pacing, as much as anything to keep from staring into the glaring eyes of JR.

"So, it's not going to be easy. We'll have to go in stages. Frankly, kinda ugly. But look," He stopped, placed his hands on the foot of Jennifer's gurney, and regained eye contact. "JR, we're going to have to slow this process down first. Yeah, we'll lose some more subjects. But we have to slow it down enough to better study it, better understand what's going on, and see what we need to change. Make sense?" he asked, almost pleading.

"Do it. Make this happen. Angelo and Drake's guys will get you all the subjects you need; just be specific. Now, get me Winfred. Then tell everyone to leave the building. Lock up, take a long lunch, whatever. Be back at," he glanced at his watch, "two. And, turn off all the cameras. Go."

Without a word, Greg left and Dr. Winfred stepped in.

"Well, uh, hello JR. Hmm. Good morning, sir," he said as he wrung his hands.

"She okay continuing on these meds?"

"Why, uh, yes indeed. Yes, sir. She's doing very well. Uh, shouldn't be any problem for several more weeks at least. Checking EEG, checking urine. Oh, yes. She's fine."

JR took a slow, deep breath, clearly not in the mood for Dr. Winfred's stammering.

"Listen carefully. Make sure that she is. Now, I want you to put her under deeper for the next few hours. Not unconscious, just deep. Safe. Can you do that?"

"Oh, uh, yes, Sir. Certainly," he adjusted the IV drips and watched. "Yes, sir. That should be just right, and the bags will be good for?" he glanced at the two IV bags on the stand. "Yes, well, they should be good for at least three hours, so . . . "

"Leave. Go off for a while. Be back at the facility with the others at two."

"Uh, yes, sir. Certainly," said Dr. Winfred as he glanced again at Jennifer, the IV pumps, and the bags. As Dr. Winfred stepped out, Greg stuck his head in. "All cameras and recorders are off, sir." He didn't bother to ask why.

Jennifer had no idea what to expect. Should she act asleep, or hungry, or moan about going to the bathroom? She had been moaning occasionally, slowly moving her head, and fluttering. But she started acting groggier to make it appear that Winfred's drugs were working. She didn't have to act much. She already felt at about the three-beer level, heading toward four.

JR just stood over her, glowering down at her.

Then he spoke.

"So, you're trying to keep all the secrets to yourself. Not going to happen. I own you." He spat the words out. "You're mine. And I will learn everything I want to know about you. All those secrets. Every last one of them."

He grabbed at her sports bra and tried to rip it off of her, lifting her up against the restraints. The material didn't tear, so he let go and let her fall back down on the gurney. Without taking his eyes off of her, he pulled out a locking knife with a six-inch blade and cleanly sliced through the material. He folded the knife, put it back in his pocket, and smiled. It wasn't pleasant.

"I have a higher calling, and guess what. You'll be a part of making that happen. I won't let anything get in the way of my destiny."

Jennifer knew this was her chance. Everyone was gone except JR. They wouldn't be back until long after she was gone. She tried to think clearly. How many days since FSAT? How much increase in intelligence and strength? How many more days until, for all practical purposes, she would max out? Questions came easily. The answers? Not so much.

*So tired . . . too many tests . . . too much from the IV . . .*

JR turned away from her and began removing his clothes, meticulously folding them and laying them on a desk. As quietly as she could and helped somewhat by the facility's noisy air conditioner, Jennifer struggled against the bonds. She knew she had to be pulling hundreds of pounds against each one, and the bed's heavy-duty metal frame began to deform.

+  +  +

Aaron Sims wasn't a focused grocery shopper. He paid for two bags of mostly microwavable meals and walked to his '88 Ford Taurus. As usual, he was distracted with his doctoral research and his lack of money, especially since his gig with Jackson Longevity Research Center was over. Yes, he had to admit, he was likely suffering a bout of depression with that as well. While he was being honest with himself, he had to admit a tinge of guilt as well. He put his groceries in the trunk, carefully stacking the cold items into an ice chest. He always tried to finish his grocery shopping early to avoid the crowds, but he still had to get the car's oil changed and tires rotated. He left the Publix parking lot and drove the thirty minutes to his appointment at the fast lube and service garage.

"It can't make any difference." He started the conversation with himself again, for the hundredth time.

"But, what if it could?"

"Ed said it was all over . . . nothing anyone could do now."

"Yeah, but . . . but what if this is what he needs to make this happen?"

Finally, "It can't do me any good."

There it was, the bottom line. The one small fruit from the strange plant, grown from a seed thousands of years old. The one he had slipped into a small Ziplock bag, and was now in his apartment freezer. Less than what Number 12 had consumed.

He thought of his grandmother. She was still with him through the words of wisdom she had shared during his early years. Her one statement ended the argument: "Do what's right. It's always the right time to do the right thing."

"Okay, Grams, I will," he resolved.

## 39. *VIOLATED*

JR's Cadillac was nowhere to be seen when the teams arrived back at precisely 2 p.m. Everything was locked up. He'd left evidence of his fury that none of them would ever forget.

"No! Oh, no. You men, out of here now. Right now!"

Medical, Security, it didn't matter. They each conveniently found something else they needed to do elsewhere, and left Lanora alone in the room with Jennifer. She had so enjoyed several hours away, to at least pretend she was living a normal life, that all was well in the world. She had even splurged and enjoyed one of her favorite buffets of Southern comfort food.

Now? Lanora felt sick to her stomach.

"Oh, honey, I'm so sorry. So sorry. Let's get you cleaned up and dressed, dear."

For the next thirty minutes, Lanora displayed a motherly, compassionate side that went far beyond anything Jennifer had ever witnessed. Jennifer was able to offer little help and even less resistance as the woman bathed her, helped her into fresh clothes, and put ointment on her chaffed wrists and ankles where she had strained against the constraints, and on the many bruises that someone else had caused. All the while, the matronly woman was gentle, using words like "honey," "dear," and calling her "Jen."

Throughout the weeks of "testing" and the drugs, Jennifer had remained strong and in control—completely unlike "college Jennifer" as she now described her former self. Now? She was physically and emotionally spent . . . and hurt in a much deeper way. She wept quietly as the woman helped her back onto the bed and stood beside her stroking her hair.

"Oh, honey, you just don't know. Just don't know." She sniffed and dabbed tears from her own eyes.

A profound realization struck Jennifer. This woman had also been abused in her life. Maybe as a child, or perhaps she had an abusive husband or boyfriend. Maybe the hardness she often projected was the result of years of abuse.

Jennifer looked at Lanora with a new understanding. For just a moment. Apparently, it showed.

Lanora startled. Just slightly. Then she quickly glanced at the cameras around the room. She bent down and gently rubbed some ointment on Jennifer's bruised shoulders.

"Honey, I think the cameras are still off," she whispered. "So. You may be more aware than what Julian says. Okay, listen. Please don't hurt me. You know JR has something on each of us. I don't care what he does to me, but he's got my little girl. His men in Miami, they've got my Jasmine. My baby's just twenty, and they've got her out on the street. Dealin' and . . . " Lanora sobbed. "Jen, your secret's safe. I'll try to help, just please . . . "

The door opened and Dr. Winfred came in.

"Lanora, uh, well, um. We all agree that I really need to check her IV and everything. You heard what the boss said. No screw-ups. Gotta keep us safe too, you know . . . "

Lanora gently squeezed Jennifer's hand as she stood up and started to back away. Without any other outward sign, Jennifer squeezed back. Firmly.

+  +  +

If anything, Aaron was even more distracted than usual as he carried his two bags of groceries up the two flights of steps to his efficiency apartment. He stepped past a casually-dressed Hispanic man and walked around the corner to his apartment. He set the bags down, unlocked his door, picked the bags back up, and walked in. The man followed him in and shut the door behind them.

"Aaron. Sit down."

The man used a very large caliber revolver to point to a chair.

Aaron sat, speechless and afraid.

"You worked for some kind of lab, researching, you know, stuff for long life. What you got, man? Look, I can walk out of here and leave you alive, or dead, or alive wishing you were dead. So, here's the deal. You got anything . . . anything at all . . . on this stuff? You give it to me. Now."

"Uh . . . "

Angelo walked over, shifted the revolver to his left hand, stuck his right hand into his pocket. When he pulled it back out it was encased in a large, heavy set of brass knuckles. He hit the left side of Aaron's head, up high, enough to make his point without knocking him out.

"You know something. Tell me now," he said, deadpan, holding his fist in front of the young man's face. A trickle of blood blended in with his red hair.

Aaron trembled. The thought that he could in any way protect himself from this muscular stranger was a non-starter.

"Uh, see, just one thing. Noth . . . nothing else. No research, no product, no . . . no . . . no notes. Nothing. Just . . . just," he glanced toward his refrigerator, just fifteen feet from where he sat in the small efficiency apartment.

Angelo followed his glance. "Get it," he commanded, backing up two steps. "And you pull out some kinda weapon? You try somethin' funny? You dead before you hit the floor. Whatcha getting?"

Aaron stood, rubbing his head. "A piece of fruit. Just one. In a Baggie. It's all that's left. Honest!"

Aaron staggered to his fridge, Angelo following several feet off to his side. Aaron opened the top freezer compartment, shifted a few things around, and pulled out the Baggie. He closed the door and leaned against the fridge.

"Give it," Angelo said, taking the bag in his knuckled hand and stuffing it in his pocket. "Anything else? You holding out on me?"

Aaron stared at his intruder, pleading. "This is all there is. It's, it's irreplaceable. Maybe it could help millions. So many, so much suffering. Please . . . "

"Nothin' else?" Angelo asked again.

Aaron stared at the floor. "Nothing."

Angelo struck him again with the brass knuckles.

Aaron no longer thought about his doctoral program, his moral dilemma, or even putting away his groceries. Not for many, many hours.

+ + +

"Hi, guys. Come on in. Got some news," Sam said as she let Ed and

Mick into her apartment. It was Thursday, 7:30 p.m.

They walked in and sat in their favorite places, while Sam stood and faced them. She already had glasses of iced tea sitting on coasters at their chairs to help with the sweltering evening heat.

"Commander Garrett called me in today. He's convinced that Jennifer's still in the area." The men's countenances immediately brightened.

"But here's the bad news. A while back he met with an informant who was going to try to find out where they were operating out of. The man's body was found over the weekend. He had been murdered and thrown in a dumpster."

"That's terrible," blurted Mick.

"It's worse. Garrett met with this guy last week, and understand, he and this informant go way back. The man knows . . . well, knew . . . the ropes, and he'd successfully survived in the shadows for many years. He said that this was bigger than drugs or basically anything he'd ever seen. Garrett thinks it's so big, so serious, that just asking around got the man killed."

"Like someone interested in the potential of a long-life formula with super strength and intelligence," said Ed.

"She is here. She's *here!*" Mick exclaimed.

"Guys, we've missed something. There has to be something, somewhere. Mick's right. And we've got to find her."

## 40. HUMILITY LOST

S everal things were different for Jennifer Friday morning. Lanora had outdone herself with a breakfast feast beyond anything she'd prepared up to that point. In her best "Stage 3" act, Jennifer groggily devoured every bite. All of her bruises had healed, at least the physical ones, and she knew she had to regain her strength. She could never let that happen to her again . . .

The Medical and Security teams seemed more subdued. For a few, or maybe just Dr. Winfred, Jennifer thought there might still be a shred of remaining decency. But the others? She suspected they would gladly do the same to her that JR had done, if they didn't fear his wrath.

They left her alone all day. Julian didn't even bother to take EEG readings. He did bring his daily news update as he changed out the IV bags, something he had to do more often with the higher "safety" dose.

"Yes, well. Okay, hope you enjoy a quiet day. Hopefully the lady next door will do much better, hmm? Yes, lowering the dose again. Just one eighth this time. Well, we'll see now, won't we?" he chattered.

Satisfied that the IV equipment was properly calibrated and feeding, he walked to the door.

"Yes, my, my. We'll see. Could all stand some good news today, hmm?"

Even the guard's chair remained empty.

+ + +

Dwayne Wilson woke up late, with another hangover. The unshaven face that stared back from the mirror appeared at least ten years older than the date on his driver's license, the one that had almost been revoked.

After his second cup of coffee, he forced himself to open the curtains, despite the pain of the strong morning sun. His eyes slowly adjusted to the light. He could see a small playground with children playing, before the hot summer afternoon would force most people back into air-conditioned buildings. The memory tapes in his mind played back earlier, happy days with his wife and kids.

*Humility.*

That's what changed. Like the old joke about the guy receiving an award for humility, and then having to give it back after taking his bow.

*I lost my humility.*

It started to be "all about Dwayne."

A boy ran after a kicked ball, toward a fence. Dwayne's radar pinged as he saw the child running toward a derelict on a park bench, hand clutching a bottle wrapped in a brown paper bag. The ball hit a tree and bounced back. The boy grabbed it and rejoined the other kids.

The man had watched the little boy, and then turned back around and took another drink from the bottle.

"Probably not a threat," mumbled Dwayne. "Just a drunk."

*Like me?*

The question wouldn't go away. No matter how many times he answered it, or how he answered, or however he tried to explain it all away.

*Like me?*

Thoughts of the hundreds of DUIs he had issued on the force, all the drunks he had put into jail to sober up, and the ones he'd taken to shelters to keep alive during Atlanta's occasional deep freezes.

The kids laughed and played on their way back into the daycare, and Dwayne realized that he might soon have grandkids.

What kind of grandfather will they have?

He went back through the mental records, everything he had heard about AA chapters, about treatment centers, counseling programs.

He remembered that it was Friday, and he had an interview scheduled for Tuesday for a possible position as a security guard. What would happen if he got another DUI and lost his license?

He thought of another program, something new that several men told him really helped them with their addictions and . . . other problems. It was called Celebrate Recovery.

Dwayne remembered that it was church based, but at this point he didn't care. He needed something that would work. His kids, potential future grandkids? He wanted them to have a man to look up to. Not some derelict drunk on a park bench sucking booze in the middle of a beautiful morning.

He reached for the *Yellow Pages.*

*Maybe it's time I admitted my life's a mess and I get some help?*

+  +  +

"Everything's documented in the report. Here's the executive summary. I wish the full team was here, but this will give you what you need to consider inviting me to your next meeting." JR handed Brazen the notebook.

Brazen, or rather, Vasilly Dvorak, now that they were meeting face-to-face in a secure location, admired the weight, thickness, and professional binding of what was obviously an extensive report. Rather than opening it, he set it to the side of his coffee cup and gave JR his full attention.

"The others send their regrets that they couldn't meet with you, Jason. As you can appreciate, our meetings are few, planned far in advance, and of utmost secrecy."

"I would expect nothing less," the former Congressional candidate replied. "I do believe they will find this helpful. I just appreciate that you were able to pick it up in person."

"My expertise is in finance. Our initiatives require considerable, well, actually exorbitant funding. I visit the U.S. at least quarterly to engage with some like-minded financiers." He picked up his coffee and took a sip, "So, let's hear where we've been wrong."

JR was careful not to take the bait. "Actually, I can't find anything wrong with what you're doing or how you're doing it," he stated flatly.

"Really?"

"You know this is all sound. It's worked everywhere else, and it will eventually work here. He began counting off points on his fingers. "For example, education has been centralized at the federal level. Sure, there are some private schools and home schooling. Not an issue, as they are well below critical mass. The federal government takes in taxes and carefully controls what goes back down to the states, and then to colleges, universities, and primary education. Directly or indirectly we regulate through accreditation, curricula, and even unions. We're keeping the appearance of free speech and open exchange of ideas, while each year we're tightening it in. Tweak what we want emphasized, and conveniently disregard what isn't, shall we say, relevant.

"Next? These kids are the vectors carrying our agenda throughout the country. They become the lawyers, news media, entertainers, politicians, and especially the civil servants who will put our agenda over the top when the time comes."

Vasily interrupted. "Civil servants? I don't follow."

JR smiled. "Oh, yes. A representative serves two years at a time. A senator? Six. Sure, many of them end up serving for decades, although that's not guaranteed. A president? No more than eight. Civil Service? A person can serve for a lifetime. By the time they reach Senior Executive Service, they can have considerable clout and influence that transcends a particular administration or even political party. Same at the state level. Best of all? There will come a time we'll be able to place them at top levels of key agencies."

Vasily smiled and considered the possibilities. "FBI. Department of Education. Department of Justice. Hmm."

"Even the IRS. Next, dependency."

Vasily nodded in agreement.

"As we discussed before, 'The Great Society.' Social Security. Welfare. Medicare. Medicaid. Even student loans. Everything that makes sense in, of, and by itself. But every benefit comes with several costs. Of course, there's the dependency issue. But you're also increasing taxes, the size of government, and the span of control. While giving the illusion of more freedom and a better life.

"One more example, and again, all these are good. Entertainment. Not just the arts that we've enjoyed for centuries, but mindless, almost mesmerizing, time-wasting distractions. At the least, you dumb down the populace so they can't think critically and evaluate what's going on all around them. Then, you add in our target social agenda while subtly attacking the detractors. Outcome? You open their thoughts to, shall we say, other persuasions."

"Granted," Vasily conceded. "So, why hasn't it worked?"

Now JR smiled. "You need a catalyst. Open to Page Four and let me introduce you to what I call, the 'Balaam Initiatives.' "

# 41.  CRISIS

*Just a little while longer.*

Jennifer's thoughts were an evaluation, a hope, and a promise. Friday had given her a needed break to recover and rest. She wanted to run or lift weights—something that involved movement and freedom. She was certain that something, somehow, was suppressing FSAT's effect on her strength. It had to be the meds Dr. Winfred was pumping into her. It wasn't the minimally conscious state that he intended, but it had the same affect. It kept her under their control. So far.

Saturday morning brought another grand breakfast. Through the day, she only saw Lanora and Dr. Winfred. At one point, after Lanora got back from grocery shopping and put everything away, the two of them were in her room together. Lanora brought in a smoothie drink, and Dr. Winfred was changing her IV bags.

"Heard the latest from Greg and Rodney, hmm?" asked Dr. Winfred.

"About the new girl?"

"Oh, my, no," said Dr. Winfred. "She's fine. Seems to be coming right along with the lower dose, yes. No, I mean, our girl here. Oh, yes. Seems like she's an antibody powerhouse. All those shots? The things they got, well, stole from CDC? Why, she not only recovered quickly but, well, she's an immunization factory. If they can make these into vaccines, well, oh, my goodness!"

"Thousands, millions of lives saved. Doubt that JR cares about that. Just the money he'd make. And it's not right," Lanora raised her voice, "Not right to keep her here like a laboratory animal!"

Julian fidgeted, even more than normal. "No, indeed. Not right at all. Hmm. Not at all."

He brightened. "Well, good news is, no more tests today or tomorrow! Let her build back up, you know, and Edgar will draw more blood and marrow Monday. So exciting," he finished as he walked to the door. "So exciting, indeed, uh huh."

Lanora took the now-empty glass from Jennifer, gently squeezed her shoulder, and also walked to the door. "Rest," she said quietly as she lowered the lights.

No EEG, no security man in her room. Jennifer napped, and used waking up as an opportunity for isometric exercises, stretching and pulling hard—but not too hard—against the restraints as she yawned. Still playing the game for the sake of anyone watching the cameras, but preparing.

*Just a little while longer.*

+   +   +

"Sir, nothing new," Skylar reported to JR on Sunday morning as he paced in his apartment. "Just wanted to let you know that I took some of the allowance you've given me. Bought some really good low-light binoculars. Hard to come by, but I go over earlier in the evenings now, and I can see a lot more of what's going on than with just the cameras."

"Initiative. Watching out for my interests. I knew I made a good choice bringing you on board. Well done."

After a few moments, when JR didn't say anything more, Skylar nervously continued.

"Well, yes sir, thank you. I, uh, I just wanted to know if you need me to do anything more. Is there something else I can be doing? I mean, like, I check the tapes daily, and I'm spending at least four additional hours there right after sunset. Anything?"

After a brief pause, "Just keep up the good work. That's all for now. Thank you, Skylar."

"Okay, yes sir. I'll just . . . " Skylar realized he was speaking to himself.

+   +   +

*Can't they just go to church and give me another day's rest?* Jennifer thought as Lanora, Dr. Winfred, and Edgar all entered her room at 9 a.m. Edgar rolled over a cart that Jennifer knew was bad news. Julian started tweaking her IV drip. Lanora touched her shoulder and spoke calmly.

"Jennifer, Edgar has to draw more blood and marrow. He was going to do it tomorrow, but he's had a brother pass away, and has to leave this evening. I've asked Julian to increase your drip a little so this won't hurt as much."

*Well, at least that's a little good news. Didn't give me anything all the other times,* Jennifer thought.

"Yes, um, well . . . " Dr. Winfred stammered.

"Look, Winfred," Edgar exclaimed as he prepared syringes. "Just get things set and get out. I've gotta go home and pack."

"Oh, certainly. My condolences. Just, oh, I'll set up a new bag and be gone." He replaced a nearly empty bag with a fresh one, watched to make sure it was feeding correctly, and left.

Meanwhile, Lanora put a cool, damp towel on Jennifer's head. "Now, I'll be back in shortly when Edgar's done and take you to the bathroom. Then I have to go out for a few hours."

"Your turn at the range?" Edgar asked, gruffly. "Ace took me there yesterday. Try the Glock 9," he smirked.

Lanora paused as she walked to the door. "Kramer's taking me. Frankly, I'm more of a Smith and Wesson .38 Special kinda girl." She smiled as she walked out the door.

It took all the willpower Jennifer could muster to keep a straight face. She didn't dare look at Edgar, even with her half-closed "Stage 3" sleepy eyes, knowing she'd smile.

+ + +

Several hours later, a groggy Jennifer realized that she'd been dozing on and off, even with the pain of the needle sticks to draw blood, and the much more painful procedure to suck marrow out of her thigh bone. She vaguely remembered Lanora taking her to the bathroom. Now she heard Julian's clock chime twice—2 p.m.—and shortly afterward she heard loud cursing in the hallway. Something about . . . had the second girl also died? She had been doing so well . . . and Jennifer nodded back off.

What was it, another hour or two? Dr. Winfred came in and adjusted the meds. Something about putting her deeper. Who was that with him? JR? Angry again? Because another test subject died? Dr. Winfred's leaving . . . JR . . . Oh, no . . .

+ + +

Lanora actually enjoyed going to the range, not only to get out of the facility for something other than shopping, but to "plink" again. It had been years. And she had to admit, Kramer knew his firearms, and gave her some good pointers. Her pattern consistently got tighter, and he had to agree with her. She really excelled with the .38 Special.

Returning at 4 p.m., Lanora was surprised to see the facility vacant and locked. Kramer drew his weapon as he unlocked the entrance door. Lanora didn't wait to follow him in. A sense of foreboding overwhelmed her as she ran down the hall, past the other room where the new subject was, or had been. She ran to Jennifer's room.

"Oh, no, honey!" she moaned as she entered. She raised her voice. "Kramer, stay out. I need to clean Jennifer up." She closed the door and returned to the naked, bruised young woman.

She tried to help Jennifer to the bathroom. Unusually, she was like dead weight. She didn't seem able to help much at all. It took twice as long as usual, and Lanora finally got her back to the bed and dressed her bruises, even worse this time. One other thing was odd. Jennifer wasn't weeping. She really did seem like she was in a deep coma.

Noise in the hallway. The others were back.

"Julian? Dr. Winfred, I need you in here now!"

After what seemed like minutes, the door opened.

"Yes? Uh, oh, my."

"Julian! It's more than that. Something's wrong with her. Check the IV!"

For once, Julian remained silent. He traced from the port, to the tubing, to the IV fluid dispensing system and its settings, to the bags. And back. Finally, he looked at the bags again, one at a time.

"No. Oh, no," he exclaimed.

"What?" Lenora demanded.

"Oh, my. This could have killed her," he said slowly, softly, with no stammer.

He immediately disconnected the meds.

"Julian!"

"Yes. Well. They gave us the wrong concentration. Far too strong. That medicine right there," he said, pointing to the bag on the right. "I never work with that high a dose. Too easy to make a mistake."

"Yeah, a mistake like this?" Lanora demanded. "Is she going to be okay? What can we do?"

"Do. Yes, well, anyone else? No. Her? Nothing we can do, except . . . " He put a bag of saline solution into the IV dispensing equipment, to help replace blood Edgar had drawn. "Dear, dear. Now we wait. Maybe give her some coffee when she's awake enough to safely drink. Don't want to give her anything else. Can't. Could end up with a see-saw effect, back and forth, even more dangerous. Oh, my-my-my."

He pulled up a chair and sat beside her bed, fidgeting. Lanora gently stroked Jennifer's shoulder, as she had started doing more often since, well, the first time.

Dr. Julian Winfred reached for Jennifer's hand and began tenderly stroking it.

"So sorry, young lady. So very, very sorry," he said quietly.

# 42. HUDDLE

For the third morning in a row, Dwayne woke up Monday without a hangover. His desire for a morning cup of coffee was stronger than his need for a drink, and he thanked God. That thought made him put his coffee carafe down. Yes, he thanked God that he was doing better.

He had found a church with a "Celebrate Recovery" program that previous Friday evening, attended, and even went to the Sunday morning church service. He had admitted to God, to some other men, and mostly to himself that he needed help. He actually felt encouraged for a change.

He shaved, put on a jogging suit, and finished his cup of coffee. He was even going to start running again, just a half mile for a couple of days, then try to increase a quarter of a mile each week.

*If I really feel good, I might add some sit-ups and pushups*, he snickered.

He poured his second cup, trying to decide whether to eat breakfast before or after his jog, and pulled open his curtains. He was surprised to see a squad car from his precinct—well, his former precinct—pull into an empty space near his apartment and Brennan, a young black man with eight years on the force, get out of the car carrying a package.

Dwayne waved through the window and opened the door before Brennan got up the steps.

"Brennan! Good to see you. Coffee?"

"You too, Dwayne. Love some, but I gotta get ready for a funeral detail. But look, I needed to get this to you. Came addressed to you last week and, well, we've had some turnover in administration, and some sickness, and Julie had her baby . . . " he handed the package to Dwayne.

"Anyways, it was supposed to have been forwarded to you, and I said, shoot, man, I'll take it. See how you're doin'. Then I got this detail. Rain check?"

"Any time, Brennan. Tell the folks I said hi."

"You got it," he said over his shoulder, as he walked back to his car.

Dwayne glanced at the package as he shut and locked his door, then froze as he saw the name of the sender.

Pat Jernigan. The last person he ever expected to get anything from, except trouble. Dwayne set the package and his coffee mug on his early Salvation Army vintage kitchen table, pulled out a chair, and sat down.

"This should be interesting," he muttered, with his sarcasm meter pegged to the right.

+ + +

"What's up?" Sam asked Mick. Mick had called both her and Ed to coordinate an emergency late-morning break at a coffee shop.

"Doc, do you recognize this stuff?" Mick handed Ed a sheet of paper with the names of several medications neatly handwritten.

Ed glanced at the list, up at Mick, over at Sam, and back at the list. "Who gave you this? Where did it come from?" he demanded.

Mick took a deep breath. "One of the medical suppliers I've been contacting each week. Melissa. She called me. Off-the-record, she told me they'd made a mistake on one of the meds, and an irate doctor called and raked them over the coals. Melissa noticed that it wasn't a doctor she recognized or a known medical facility, so she got to checking. She saw that they'd gotten a lot of orders for this stuff for several weeks. But not this much. The same meds, ordered by the same doctor and going to the same place, and gradually increasing!"

"Sam," Ed exclaimed, "these are IV meds. They can be used to induce long term comas, typically to treat brain and spinal injuries. Likely what was used to knock her out at the hospital."

"And keep her sedated? Like, for several weeks?"

"Exactly. And if they're supplying more, it may be enough to also sedate another person or two!"

"Where to?" Sam asked Mick, grabbing her things.

"She wouldn't say, not to a lowly citizen like me. Think she needs to see a badge."

A young couple quickly stepped aside as two very determined men and a not-to-be-messed-with young woman nearly ran for the door.

+ + +

Sam hoped she, Ed, and Mick could get in to see Major Garrett on such short notice. To her surprise, as soon as he saw them walking toward his office, he urgently motioned for them to enter and close the door.

Her next surprise was seeing Dwayne Wilson.

"Seats," the commander said. "Dwayne doesn't know much about Jennifer, and that's okay. He has some important information from a very unlikely source. Guess you have something, too?"

Sam recognized the invitation and went straight to it. "We believe we know where some medicine is going; the exact medicine it would take. . . the, ah, well, exactly what a kidnapper would use to subdue a young woman for a period of several weeks."

"Where it's going. Does that happen to be in our Zone, out to the west?" he asked.

"Exactly," Sam stated, and gave the address.

Garrett glanced down at some paperwork on his desk, then at Dwayne. "Matches. Okay, we brief SWAT in ten minutes, roll in twenty. Gentlemen," he glanced at Ed and Mick, "Can't have any civilians. I know you understand. Sam will let you know how it goes."

Ed and Mick nodded, and Ed spoke to Sam, "We'll go to my place and wait to hear from you."

Garrett continued. "Dwayne, that goes for you, too. You want in on this? 'fraid you'll have to let me give you back your badge. Got your firearm in your truck? You in?"

Dwayne smiled. "Sir. Thanks." Sam cocked her head slightly, noting a humility she didn't remember seeing from the man.

"Got a vest?" Garrett asked Sam.

"Ready to go, sir," she responded.

"Let's go save Supergirl."

Sam gave him a look.

"What?" he asked. "You think I'd sit this one out?"

## 43.  BREAKOUT!

*N*ow.

The deep meds had forced Jennifer into a deeper sleep than any she'd experienced since her kidnapping. Dr. Winfred had completely shut off the medical IVs and was just dripping saline to provide hydration, following the two units of blood—not one—that Edgar had drawn the morning before.

She had been off the meds for hours, and the saline and a few extra trips to the bathroom with Lanora's help, had helped flush it out of her system. Now she was alone. And she was upset. Really, really upset.

*Now.*

Jennifer focused all her attention and strength on her dominant right arm. She pulled hard, steady, twisting her body. The wrist strap snapped. She quickly unbuckled the left wrist strap, and then both ankle straps. She was careful not to pull loose her IV and cause an alarm. It was bad enough that someone might already see her breaking loose if they were monitoring the camera feeds. But then again, perhaps they'd become complacent.

Jennifer was clothed in a stylish, jogging suit. Red, with black stripes. Actually, very attractive; Lanora had good taste. No socks or shoes, which would be the least of her worries. She had to storm the door, take out one or two guards, appropriate their guns, and be ready to shoot anyone who stood between her and escape. Except Lanora. And, maybe, Dr. Winfred. Unless they drew a weapon against her.

She knew little of the building's layout. From the parts she had observed, in her Stage 3 coma ruse, it appeared to have originally contained the factory's reception area and main office, and it might have served as shipping and receiving for smaller, non-forklift items. There were large rooms like the one she was normally kept in, and where the chamber had been built. She assumed the room next to hers, where the other test subjects had been kept, was likely around the same size; roughly twenty-by-forty feet. They may have originally been conference rooms.

Beyond that slight amount of intel, she didn't have a clue.

Only seconds had ticked by. They felt like minutes. She knew as soon as the alarm went out, everyone would shoot to kill, and face the consequences with JR later.

Ready to sprint for the door, she pulled loose the IV.

A klaxon sounded, followed by the last thing she expected to hear, and perhaps the only thing that would cause her to pause.

Someone, maybe Drake, shouted: "Police and SWAT! Heavy attack! Places, and open fire!"

Within seconds, she heard running footsteps and windows being smashed. High caliber, rapid-fire rifles opened fire. First one, then two, then it sounded like four separate weapons firing from inside the building.

Jennifer couldn't see how effective the defensive fire was. For now, but it sounded like the gunfire was all one-way; perhaps the police were afraid of hitting her.

Then, between the defensive bursts, she occasionally heard a round slam into the building.

*Snipers!*

She heard a man scream and then fall silent.

More defensive outgoing bursts. Several more inbound sniper rounds. Then what sounded like a large gauge shotgun went off outside, followed by breaking glass.

"Grenade!" someone shouted, followed instantly by a loud explosion. That flash-bang round was quickly followed by another.

"Ace, we gotta hold them off, man," Angelo shouted, as loud as he could. Jennifer knew they had to be nearly deaf from the concussion rounds. Then he shouted down the hall. "Yo, get your butts in there and take the woman! Car off the side. Get to the reconstitution point! Go!"

Jennifer heard more footsteps . . . nothing wrong with her hearing . . . and the door swung open. In ran Lanora and Dr. Winfred, in that order.

*Perfect.*

Lanora ran only three steps into the room, and froze, staring at the empty bed. Dr. Winfred bumped into Lanora, knocked her down and tripping over her.

From behind them, a strong, clear young woman's voice spoke calmly as she closed the door.

"Both of you stay on the floor. Lie down. I do not want to hurt either of you."

Dr. Winfred cowered and huddled into a fetal position, quietly muttering. "Oh, oh my. Oh no. No. Please? Oh, dear."

Lanora? She chuckled. "You go, girl. Want my gun? Ankle holster. Left leg. Julian refused to take one."

"Thanks," Jennifer said, quickly stepped over to her, retrieved the revolver, and stuffed it into her right pocket.

"Honey, please remember my little girl. Jasmine Wellston. In Miami. Just 20. If something happens to me?"

"I'll do what I can, Lanora. I promise. Stay down. Tell them I threatened you."

She ran back to the door and opened it.

+ + +

Sam was grateful that the team took her seriously. She knew without a doubt that this would not be easy. Everything had been too professional, and too well-organized and funded. If anything, she expected even more resistance.

The armored SWAT vehicle had led the way in, with the other vehicles safely shielded behind. Heavily protected SWAT personnel had exited from the rear of the vehicle and advanced behind large shields. Many of the kidnapper's rounds had found their marks, yet no one had been hurt. Within seconds, sniper fire began, with at least one round finding its target.

As intended, the flash-bang concussions temporarily halted gunfire from inside the building. SWAT personnel quickly advanced and spread out, several running around to the left and right of the building. Two police cars also circled the building, each parking thirty yards behind exit doors. Dwayne was in one; Brennan in the other. They left the engines running, and kneeled, weapons drawn, behind the driver's door. Major Garrett in his cruiser, and Sam in her Mustang, parked near the single, large entrance to the complex. They also stood behind their running vehicles with weapons drawn

"Come on, come on . . . " Sam said, waiting for SWAT to storm the building. "No knocking on doors today."

"Front door ready," the radio crackled.

"Gotta large rear door ready. Other doors under observation," another voice responded.

"This is Lead. On my mark. Three, two, one, now!" A third voice commanded.

Two explosions sounded almost simultaneously, and six SWAT men stormed into the facility, three into the front entrance and three through the back. Each team was led by a man holding a full-length shield with his weapon strapped to his back, followed by two more with rifles drawn, ready to engage.

In the front entrance, Ace unloaded his rifle in "felony" mode; fully automatic. Andre was running to the side for a clear shot, but before he could get in place, several high-power rounds slammed him back against the wall, dead.

The noise from Ace's weapon was deafening, yet the rounds were ineffective against the shield. He was highly skilled with the weapon and reloaded within two seconds, but his life ended before he squeezed off a single additional round. Within mere moments, the team had cleared the lobby and were into the main hallway.

At the rear entrance, the team tossed in a flash-bang. The lead man ran four steps inside holding the shield, and his two teammates followed and squatted behind him, one facing left, the other right. As expected, there were gunmen on either side. Before they could recover from the flash-bang and acquire their targets, Drake and Kramer were dead. A third gunman faced them and opened fire, his shots wild. In a moment, Thomas was also dead.

"Front entrance, one hostile dead; we're moving down a hallway," Sam heard over the radio. Then from the rear, "Three hostiles dead in the back. We're also entering a hallway. Watch the exits."

## 44. CONFRONTATION

Jennifer, barefoot, quietly but quickly moved down a long side hallway toward an exit. She wanted to be close to an outer door and wait for the gunfire to end, one way or another. If the good guys won, she would speak up and reveal herself to them. Otherwise, she would bolt out the exit and take her chances. She'd never shot a firearm, but she knew she would learn a lot after the first trigger pull. She would then have, what? Five more rounds to get it right.

She stopped and listened intently as she heard a strong, commanding voice from around a hallway intersection she was approaching: "Get the girl out of here or I will kill you myself."

JR.

She fought the desire to abandon everything for the single objective of taking him down. She hesitated only a moment, when Jake, Rodney, and Greg suddenly appeared around a corner running toward her, less than thirty yards ahead.

Greg was the first to see her. "Oh, crap!" he shouted, then turned and ran. Jake, on the other hand, pulled a 1911 from a side holster as the young woman charged at them.

Jake's draw was slow, his two-hand stance shaky with the heavy gun. His first shot was high and right. Rodney had also drawn his firearm and appeared to be steadier.

There were no rooms to duck into. Jennifer had a good chance of neutralizing both men before they could get off a decent shot. If she was hit, there was also a fair chance that she would survive and, eventually, recover. But if the rescuers . . . at least, that's what she hoped they were, and not some foreign government or competing crime group . . . if the rescuers failed? She would again be a prisoner. She was certain she would never have another chance.

The clincher was the intensely painful memory of the close-range gunshot that had almost killed her.

Now fifteen yards and approaching at a world-class sprint, with Rodney's large caliber revolver almost in position and Jake having recovered from his .45's recoil and ready to fire again, she whipped out

Lanora's .38.

Jennifer didn't know the dynamics of load, muzzle velocity, bullet mass or anything else. Her first-ever trigger pull startled her. And firing the gun single-handed at a hard sprint sent her round to the right of Rodney. In a split second, she overcompensated and shot low and left of Jake.

Both men fired their weapons, but they had lost their aim points when startled by her return fire. They missed.

The five concussions in the confined width of the hallway, even as long as it was and with a high ceiling, were deafening. But Jennifer's mind was clear and, unlike the men, she kept her focus.

In less than two seconds, multiple events occurred. None were in the favor of her tormentors.

Two .38 rounds slammed into Rodney's chest, slamming him backward. Two more slugs slammed into Jake's chest with the same result. Their guns went flying up and back as Jennifer's sprint took her between the two men. She started to toss the empty revolver aside, but for some reason decided to hold on to it. She stuffed it back into her pocket and grabbed Jake's .45 out of the air. She continued down the hall after Greg.

+   +   +

"Rear Team, you guys okay?"

Sam, Major Garrett, and the other officers had the same question as the Front Team's radio call. Their trained ears heard the five gunshots, clearly from pistols, without return fire from tactical rifles.

"Affirmative. Shots were not from or directed toward us."

"Jennifer!" Sam exclaimed. She reached into her car and grabbed the mic. "All: The captive may have escaped and is engaging her kidnappers. Be careful!"

"Roger that; Front Team continuing to clear forward office spaces."

Another voice: "Rear team clearing storage areas."

The spurious gunfire meant they had to not only had to engage armed resistance, but also to ensure that Jennifer wasn't injured by "friendly fire" if she was now armed.

"This is Garrett. Kill the power."

He returned his mic to its cradle and resumed his position outside his cruiser, glancing at Sam. She nodded about the time they heard a small explosion from the back corner of the large building, where the very substantial electrical service entrance was. A SWAT ordnance expert had just severed the power feed.

Sam turned back toward the building. "Come on, Jen. Hide. Let the experts take them out." Reducing light inside the building to any that filtered in through the window, and any remaining emergency lights that still had good batteries . . . providing only a few minutes backup lighting at the most . . . would give the well-prepared SWAT members the advantage as they methodically swept through the entire facility, one room at a time. It would also give Jennifer her best chance to find a hiding place and wait. "Just hide," Sam repeated.

+ + +

While the other men tried to stand their ground against Jennifer, Greg continued running back down the hall, and then turned and ran down a side hall. He was remarkably fast for a man in his late-sixties, but he knew he was no match for genetically enhanced Jennifer. He ducked into the large breakroom just as the building power went out. It still housed an old refrigerator, still functional. It also now housed a new, large side-by-side, along with two large upright freezers. A single emergency light provided dim light, but it was fading by the moment.

This is where Greg chose to take his stand. He, too, would rather take his chances with JR in the future, than to die in the next several seconds at the hands of a crazed superwoman. Perhaps, he hoped, his genetics expertise and ability to continue working from the frozen blood and marrow they'd extracted from the woman, would keep JR from carrying out his threat if he shot her in self-defense.

Greg pulled a compact .380 semiautomatic and took aim at the door.

+ + +

JR had two remaining objectives.

First, he had to "live to fight another day," as they say, which meant he needed to escape to a small storage warehouse off to the side of the building, originally used to store and recycle scrap. Its main advantage was that it had a roll-up door, and it faced into an alley between several other buildings. He then had to reach a high performance, four-wheel drive Subaru sedan he had pre-positioned as an escape vehicle. JR realized that he would likely lose his test subject, the last living link to the longevity formula. He would also likely lose access to his geneticist and to the blood and bone marrow that were so essential to continue Greg's work, all stored in the new refrigerators and freezers in the breakroom. He might even lose Greg. But he could hire someone else and use some of the samples safely stored off-site.

The second objective, before he could flee, was more subtle.

After he gave the command for the three men to escape with Jennifer, he entered the door to the breakroom and strode to the right-hand freezer, nearest the sink and cabinets. There, on the top shelf, was the Baggie that Angelo had seized. The man had privately explained to JR everything he'd learned about the frozen fruit. JR had not yet decided whether to turn it over to Greg, or, more likely, to the greater resources available through Brazen's organization. Now? He couldn't leave the facility without it.

When the gunfire started, JR hid behind the freezer. A few moments later, the door opened. In the dim light, he recognized Greg as he entered, stepped off to the back side of the door, squatted, and drew his pistol. He couldn't see clearly enough to tell that the older man was sweating and shaking profusely, trying to catch his breath.

"Greg . . ." JR whispered, and immediately wished he hadn't.

## 45.  FRESH AIR

Greg was in full panic mode. He swung toward the unexpected voice and began firing.

With adequate lighting and a steady hand, an individual well-trained with the short barrel and recoil characteristics of the compact .380 could consistently put a tight pattern of bullets in a man-size target at twenty feet.

Terrorized, Greg fired four rounds in rapid succession before coming to his senses and realizing that his target was not Jennifer; wasn't even a woman. All of his shots went wild. But one round hit the stainless steel sink off to the side of JR, ricocheted, and struck the man in the back of his head.

JR fell face forward. A pool of blood began covering his head and dripping onto the floor.

"Oh . . . oh no . . . no, no," muttered Greg as he scurried the twenty feet to the bleeding man and recognized his boss. Greg was still trying to catch his breath. His left shoulder ached. He had trouble thinking clearly, and struggled to see in the dim light.

Forgetting about Jennifer, he raced for the door, ran into the hallway toward a side exit, and all of about thirty more feet before he collapsed.

JR didn't think. Didn't analyze, or plan, or try to manipulate. He had just one task, one urgency that he performed without any conscious thought, before entering into a painful, deep darkness. He rolled over, now facing up. His left hand reached over to the plastic bag in his right hand, opened it, extracted the frozen fruit, and brought it to his mouth. As he chewed, warm affectionate feelings overwhelmed him. His deep love, his passion and concern for the most important person in all of his existence. Himself.

+ + +

Just under an hour later, and the SWAT team gave the all-clear, along with some very good news.

Sam nearly abandoned her car and ran to the building in her excitement. Almost. As it was, she hardly turned the engine off and got her keys after she skidded up to the front door.

"Jennifer? Jen!"

"Sam?" Jennifer stepped through the doorway, into the bright summer afternoon sun, shielding her eyes. She just stood there, as Sam ran up and hugged her, then collapsed into her arms and wept uncontrollably.

"Jennifer . . . it's okay. It's over. It's over," Sam said, holding her tight. Major Garrett had also driven up to the gate. He smiled to Sam as he walked past the young women, and into the building to receive the SWAT team's verbal report.

"Commander, we found a man and woman in good shape in one room. They apparently were noncombatants, in some kind of support capacity. Everyone else? Dead. We took out six. One older man had an apparent heart attack. Three other men were shot, but not by our team. Two men in a hallway each had two chest wounds. Another man in a kitchen area was shot in the back of the head."

"Okay, follow protocol. Mobile crime lab should be on their way."

"Yes, sir. We're leaving all the bodies where they are. You may want to call utilities to have them reconnect power."

"Dwayne already did. But most local teams have deployed out of state to help with the storm damage from last week. They probably won't have anyone here for several days, maybe a week. He told the lab to bring generators, cords, and a lot of lights."

Major Garrett walked back out to the women. They were side by side, leaning against Sam's Mustang. Jennifer was composed and dabbing her eyes with a tissue Sam had pulled out of her car.

"Jennifer, Major Steve Garrett, our Zone One commander. He's one of few . . . very few . . . people who knows everything. Your secret is safe. He pulled this together to get you out."

"Thank you." Jennifer shook his hand, smiling weakly. She chose not to reveal that she was in the process of breaking out on her own. She was out, and free. In retrospect, realizing the security JR had, Jennifer knew that her chances of having escaped on her own, uninjured, would have been well under twenty percent. "Thank you," she repeated.

"Jennifer," he said calmly, "I can't imagine all you've been through. Normally I'd recommend hospital evaluation, professional counseling, you know. But," he smiled warmly, "let's just say that your situation is unique. Haven't talked to Sam about this, but . . . "

+  +  +

Mick and Ed drove up at the same time and tried to look cool and composed while getting inside the house as quickly as possible. Sam met them at the door of the pleasant two-story safe house in East Atlanta. There were no words, just huge grins all around.

The men's smiles continued along with many tears as they dropped their bags and ran into the living room and surrounded Jennifer with long affectionate hugs.

Garrett had arranged the Zone 6 location since his own safe house had been compromised. Jennifer had preferred the old house because of the memories of her "growing up" experience, as she called it. Garrett understood her feelings but was adamant that the risk was too high.

When Sam called Ed and Mick with the news of Jennifer's freedom and Garrett's offer, they enthusiastically agreed and began packing and getting time off from their jobs. She had cautioned them to let Jennifer open up and share anything she wanted to, but only when and only as much as she chose.

Sam watched and listened as the men each brought Jennifer up to date on what they had done to try to find and help her, their new jobs, and how they had tried to rebuild their lives, which they gratefully acknowledged they owed to her.

Sam smiled. She was glad that she had already spent some girl time with the young woman, who physically appeared to have removed two years off the calendar even with her traumatic ordeal. Yet, she somehow also seemed older by several years. Sam couldn't figure it out, so she attributed it to the FSAT. It was like the twenty-two-year-old looked twenty and acted thirty. She would need to discuss her impression with Ed later, in private.

The doorbell interrupted her thoughts, and she heard "It's me," as

Garrett opened the door with his arms full of Chinese carry-out. The aroma quickly filled the room and Jennifer exclaimed, "Oh! You didn't!"

"Yes, I most certainly did, and I hope you've got an appetite. Sam insisted I order just about everything on the menu."

Sam shrugged. "Well, he said he was buying. Come on in, boss, room at the table for five!"

They all filled their plates and were about to dig in, when Jennifer spoke up.

"Wait. No. This is all wrong." Jennifer's urgency startled them. "Well, I mean, look. I thought we were all dead. Then I thought I was dead. And for weeks now, I thought I would be experimented on . . . ." She paused. " . . . Experimented on and never escape. And, there was more . . . " her voice trailed off.

"Okay, what I'm trying to say is, I have a lot to be grateful for. While I hid in a bedroom while the FSAT took over, I changed from a girl to a woman, then some kind of superwoman. But mostly, I became a Christian. I would like us, as a group, to give God thanks. Without His divine intervention, at least we four wouldn't be here today."

Garrett didn't hesitate. "Make that five for five. I could tell you stories."

The others nodded in agreement.

"Ed, would you lead us please?

Ed prayed sincerely, fervently, giving thanks. They enjoyed a great meal together, and there weren't many leftovers.

Everything was pleasant, positive, even relaxing. Until Dwayne called.

# 46.   UNACCOUNTED

After putting away the few leftovers and throwing the trash away, the five walked back to the living room. Garrett let the others choose their favorite seats, and then walked toward the remaining seat, a rocker in the corner. As he was sitting, he received a call.

"Major Garrett." Pause. "Yes, Dwayne."

The others watched as his face changed to a look of disbelief.

"Corpses don't get up and disappear. He's gotta be there somewhere. Who checked his vitals? What . . . " Pause. "What!?"

He looked at Sam as he waited for an answer, saying off to the side, "Dwayne stayed and is helping the Crime Lab. They've been there for a couple of hours. The body they found in the kitchen? With the head wound? Gone."

He returned his attention to the phone call. "You're kidding?" Pause. "Okay, alright. Nothing we can do. Remember the guy's description?" Pause. "Yeah, okay. Thanks."

He hung up, looked across the room, and focused on Jennifer.

"Jennifer, I didn't want to trouble you with anything for another day or two. Unfortunately, we have some loose ends, and now another one that could be serious. Can we talk together here, would you rather go to another room, or do you want to come down to the station? I'm very sorry."

Jennifer sat quietly in what had been her favorite chair when they were there before.

"Frankly, I'd rather have my friends here with me. I'll try to help. What, uh, what in the world just happened?"

"The two people you left in the room? Safe? They agreed to help identify all the bodies. Apparently, the entire team can be accounted for. Two alive, the rest dead, except for one person who was called away out of state for some reason."

"Edgar," she commented.

"Okay. But one of the bodies, the one that went by initials . . . I guess he was the leader . . . "

"JR?" she asked.

"Yes. He was found alone in the kitchen area. Head wound, a lot of blood. No pulse according to my team. They're pretty good; no, they're really good. Got no reason to doubt them. But Dwayne calls and says that now, they can't find the body. Then says they heard a car start, drive away, and bust through a section of fence in the back of the plant. Apparently, there was a whole section that had been modified to look secure, yet could easily break away. Anyway, they're certain that they missed someone. Someone got the body and escaped."

Jennifer's face showed a kaleidoscope of expressions as Garrett spoke, from anger, to fear, and hurt, and amazement, to sadness.

"Jennifer, I'm sure a lot went on while you were there. Much of it may be very difficult to talk about. We'll need to interview you and write up a formal report. We all know it has to be worded very carefully. That can wait. Stay here for several nights. If you have to go anywhere like back to your apartment, go with Sam. Let's just be careful for a few more days. Okay?

+ + +

Garrett left just before 9 p.m. After a good night's rest, the four enjoyed a hearty breakfast at a hole-in-the-wall restaurant known for its killer omelets. The men went to work and the ladies went shopping. Not what they really wanted, which would have taken all day and involved every mall in a fifty-mile radius. But they found enough to get Jennifer by for a few days. She now had a physique that matched Sam's, and the only clothes from her "pre-FSAT" wardrobe that still fit were her bathrobe and shoes.

Then to headquarters.

"Sure you're up to this?" Sam asked.

Jennifer, casually dressed in new blue jeans, a black pullover top, and comfortable sneakers, stood in front of the door to the interview room. Inside was a nervous and unsuspecting Dr. Julian Winfred. An uncooperative individual, according to Garrett. He wouldn't ask for an attorney or accept one when offered. He just wouldn't talk. Sam shared a suggestion.

"Wouldn't miss it. Let's go," Jennifer responded.

"Just, you know, don't make any direct threats, and whatever you do, don't touch him."

Jennifer smiled. "Don't think I'll need to do either."

The two walked in. Jennifer walked to the table and stood across from a wide-eyed man who suddenly seemed to diminish to half of his size. She put her hands on the table and leaned across to face him, her face less than eighteen inches from his. He started to speak, to stutter. She held her finger to her lips and he shut up, leaning back as far away as he could from her gaze.

Jennifer slowly straightened up and looked around the room. Steel table, bolted to the floor. Heavy steel chairs, with legs and backs made of thick gauge welded tubing. They were also bolted to the floor, so a prisoner couldn't use them as weapons.

She slowly, casually walked behind a chair across from the table from the man, now shaking and sweating profusely, put her hands on either side of the chair's back, and ripped it out of the floor. She slowly raised it so her hands were chest high, and bent the tubing apart.

Sam spoke to Jennifer in a matter-of-fact tone, as if passing on information about a good nail spa. "You know, we really don't have any witnesses of what went down those weeks at that facility. Well, of course, there are the other felons who may or may not want to cooperate. They could cop a deal and put everyone else away for life. But short of that? Well, Jen, it really depends on you. I guess if you didn't press charges, we'd just have to let this guy go. He'd have to fend for himself. Bad world out there. Hope nothing would happen to him. But, well . . . "

As Sam's voice trailed off, Jennifer set the chair on the table in front of Julian, locked eyes with him in an expressionless gaze, and then turned and walked out the door. She casually walked to a waiting area, drank some ice water, grabbed a magazine, and waited.

An hour later, Sam walked out and stood in front of her friend, motioning for Jennifer to follow her into a private room. Inside, with the door closed, Sam's professional façade was replaced with a look of complete amazement. "Full confession. I mean, like, details. He just begged me to keep you away from him. I warned him that if he breathed a word about you to anyone, we could not be responsible for any actions you might take. He said he didn't care if he went to jail,

Witness Protection, whatever. He just wanted to forget that those weeks ever happened, and never see you again!"

"Thank heavens. I so hoped I could get a normal life back." Jennifer sighed. Then her shoulders slumped.

"JR?"

"JR. If he's still out there. He probably doesn't know anything about you, or the commander, or even Mick. But me? And Ed. We're in mortal danger if that man is alive."

"Wish there was something I could say. That it wasn't so," Sam said. "But you're probably right. Maybe not mortal danger. He needs you. Both of you. But if he ever gets you again . . . "

"Neither of us will escape," Jennifer finished. She paused a moment. "I'd like to talk with Lanora."

# 47.   LANORA

"**S**ir, uh, I really need to report what I've observed. It's, uh, it isn't good, Sir. I'll await your call and instructions. Um, I really can't go back and observe anything. I'll tell you all when you're able to call. Goodbye."

Skylar had never left a message for JR before. Then again, he'd never tried a dozen times, every half hour since 8 a.m. that morning, without a response or call-back. So, fearing that the phone could be out of order or compromised, he was intentionally vague.

He was worried, terrified even. His stomach was in knots. He hadn't eaten since seeing the police crime scene presence the evening before, though he'd had the presence of mind to sneak into his shack and retrieved the videotapes.

The facility had been raided. SWAT and a few others came out, but none of the rest of the team. At least, they didn't walk out. He saw a young woman walk out, join up with another woman and drive off together. Was that the same person he saw on the stretcher at the safe house? Had he been manually controlling the cameras, he might have been able to zoom in enough for more detail, but clearly identifying individuals from that distance with the equipment he had from an enlarged videotape image? He just couldn't be sure.

Later, he saw the SWAT vehicles leave as several patrol cars and Crime Scene vans arrived. He watched them set up generators and mobile lights outside and inside the building as night approached.

Then a small sedan, maybe a Subaru, appeared from around the building and sped erratically to the back side of the complex before disappearing from his field of view. That drew several people out of the building, with an officer running to his cruiser, but the small sedan had a significant head start before the officer could give chase. The sedan didn't reappear, so it must have had an alternate exit path—one that Skylar had missed when he initially surveyed the property. That escape route apparently caught the officer by surprise as well, as Skylar saw the cruiser reappear several times driving between buildings.

He paced his apartment. He wanted to have a drink, go shoot pool, take in a movie. He wanted to hear from JR and know what he was supposed to do next.

+  +  +

Sam and Jennifer sat in silence at a table in one of the precinct's break rooms, drinking coffee they brought back from their lunch. The latest update was that Lanora should be brought to the interrogation room within an hour. Jennifer got up and excused herself to the ladies' room.

Sam watched Jennifer walk away and mentally played back the "before" and "after" images.

*How everything has changed,* Sam thought for at least the hundredth time since they were reunited. Obviously, the outward effects of FSAT were unparalleled. And there was the significant enhancement to her intelligence. But there was more. Maybe it was her near-death experience; maybe, the things she experienced during her captivity. She hadn't shared much beyond a few vague comments. Not yet. Sam's intuition suggested that some of the details would be very hard for her to speak about.

Yet, here she was. Coping, planning, even wanting to see Lanora. As they waited for guards to transport the woman from her holding cell, Sam tried to figure out how to help her friend, or if she even could. Yes, the FSAT and all those experiences were significant parts of the change she saw in the young woman. Still, there was something more. Something that tied it all together and kept her from flying apart.

Sam remembered a problem-solving technique she'd heard of in college, which had helped her as a young police officer on multiple occasions. Occam's razor, simply stated, was that the simplest solution tends to be the right one. It made sense that in spite of, and in addition to everything else, the one significant change that focused everything else was what Jennifer had described just the previous evening. She had committed her life, all of it, to Jesus Christ.

Sam had attended church sporadically, along with her older brother and younger sister. Growing up, they were there just about every Sunday morning. Their single mother would also take them to one or more Vacation Bible Schools every summer, to give herself a break as much as anything, Sam suspected.

The church wasn't bad, for the most part. Sam had some good memories. But it seemed so formal, so traditional, so . . . well, so dead. By the time they were all teenagers, they presented a united front against their mother, who got tired of fighting. No more church. Not for years.

In college, Sam was attracted to a group that really seemed to get into "the church thing." They were exuberant over the music, the dynamic preaching, and all the activities. Sam attended for almost a year. Gradually, though, she suspected that it was also dead, just in a different way. There was a lot of outward activity, a lot of emotion. But she had to ask herself, was it really changing lives? Ultimately, as she took a hard look at herself and her friends, were their lives any different from their non-church peers? Gossiping, partying, immorality; the word 'carnal' came to mind.

She stopped going.

*But Jennifer. There's a real change. And Ed . . .*

Her analysis was interrupted as Jennifer returned, and as a woman guard approached.

+  +  +

"Jen!" Lanora jumped to her feet, almost falling over because of the unforgiving metal chair bolted to the floor in the interview room.

"Hi, Lanora." Jennifer smiled, then turned to Sam, "Can I hug her?"

"Just a hug, right?" Sam asked. Jennifer was already around the table giving the middle age woman a warm embrace. Lanora couldn't fully reciprocate with her hands cuffed, but she buried her face in Jennifer's shoulder. "I was so concerned, Hon, so concerned," she sniffed.

"Lanora, please have a seat and let's talk," Sam said after several moments. The ladies all sat, and Lanora's smile quickly faded. Her worried expression made her appear ten years older.

Sam smiled warmly. "Lanora, please try to relax. We'll handle the official stuff later, so you don't need a lawyer—though you are welcome to one, of course. So only talk to the extent that you're comfortable. Okay?"

Lanora looked perplexed. "Uh, yeah, I guess so . . . "

Sam continued. "Jennifer is giving us a sworn statement about all you did to care for her, protect her, and even help her escape. Later, we're going to ask about some specific things you can help us with, and along with Jennifer's statement, we're not going to press any charges against you."

Lanora's mouth opened and closed, but no words came out.

Jennifer leaned forward. "Lanora, does JR have anything else over you, anything other than Jasmine?" she asked, concerned.

"Money. Yeah, money. He had money over all of us. Loan shark kinda stuff. He'd lend money anytime, for anything. Me? Paying off a DUI and stuff for Jasmine. When I couldn't pay ? He needed a nurse to . . ." she sniffed.

"It's okay, Lanora. It's okay," Jennifer said. "What? To help with me?"

The older woman began weeping. Sam gave her some tissues from a box on the corner of the table.

"Oh, honey, I'm so sorry. So sorry. They took my Jasmine. Said they were taking her to Miami, they'd put her on the street . . ."

"Lanora." Jennifer's tone of voice was firm. "Lanora!"

She slowly lifted her head, clearly afraid.

"I'm going to try to get your daughter back," Jennifer said gently.

"Lord, have mercy."

"Correction," Sam added. "*We* are going to try to get your daughter back."

Jennifer raised her eyebrows. "Still wanting to make a difference?" she smiled.

"More than ever."

## 48.  FULFILLING A PROMISE

"Look these over. They're copies of the SWAT reports. See if anything comes up." Garrett handed copies to Sam and Jennifer. They were seated in his office, the door shut.

After three minutes, Jennifer looked up and smiled. "Commander, I believe I see an alibi."

Sam cocked her head. "Got me. What am I missing?"

Steve Garrett smiled. "I studied these all afternoon. Let's see what you came up with in under five minutes."

"Drugs. Forget what we know; look what the evidence lays out for an impartial team of otherwise clueless experts!" She sat back in her chair and tossed the report on the commander's desk.

"And? It's even bigger than that," she continued. "What do you have on the Security team, as I called them? I think one came up from Miami, where Lanora's daughter is, and the other came down from Chicago. What could that indicate?"

"Even better," Garrett added. "The green Cadillac was owned and insured by one Louis Thatcher, aka, "Bull." Wouldn't be surprised if he's the one who did JR's dirty work as a loan shark with Lanora. She also might be able to finger the guy from Miami, Angelo, as the one who kidnapped her daughter and recruited her to help with you."

"And if they're both involved in drugs back home . . . " Sam caught on.

Jennifer continued the cover story. "Came up here to build a large presence in Atlanta, home of numerous interstates spreading across the country. They set up a lab, brought in some medical professionals, and were experimenting on . . . "

Sam exclaimed, "A stronger form of heroin!"

Garrett held up a hand and challenged, "Explain the death of the non-combattants?"

"A missing person. Someone who got away. It was probably a plant, an infiltrator from another crime group that wanted to shut it all down. He shot two men in the hallway, then followed JR into the kitchen and shot him. He had to hide till he could sneak back into the kitchen, take the body to his pre-positioned escape vehicle, and the rest is history.

JR sure isn't going to show up to discredit the story."

Garrett stood up and looked out his window. The sun was setting. He turned back to Jennifer.

"Explain who needed JR's body."

"Proof," she said. "Proof to his own mob that he'd broken up the operation."

"And you?" he asked.

"Just, just one of the poor, hapless test subjects."

"Well, I'm impressed," said Sam.

Garrett nodded. "I am too. In minutes you came up with what took me hours. And made it sound even more believable." He smiled and leaned on the corner of his desk. "Whatever happens here, I hope we'll stay in touch. We may need you in years to come."

Jennifer smiled and offered a quiet, "Thanks."

"Now the next step," said Garrett. His face was stern. "Sam, you're not about to go down to Miami on vacation. Not going to happen."

"Sir?"

He smiled, proud of what he had pulled together. "You're going there on special assignment. It's all arranged."

"Uh, a paid business trip to Miami, F-L-A? Really?

"Got a contact who would be very interested in what we have on Angelo and JR's operation down there. I suspect Angelo never thought the medical folks would be allowed to live, so he and the others talked a lot. Can't believe some of the stuff Dr. Winfred shared with Sam. Incredible."

The women shared a knowing glance and smiled. Garrett raised a hand. "Don't even want to know."

"All that, along with Jennifer's perfect memory?" he continued. "Yep, they'll want to hear from both of you. Same with Drake's Chicago operation. I'm sending Dwayne up there. He's itching to do some real law work, and he may just make detective if he pulls this off."

"Commander?" Jennifer asked.

"Yeah, I know. You wouldn't miss this. You're a civilian. Can't keep you from going. Want my recommendation?"

"Of course," Jennifer answered.

"You'll go as a witness, wanting to help as part of your recovery, to help you deal with all you have been through. Not unprecedented.

We'll send you with a doctor's statement clearing you for that. It will instruct them not to put you under oath or interrogate you. Nothing beyond what you're willing to share."

Jennifer nodded and smiled at the wisdom of his plan, which would protect her both personally and professionally.

"Just understand," he added. "I can't give you any legal cover. Not to be harsh, but, if Supergirl here does something foolish, you're on your own. And you could put all of us in trouble. A lot of trouble."

Jennifer nodded. "I'll try to stay on the right side of the law. Or, at least, not get caught."

"Sam, ya gotta help me here with this one," he chided.

"I'm on it, commander." Then she added thoughtfully, "Back to the cover story? I can talk with Julian and Lanora and see if they'll agree. We should be able to honestly word it in general but leave out the 'difficult specifics.'" She smiled again. "Julian will agree to anything to avoid another encounter with," Sam nodded toward Jennifer, "this one."

"Lanora? She just wants her little girl back, and her life," added Jennifer.

"Sounds like we have a plan," Garrett said, and grabbed his coat. "Let's go. It's been a long day. We need to do some more interviews, tighten up our intel, and work on getting our story straight. Think you ladies will be ready to leave, say, in time to be there Monday morning?"

They looked at each other and both nodded.

"Commander?" Now it was Sam's turn to ask a question, one which she knew didn't need elaboration.

Garrett sucked in a long breath and chuckled.

"Yes, Samantha Knowles. Yes, you may take the Mustang."

+ + +

Dr. Ed Richardson was grateful for the job, the income, and the opportunity to help people at the urgent care clinic. He realized, of course, that his tenure there would be limited. He would eventually need to get back into research, join the clinic or a hospital full time, or work for a private practice. He had no interest in starting his own. Regardless, everything depended on his safety. Even more, on Jennifer's. Part of her safety was for him to be available to help her in any way that he could.

"Everything's so complicated," he muttered as he entered his car, rolled down the windows to let the heat escape, started the engine, and turned the AC to maximum. His shift at the clinic was over, and he was looking forward to an evening with the team. Especially now that Jennifer was back and safe.

Before he drove off, he needed to make a call. He closed the windows, lowered the AC fan speed to cut down noise, and dialed a number from his "Favorites" list.

"Hello?" a voice answered after four rings.

"Aaron. Hello. It's Ed Richardson. Just wanted to call and see how you're doing."

"Dr. Richardson? Uh, hey. Hello, sir," a quavering voice answered.

"Aaron? Are you alright?

The young man sighed so loud Ed could hear it. "Sir, I'm moving. Across the country, back home. Dr. Richardson, I knew the stuff you were working on was important, and you told us that, well. . . " his voice trailed off.

"Aaron, what's going on? Do you need someone to talk to? I've got a contact with the police."

"No!" Aaron exclaimed. "Look, I got roughed up, okay? They wanted anything I had on your stuff. I said it was all destroyed, okay? I can't hang around and wait for something worse to happen, you know? I'm just getting away. I'll find something else to do with my life. Goodbye, sir."

Ed tried to think of something reassuring he could say, a way to encourage the promising grad student, or at least to promise that he'd pray for him and ask him to stay in touch. But before anything came to mind, the line was dead.

He would need to report the incident to Sam. And, of course, he'd have to share it with Jennifer, but carefully. When the time was right.

# 49.   ROAD TRIP?

"Jason? Jason, what's wrong?" Brazen asked, abandoning usual protocols.

JR spoke low and slow. "Need help. Medical. Discrete. Facility compromised, many casualties. Don't know about Jennifer. I have a head wound. Got away. But . . . out for almost two days. Had to pull JR disguise off . . . need someone we can trust . . . who I am. . . "

"Time for JR to die. Not worth the risk. We can find someone in Georgia to help you. Is there anyone you can trust to get you to him? He's in . . . uh, he's in Macon. Is that close to you?"

"Yes. And, uh, yes. Not too far. Give me the address. Ohhh . . . "

"Leave your phone on in case we have to find you. We have ways to triangulate your signal from area cell towers. Call when you can. Head wound, you say?" It was a comment more than a question. "We'll talk again soon, Jason."

A few moments later, Skylar Brown received a call that changed everything. Again.

+ + +

"So, that's the plan," Sam summarized at the safe house that evening. "Jennifer has no law background at all, but she figured out more in minutes than Garrett could in hours and made me look like a rookie."

"I've prayed so hard that I could get back to some kind of normal life," Jennifer said.

"That's the other issue," added Sam. If we can contain Julian and Lanora, and we think we can, that leaves Edgar and JR."

"Especially JR," Jennifer said.

Ed noticed the slight tremble in her voice and a shudder like she had been hit by a cold wind.

"What do you mean, it 'leaves them'?" Mick asked.

Ed spoke up. "Mick, since all this started, there's nothing about you to set off alarm bells with JR. With Bull, yes. But he's out of the picture. Permanently. Same with the guys at the safe house."

"They could have told JR, or someone?" Mick asked.

"If any of them had, you would have had more company by now. Sam? He probably isn't aware of her as a threat either. A very serious one, I'd add."

Sam blushed.

"Me?" Ed continued. "I'm sure they're watching me. Maybe not so much recently, because their attention was on Jennifer. And JR heard what our captors said here in this house. They told him that I didn't have anything except the one capsule."

"The one pill . . . " Jennifer mumbled, staring at the floor.

They waited in respectful silence for her to continue. She nodded, looked up, and smiled. "And, well, here we are. By the way, how in the world did you find me?"

The three tried to outdo each other in humility, but Jennifer kept asking pointed questions until she pieced it all together. After thirty minutes, she was noticeably impressed.

"Sam, you've got a great team here. I think Steve Garrett needs to put you all on payroll!"

Sam chuckled. "I'd put that in my report, but . . . " she paused and looked bewildered. "Wait a minute. We didn't just find you. You, you were breaking out?"

The men glanced at Sam, and then at Jennifer.

"It was bad in there. Really bad. And if JR succeeded? He was after more than just making money. A lot more. Test subjects died. Horribly. I overheard some really creative and disgusting ways they disposed of the bodies. And, well, they ran a lot of tests on me."

She paused to regain her composure.

Ed said, "Jennifer, if it's too much . . . "

She waved him off. "From the moment I woke up, I was planning to escape. But they were careful, and thorough. Finally, I knew I couldn't let them get away with this. If I couldn't escape, well, at least they wouldn't have me anymore as a lab animal, or . . . " her voice trailed off. "So yes, I broke loose, right about the time you stormed the place. I got the .38 from Lanora. Two men tried to kill me. I shot them, then hid until I knew whether I was being rescued or kidnapped by someone even worse."

Now Sam looked impressed. "Okay. That fills in some gaps. And they never found the .38."

Jennifer smiled. "They never will. I also wiped the .45 clean."

Sam laughed. "Jen, this is going to work. We're going to have us a cover story!"

The ladies tag-teamed their explanation of the plan, to use the known drug trade and anything else they could find, as a cover for all that had occurred and was discovered at the otherwise-abandoned facility on the outskirts of Atlanta.

"So," Jennifer concluded, "we're taking a road trip. Sam!" She blurted out, "I don't have any clothes! Just the couple of things we just got."

"Why do you think Garrett wanted to give us till Friday?" Sam grinned. "Don't plan to sleep in tomorrow."

"Let's do it. Girl's day at the mall," Jennifer replied.

Ed had failed to think of an appropriate way to say how good Jennifer looked, two sizes smaller, yet about the same weight because of the added muscle mass. He had wisely remained silent. Until now, as he saw Jennifer's smile fade. "I'm buying," he said. "Sam and Mick have helped with some other things, so this is on me, and 'no' is not an acceptable response."

"Thank you. Thank you all," Jennifer said, her eyes misty. "I really hadn't given much thought about what . . . when . . . if . . . "

Ed spoke up. "I have some ideas we'll talk about when you're ready. But as soon as you feel up to it, I'd like to talk about how you're doing medically."

"Yeah, well, I guess you're the closest thing I've got to a primary doctor now. Actually, I guess it would be a problem if I ever went to anyone else. Hmm. Yes, I need to talk to you about some concerns. And I really want to pick your brain about my faith! Goodness, I hardly know where to start."

Ed and Jennifer shared a lingering, silent look. It was subtle, but it was there. Then Mick and Sam unexpectedly glanced at each other. They were startled and looked away for a beat, and then back. And smiled. It had been many weeks since their last date. Their smiles grew wider.

The four of them continued talking, sharing, joking, and enjoying each other's company for several more hours. Finally, Mick and Sam went to their former rooms, showered, and went to bed. Jennifer and

Ed stayed up until after 2 a.m. In her bed alone, Jennifer was awake for several more hours.

+ + +

"Yes sir, I'd say it's pretty close to a miracle," the retired combat medic said, watching the sleeping man intensely. "Highly unlikely. Especially that he was able to escape, get somewhere safe, and then make the call, what? Almost two days later?"

He listened to the voice on the other end of the phone. "Certainly. Go ahead." A few moments later he nodded and repeated what he had told Brazen.

"He lost a lot of blood, and usually with a wound this severe, he would have bled out. The bullet didn't penetrate directly into his skull. It was more than just a grazing hit. There doesn't appear to be any need for bone repair, I don't detect any cranial swelling, and I've stitched up the wound. His hair should eventually cover the scar, except perhaps when it's wet. And I've got him on IVs to build his fluid back up. Plus, some antibiotics to make sure no infection sets in. He's resting peacefully. Any questions?"

He listened for a few moments. "Yes, his heart is beating strong and regular, good rhythm, and both EEG and EKGs look good. Remarkably good, for what he's been through."

Several more seconds. "To all of you as well. Glad to be serving the cause. Let me know any time I can assist."

He hung up the wall phone—his cell phone couldn't get a solid signal down in his converted basement—and smiled at his quietly resting patient.

"So good to meet you, Jason Matthews. We've been waiting a long time." Looking over to the corner, "Need another cup of coffee?"

Skylar Brown nodded and followed the doctor upstairs. He hadn't asked any questions, beyond concern for his boss. He knew he'd be told what he needed to know when it was appropriate. He also knew, more than ever, that he was just a small fish. A very small fish, in an unimaginably large ocean.

## 50.   PREPARATION

Jennifer and Sam could barely fit in the Mustang. It was loaded down with bags from their hours of shopping. Sam had taken the afternoon off, and they had covered all three levels of Atlanta's Lenox Square from end to end. An hour later, while there was still daylight and after carefully surveilling the complex, they made a quick visit to Jennifer's apartment. Just passed the stairs, Jennifer noticed that the bullet holes had been patched but said nothing.

"Hate to imagine what this dump looks like after all this time," Jennifer moaned as she unlocked the door to the apartment she hadn't seen in well over a month. "I just can't imagine . . . " Her voice trailed off as she entered, turned on the light, and looked in amazement.

"Well, don't just stand there!" exclaimed Sam as she nudged Jennifer aside and walked in.

"Uh, Sam?" Jennifer slowly walked around the living room.

"Look, we were worried sick. We had to believe we would find you, that you'd be alright. I handled all your 'girlie' things; Mick cleaned everything else. I had the full-time job and made sure your bills got paid. Doc started working at an urgent care clinic part time, so that's why he was adamant to update your threads.

"Apartment hasn't been this clean since I moved in. Never." Her eyes were moist. "It's, well, it's like a new world. A new life."

"Did we do good?" Sam smiled.

"You have no idea. I'm so ashamed of the, well, what I was. I already feel like that was a lifetime ago. This helps even more. Thank you."

"You're paid through the month, utilities are up-to-date, and Mick even drove your car some to keep it charged. I think he even cleaned it up and fixed a couple of things for you."

They had walked into her clean, organized bedroom, and bathroom. Fresh linens lay on the bed and clean towels were neatly hung, with the others folded on shelves in the closet. Dead light bulbs had been replaced and the fixtures cleaned. Jennifer pulled out a tissue and dabbed her eyes. Then just reached over and hugged her friend.

"Got another surprise," Sam said after a few moments, as she stepped back, holding Jennifer by the shoulders, and smiling broadly. "Hope you're hungry. The guys are grilling. They're expecting us back at the house in an hour."

"What a send-off," was all Jennifer could muster.

"Girl, we've got places to go and things to do. Miami, F-L-A here we come. Oh!" she exclaimed, "Don't let me forget to pack my bikini. Hope it still fits."

+  +  +

"What an incredible send-off and goodbye." Jennifer sighed and smiled. As promised, the men had grilled them an incredible dinner. Now with everything cleaned up, they were relaxing in the living room.

"Goodbye? Nah, we'll work something out," Mick said.

Jennifer shrugged. "Ed and I are marked. If there's any chance that JR is alive, then we're targets. You two," she nodded to Sam and Mick, "are not."

"And . . . ?" Mick still clearly didn't understand.

"Mick," Sam spoke not as a woman in charge, but as the bearer of bad news. She took a deep breath and blurted, "Mick, it means that they have to go in hiding. Maybe . . . for the rest of their lives."

"But . . . you just said you're going to Miami together?"

Jennifer summarized. "First, I have a commitment to try to find Jasmine. Then, we need to add more to our cover story and make sure it doesn't draw the wrong kind of attention, and I end up with the entire world and half of the known universe after me. Finally? I'd sure like to take down JR's teams. I want to cause that scum to suffer any way that I can. That might also slow him down, at least 'til he re-groups."

Sam added, "When we're done, hopefully Dwayne can also have some success in Chicago, then . . . "

"She's right," Ed interrupted, catching everyone by surprise. "We endanger anyone we're around."

"But we should be able to find some way to at least stay in touch?"

Mick asked quietly.

"You've heard of the Witness Protection program?" Sam asked. "Kinda like that." She spoke to Ed and Jennifer. "Garrett was a Fed before he took over as our Zone commander. I'm sure he had his reasons to leave. A lot of folks thought he was set to go up the food chain very quickly there. Guess he needed to be back down here for family or something."

"CIA?" Ed asked.

Sam smiled. "Nope. One more guess, and the initials are FBI. Several years managing part of their . . . drum roll, please . . . Witness Protection program. We've already talked, and he's going to show you two all the tricks."

An uncomfortable silence followed. They each stared at the floor. Jennifer heard an owl hooting in the darkness outside.

Sam looked at Ed. "If he is alive, there's no telling how soon JR might focus back on you. I'll ask Garrett to give you a point of contact to go with you back to your place. Get enough of everything you need and check into an "extended stay" somewhere for now. We should be back in a few weeks. We'll take a crash course under Garrett and help launch you guys out into a new world. That's my best suggestion."

"Well, for now?" Mick spoke sadly. "I'd say it's time for dessert."

Smiles returned, helped in no small way by in-season peach cobbler and ice cream. Later, Mick and Sam both went to their rooms. Ed made a pot of decaf coffee and brought out two large cups. He set them on the coffee table in front of the couch and sat down. Jennifer returned from her shower, wet hair wrapped in a towel and wearing new pajamas, along with the one clothing item she was so grateful that still fit; her favorite pink terry cloth bathrobe. She sat beside Ed, close, and sipped her coffee.

"Something else I didn't tell you about last night," she began. "Ed, I haven't had, well, my womanly time of the month," she said. "Not since I took FSAT. And, well, of course it's all been an emotional roller coaster. But strange thing is? I haven't noticed any hormonal changes. Nothing."

"Not unusual for that to become sporadic or even stop during periods of high stress, illness, dramatic weight change," replied Ed. "You've been through a lot, so that should get back to normal. I know it's the last thing you want to consider, but if you're interested and when you're ready, I could run some tests."

Jennifer smiled and touched his arm. "You? I trust." She removed her arm and retrieved her coffee. "That's not a bad idea. I think I need to know more about what's going on with the new Jennifer. I picked up some things from JR's people, but not to the detail I'd like to know."

Ed raised his eyebrows.

"What I learned from them? Stuff like, I recover quickly from heat stress, I'm very resistant to cold, I don't seem to develop altitude sickness. And they exposed me to a lot of stuff, some that they apparently got from CDC, and I was able to fight it off."

"What?" Ed exclaimed.

"All of it. They sealed the room, came in wearing special suits, and did a lot of skin pricks over many days. They said that I'm an antibiotic factory. Just wish I knew what some of that was."

"Incredible," replied Ed, though he didn't press for details.

Jennifer continued. "What they never learned about me? You know about the strength thing. Apparently the IV they used to keep me under? It didn't work. I just played along so they didn't give me even more. I thought of it as a beer level, whether I felt like I'd had one, two, or three beers. But it did slow the acceleration of strength. I never lost any, just didn't gain as quickly. Probably wouldn't have any affect now that I've caught up. But . . . " she sat up, set her coffee down, and turned to face him. "Ed! The intellectual stuff!" She grabbed his arm. Firmly.

"Careful," he smiled, and winced.

"Oh, sorry," she lightened her grip but didn't let go. "Ed, I see patterns. I mean, I can look at numbers and I can just see how they would add together, or multiply, or divide; whatever! I'll probably be able to do the same with higher math. And I remember things. It's like all my memories are laid out in front of me, and my mind is continually cataloging them for better recall, and I'm putting things together that I never even paid attention to!"

"Jen, let me tell you what's more amazing."

She looked at him quizzically.

"In spite of everything—all the changes, your uniqueness, all of it— you are an amazing person."

Her eyes became moist. He reached out and gently drew her to him. She cuddled in his arms, head against his chest. They sat together like that for a very long time.

## 51.  HEADING SOUTH

The weather was already hot at 10 a.m. as Sam and Jennifer merged onto I-75 South out of Atlanta. The deep exhaust tone was loud, but not unpleasant. The ladies both wore spaghetti-strap tops, shorts, and sandals, well-prepared for the hotter and more humid weather expected in Miami.

Plans were to drive the long leg today, make it to Orlando, then drive the short leg Saturday and get to Miami in time to sit by the pool. Finish the day with seafood at a restaurant Ed had recommended, and a new movie they both wanted to see. Sunday? Hit the beach.

Monday, it would be back to work, meeting with the police contact Major Garrett had set up. Beyond that, no clue.

"Mind if I check out Angelo's cell phone?" Jennifer asked.

"Go for it. Our team got a list of calls and will fax us the account info as soon as they get it from the carriers. Obviously, they didn't try to call any of them. And they said the voice messages have to be some kind of code. Made no sense at all. They'd never heard anything like it."

As they drove though Macon, Jennifer asked if Sam had Dwayne Wilson's cell number. Dwayne was scheduled to fly to Chicago on Sunday and meet with the police there to follow up on Drake Cavanaugh's criminal activities in the Windy City. He answered on the third ring.

"Dwayne? Sam. Jennifer and I are on our way south. Got a minute? She's got some questions." Sam passed her phone to Jennifer.

"Hi, Dwayne. Any chance you have Drake's cell phone close by? Wanted to see if you could play back his voice messages. It looks like there's a pattern." Several moments passed. "Yes, if you could just start with the most recent and play it back. Hopefully it'll give a date and time stamp for each one."

She listened intently for several minutes. Sam would occasionally glance at her. Jennifer's eyes were closed as she held the phone against her ear. "Yes, I'm tracking," she said eventually. "Please keep going. Maybe two or three more."

After several more minutes: "Dwayne, thank you so much! I'll think through this, and I may need you to share some more later." Pause. "You, too. Have a good flight."

"What in the world?" Sam asked.

Jennifer turned in her seat to face Sam. "Okay, some really dumb questions. So just humor me. If you were doing whatever it is these guys do—getting stuff in, sending stuff out—what would that look like? Really high level. Like, start with stuff coming in."

Sam glanced at her, then back at the interstate.

"Miami. Our contact can tell us more. I assume most of whatever they get comes by ship or private boat."

"What stuff? I mean, is it just one drug, or several? Other contraband? I don't know, Cuban cigars?"

Sam only pondered a moment. "Again, our contact can verify, but I'm pretty sure it's cocaine. JR's too organized to go after low-dollar stuff. It's gotta be coke."

"Next, do you think there would be a lot of pick-up places, like twenty, maybe? Or just a few, like between four and ten?"

"Let's say JR's team is at the high end. Probably a few really big suppliers, and only a few well-concealed and guarded drops. Same with ways to ship out. By that I mean, highway transport by truck, van, or SUV. Different locations, probably. JR seems to keep things compartmentalized."

"So . . . " Jennifer mused. "In by several ways, out by several more. Do you think they were into prostitution or anything like that?"

"Doubt it. High legal risk for low payback. Surprised he was even a loan shark. Maybe that's how he started, and he just kept at it not so much for profit, but for control."

"Like Jackson Longevity Research, and various medical-related personnel he could call in?"

"Yep. Whatcha thinking, Jen?"

"Give me some time to let it sink in."

Jennifer turned back forward and let her seat back down a few clicks. She closed her eyes and appeared ready for a nap.

"Mind if I play the radio?"

"Go for it," Jennifer smiled.

+ + +

A few hours later, it was time to refill. The Mustang still had a quarter tank of gas, but Sam had been warned of possible delays from below Tifton until they reached Lake City, Florida. I-75 had been under constant construction along that stretch for years, and they certainly didn't want to run out of gas.

Next, their late breakfast was followed by a 2 p.m. lunch at a Shoney's in Ashburn. Jennifer ordered off the menu, Sam tackled the buffet. When Sam came back with her two plates, Jennifer was smiling.

"High school English. Writing a news story. What's important about the first paragraph?" Jennifer asked.

"Other than making sure your facts are correct, I always heard it's to lead in the story with who, what, when, where, and why. Right?"

Jennifer's grin grew, and she took a long drink of ice tea.

"Patterns?" Sam ventured.

"Patterns," Jennifer stated. "Look, we'll be able to get cell phone records. And they know that. They likely suspect that even cell phone calls can be tapped and traced. So, they have to organize in a way that's hard to track and harder to prove in court. What puts JR's teams at the top of their game? They communicate clearly, effectively, and privately."

"And similarly?" Sam asked.

"Yep. Seems Drake used the same method to coordinate his activities as Angelo."

"Which is?" Sam asked, as she started eating her salad.

"All the crazy voice messages, with someone just reading random letters and numbers? Each alphanumeric stream is separated by a pause. So, the stuff in each sentence has to make some kind of sense, but of course it doesn't. Not until you take the number for the day of the month and add it to the numeric value of each alphanumeric. Start with A as one, and if it's the 30th day of the month, then the first letter is 31. Since there are only 26 letters, you count zero, one, two, three, and four. That's the first character, followed by a space. So, toward the end of a month, all characters are represented by numbers. At the beginning of a month, there are a lot more letters. On the 10th day, for example, A would be one plus ten, which is eleven, which is K."

Sam stared, then asked, "And . . . it takes how many hours to figure out, make a call that isn't answered, and leave an encoded voice message? I mean, these are thugs, not military cryptographers. No offense, but . . . "

The waitress brought Jennifer's lunch and refilled her tea. Jennifer bowed her head in silent prayer, then picked up her fork and smiled.

"None taken. Answer? Computers. Type in your who, what, when, where, and . . . in this case, how. Add in the date. The computer has a line of alphanumeric characters for you to carefully read. They transcribe it back out at the other end."

She paused long enough to enjoy a bite of country fried steak, then continued.

"Several names keep repeating and the 'what' is mostly coke from several suppliers, and occasionally pot from a couple more. At least, that's based on what I've seen so far and the ones that Drake shared. 'When' is a three-letter day, like MON or WED, and a time on a 24-hour clock, like 0800 or 2000. 'Where?' I don't recognize the locations. Hopefully our contact person will."

While she took another bite, Sam spoke up. "How, Jennifer? How?"

Jennifer relished her mashed potatoes and carrots, washed them down with more iced tea, and smiled again. "Some of the locations? Inbound. Ship or, more often, yacht. Other locations? Outbound. Semi, truck, van, or SUV."

Back in the Mustang, refreshed and excited, Sam asked: "Jasmine?"

Jennifer nodded. "Jasmine. If they're not into prostitution, and they're at the higher end of the food chain, not the direct dealing? Whatcha wanna bet that they're using her for transport? Threatening to kill her mother if she doesn't comply."

"Just like they used her to threaten Lanora. I think I'd lose that bet."

"And the good news is?" Jennifer asked.

Sam nodded. "The fantastic news is that she's probably okay!"

## 52.    LIAISON

Pools, beach, malls, restaurants—so far, seafood and Cuban—a movie, and some serious planning of other things they would like to do. But now it was Monday morning and time for business.

Sam and Jennifer arrived at the police precinct right on time, 9 a.m., both professionally dressed in dark colored, lightweight pantsuits. Sam sported a modest tan she'd acquired the past day and a half. Jennifer? A healthy glow, but no significant tan despite no sunscreen and a lighter complexion.

The women were introduced to Sargent Mia Gonzales. The no-nonsense Hispanic woman was in her mid-forties, stood five-feet-four inches, and a stocky 160. She loved her city, and it showed.

"So concerned," she said, as she gave them an overview of crime in Miami. "Heading toward a crime rate per 100,000 people that would bring us to twentieth in the nation in the next year to two. And drugs? We're a major point of entry for cocaine. Comes in from Colombia, Bolivia, and Peru. It's bringing in billions of dollars into front organizations that launder the money and pump it into the local economy. Lot of the newer top-end hotels, condos, nightclubs, luxury car and boat dealerships, stuff like that? Blood money. And bringing in violent crime. Can't keep up. Let's get coffee. I tell you more."

She led the way to their breakroom, where they filled tall cups with coffee, then followed her to a small conference room.

"Any progress at all?" Sam asked.

"We work closely with FBI. Biggest bust so far, four years ago. FBI scored their largest-ever direct seizure of cocaine, a large yacht. Few months later, they find a stash house used to distribute and transport cocaine and marijuana. Confiscated almost four million in cash."

"Wow," Sam exclaimed.

"Did it make a difference?" Jennifer asked.

"For a while. But you know? Supply and demand. If there's a demand, someone keeps stepping up to supply. The very next year, a big case. A big win. Thirteen convictions pretty much shut down Dangond

Columbian Drug Organization. They'd been importing and distributing multi-ton shipments of cocaine. Part of what got confiscated? A 400-foot freighter."

"That had to have helped," said Jennifer.

"Again, for a while," agreed Mia. "But, you know, you take out the big dogs? Give more room for small dogs to grow up. You got a way to help us knock some of them off? We're listening. Get all the help we can. Save my Miami."

"Mia, my commander probably told you about Jennifer, here," said Sam. "She got pulled into an operation by someone who goes by the initials, 'JR.' His main person in Miami is, or was—he was killed in our raid to rescue Jennifer—Angelo. No last name we know of, just Angelo. Anyway," she began opening her briefcase, "here's what our CSI team found. Here's all the other material we collected. You should get some more records, like cellular phone records, faxed here within a few days."

"They were on my desk this morning," Mia said.

"Excellent. So," Sam continued, and pulled out a cell phone, "Part of Jennifer's recovery is, she wants to help. We'll go over all the other stuff, but I think this will blow you away."

The three women spent all day poring over the reports and records, and carefully transcribing the messages. All of them. Sam had made the mistake of mentioning her love for Philly cheesesteaks, and Mia took her to a local deli that beat anything she'd had in Atlanta. Jennifer was likewise impressed with her Cuban sandwich. Mia shared the code Jennifer had broken of the various locations with her team.

"Now?" Mia smiled as they walked to their cars at the end of her shift. "Now, we wait."

Angelo's phone was on and fully charged. Evidently, from the phone records and the fact that it hadn't received any calls, it was used infrequently. For other calls, he likely used a standard phone or even a pay phone. Or? Maybe someone in the organization had learned about the raid and Angelo's death. If so, they would assume that his phone was compromised and delete its contact information. *Possible,* Sam thought, *but doubtful.*

Sam and Jennifer followed Mia's advice and enjoyed a Polynesian dinner and show that night.

+   +   +

"Hey, Mick!" Sam answered her cell. She had just parked her car and the two women were walking into the motel.

"So, have you taken down the Godfather and his organization yet?" Mick asked.

"Funny. No, but soon. You know what I've been telling you about Jen's code? Our contact here is very impressed. She recognizes some of the locations, and her team's looking into other details. It went really well today. We're about to get in the elevator, so I might lose you."

"Okay," Mick said. "Well, call back if you've got a minute. Just interested. Concerned. And, Sam?"

"Yeah?"

"I miss you. Please be careful."

"I miss you, too. You still owe me a concert. I'll call you after I get a shower."

The women were alone on the elevator. Sam's room was on the eighth floor; Jennifer's on the tenth.

"He's a good man, Sam. I am so embarrassed that I was such a jerk."

"He is a good man. When Bull tried to take both of you down? I told him at the hospital how impressed I was. He held everything together better than men twice his age, including some macho-types I've seen fall apart like whiney babies. And all that he did trying to find you? Yep. He's a keeper."

"I'm really happy for you two," Jennifer said as she touched her friend's arm. The elevator door opened on Sam's floor.

"Thanks. And tell me, girlfriend. You and Ed staying in contact?"

"Every single night." Jennifer smiled as the elevator doors closed.

+   +   +

"JR is dead."

Skylar's mouth dropped open. Wisely, he said nothing.

"You're one of only a handful of people who know who JR really is. Or, *was*. I'm Jason Matthews. JR was a cover for, shall we say, some after-hours activities."

Skylar nodded. "Yes, sir. Looks like Bull tried to follow your example. I didn't know a thing about his 'normal' life."

"Yes. Well, you've served me well, and I want that to continue. Will that be a problem?"

The older man was intimidating, even with his head still wrapped in bandages. But Skylar looked at him straight in the eye and responded firmly. "No, sir. It will be an honor."

It was ever-so-slight, but Skylar noticed. Jason smiled.

"So, tell me, Mr. Matthews. How are we going to kill off JR?"

"Didn't you notice? He already died. I just need you to send out the word."

## 53. SETUP

"**S**o, what's with this girl? Is she some kind of savant?" Mike Jernigan was one of the technical specialists who provided support to the various Miami police teams as needed. He was in a conference room with Mia and Jose Morgalo. Mike was an office type; early twenties, light complexion, tall, and thin. Jose? He looked like a man ready to do business, if the business involved being a bouncer at a high-end night club. Dark complexion, black hair, tattoos on muscled arms. At six feet and over 220, he was one of the precinct's most successful plainclothes investigators.

"Don't know. But she's smart. She's here to help, but we've got to be careful. Gentle. She's been through a lot." A moment later Sam and Jennifer entered.

"Ladies!" Mia exclaimed. "Introductions, and then some very interesting news."

Two minutes later, Mia handed Angelo's cell phone to Jennifer. "Listen to what came in at 6 a.m."

Jennifer replayed the voice mail, closed her eyes, and sat still a full minute as the others remained silent. Finally, Mike looked at his notebook and started to speak. "I have the transla . . . "

Jennifer motioned him off. "No, no, it's not that. I just don't understand why they'd do a drop-off from a yacht in a harbor at 6 p.m.? Why not 10? Or after midnight?"

Mike's draw dropped. "It took me an hour . . . "

Sam spoke up. "Is it to mask what they're doing? Hiding it in plain sight?"

"Busiest time of day," Jose agreed. "Pandemonium. Everyone trying to get through and get home. Boats and ships trying to leave port. Lot less conspicuous."

Mia smiled. "Time to host a welcome party?"

"Time to call Travis Johnson," Jose responded.

"He's on his way," Mia replied, then smiled at Sam and Jennifer. "FBI."

+  +  +

"Hey, Jen. Didn't expect a call this early. Everything okay?"

"Yeah," Jennifer replied from her hotel room, smiling at hearing Ed's friendly greeting.

"Just odd girl out for the evening. A call came in this morning. We didn't answer it, of course, so they left a voice message. We transcribed and decoded it. There's a shipment arriving in under an hour, at one of the docks. Mia, our police contact, called in the FBI. They've invited Sam to be another pair of eyes. They just want to observe, get pictures, and see if they can track it. If it matches other drop-offs I've seen, it'll be out for delivery tomorrow evening. That's when they want to do the raid."

"That soon! They don't wait around," Ed replied.

"Nope. What have you been up to?"

"Not much. Going through the apartment, deciding what to keep, what to store, and what to give to the Salvation Army."

"Well, it's like a well-rehearsed play here. Good thing, too. Normally, they might just monitor and track, until they understood the network and could work their way to the top. But we don't know how long before the natives get restless with no word from JR or Angelo. If they also learn that Drake's gone silent, all JR's operations could shut down and go into hiding."

"Jen, are you okay?" Ed asked. Her heart skipped a beat at the sound of his genuine concern.

"This has really been good for me. I feel I really have a friend in Sam. She's like the sister . . . well, full sister . . . I never had. She's a rock. We're having a great time, but we also have a strong purpose. Ed, people are dying. JR and his poison? This stuff is killing people directly, and far more through violent crimes. And there's Jasmine."

"Any word on her?"

"Nothing yet. We suspect she's part of the transport team; a mule. So anyway, yeah, this trip is just what the doctor ordered."

"Told you so."

"Alright, wise guy," she retorted. Then her tone turned serious. "Just, well . . . "

"What is it, Jennifer?"

"So many changes. And I finally get close, I mean, have some real friends, and I have to go into hiding . . . " her voice trailed off.

"We, Jennifer. We have to go into hiding," he corrected her.

There was a long pause. Finally, just above a whisper, she asked, "Together?"

No pause at his end. "I certainly hope so, young lady. After all, I'm your doctor. And more." He didn't elaborate. "Let's see what we can learn from Garrett. You just take good care of yourself and get back here soon. I miss you."

+  +  +

"Sam, so how'd it go?"

"Amazing, Jen, just like a real FBI Op. They gave me a tactical radio, binoculars, and placed me into position. We had to report status, everything. And pictures . . . they had two different cameras set up, shot several rolls with massive telephotos. They'll have a lab process them overnight. I mean, this is huge."

"Way to go, Agent Sam!" Jennifer chuckled. "The next messages should go out in the morning for pickups tomorrow evening, if they follow the pattern. They'll set up the location for mules to load up and transport."

"That's when we draw in the net," Sam said.

"And find Jasmine."

"Her, and perhaps dozens of others who are risking their lives out of fear or blackmail. Hungry?"

It was 8 p.m.

"Starving I've been sitting here by my phone waiting to hear from you."

"See you in the lobby in thirty."

+  +  +

"So, it's on," Jennifer said somberly as she set the phone down.

Mike nodded. "Message came in at seven this morning. Mia called in the team."

Jennifer and Sam met Mia at 9 a.m. Mia already had Mike, Jose, and now Travis, waiting in the conference room.

Travis spoke first. "FBI photo analysts estimate this is a lot of cocaine, one of the larger shipments that's come in over the past several years. We're talking huge; tons. This could go all over the country. Street value in the tens of millions. Maybe over a hundred million. We bust this, and the people behind it, and we could put a serious hurt on the drug trade."

Jennifer glanced back at the transcribed message. "Where's 'Little Haiti?'"

Mike just shook his head. This morning, it had taken him 45 painstaking minutes to decode the message. Ms. Lane did it almost as fast as reading the raw transcription.

Mia walked to a projector screen on a large side wall and pulled down a detailed map of Miami and the surrounding area. She stood to the side and pointed. "Lot of immigrants came here starting last decade. Haitians? Most of them settled in an area out from Northeast Second Avenue and 54th Street."

Jose looked at Travis. "So, we've got till seven tonight to find someplace in all of Little Haiti, that they might use to transfer and ship out all this?"

"Gotta be big. Look at the message. Semi's, plural. SUV's, plural, Vans, plural. If this is as big as you guys said," motioning to Travis, "this place has gotta be able to handle a lot of traffic in a short time."

"Still gonna take a long time to narrow this down," muttered Jose.

"May I help?" Jennifer asked.

## 54. TAKEDOWN

Al Frederickson paced the floor. He took a last drag off an unfiltered cigarette, tossed it underfoot and stomped it out on the warehouse floor, and then lit another one. The balding, heavyset man was sweating, thanks to Miami's early afternoon heat and humidity. The clouds helped, and the promise of rain might also help for a while—but only if it lasted long enough to lower the temperature before the humidity shot up even higher. Huge warehouse ventilation fans were all that kept Al from passing out. But none of that was unusual.

Al was Angelo's "Number Two." A distant Number Two, but he's the one Angelo fingered to keep things going when The Boss had unexpectedly called him to Atlanta weeks earlier. And now, Number Two had some decisions to make. Make them right, he'd be a hero. Wrong? No one would ever find his body.

"Tell me again, Marcos," he barked to the man pacing beside him.

"Sir, I already . . . "

"Tell me again," he snapped as he deeply inhaled and slowly blew out.

"The guy that Bull sent to us? What, six or so weeks ago? And we had no idea what it was about? He called me this morning. Said the operation failed. Raided by a SWAT team. Couldn't confirm anything about Angelo, but he said JR and lots of his men were killed. That's it, Al. That's all I know."

Al let out a string of profanity. He turned and faced the young Hispanic, his own "Number Two," but looked right through him. "The largest shipment we've ever taken on. Six months of planning. Over a hundred million dollars. Pickup's tonight. And Angelo might be dead." He didn't mention JR. The man was rarely mentioned, and then only by the very top echelon of the organization.

"Can't reach Angelo?" Marcos asked.

Now Al did look directly at the younger man and scowled. He pulled out a handkerchief, already soaked with sweat, wiped his head, and stuffed it back in his pocket.

230 Five Score and Ten

"You don't call the man unless it's an emergency. He calls you. But yes, I've tried to reach him this morning. And no, I can't."

Marcos remained silent as they continued pacing.

"Okay, here's what we do. Call in everybody. Armed to the teeth. Spread them out everywhere. We clear out this shipment, then put everything on hold until we find out what's going on. Got it?"

"Yes sir," Marcos responded and started to walk away to make the calls.

"And Marcos?"

"Sir?"

"Tell 'em to get here an hour early!"

+ + +

That day, everyone worked for Jennifer. It only took a few minutes for them to all realize that if they were going to identify target zero by that evening, she had to be the lead analyst. Detailed maps were brought in so she could analyze streets. Pictures and development surveys were brought over, thanks to FBI resources, so she could estimate warehouse floorspace along with truck access and turnarounds.

Many warehouses were well-known and had been occupied by legitimate businesses for years. Others? Not so much. As she would call out possible locations, plainclothes officers in unmarked cars would drive by and report. Only one warehouse stood out as a likely location.

By 3 p.m., they were each certain of one specific location. Travis took over, as it would be an FBI Op, with Miami providing SWAT backup. Jose was dispatched to wander around with eyes on the facility and report anything unusual between his arrival and 6:30 p.m., and then to clear away to protect him from 'friendly fire.' Mia and Sam would be in the unmarked Mustang a block away, ready to trail but not engage any vehicle that escaped. As before, Sam took Jennifer back to the motel to wait it out.

Before they left, they made sure Travis had pictures of Jasmine to hand out, with instructions that some of the mules were likely unwilling participants.

Sam was back at the precinct by five to pick up Mia, who didn't even try to hide her admiration for the confiscated and converted car, and how Sam was responsible for the drug bust that took it away from the criminals.

"Hope we see more of that tonight," Mia added. "Just wish we had more time to spread the net."

"Yep," Sam agreed. "But if we don't move while we have the intel, it could all go underground and out of sight." She adjusted her radio channels to match the team, performed a radio check, and drove to Little Haiti to familiarize herself with the layout, just in case.

+  +  +

It was 6 p.m. Jennifer had looked up the number for the cab company and started to place the call. No way was she going to sit this one out. Too much was at stake, and she had the brains and the brawn to help make sure it went down correctly. She wanted to hurt JR any way that she could.

But then a strange impression came over her. At exactly 6 p.m., she set down the phone and knelt beside her motel bed and began praying. She earnestly prayed for the specific protection of Sam, the team, Jasmine, and all the other innocents. She prayed that the raid would be accomplished successfully without violence and would result in a major, successful bust that would cripple the drug trade and put many criminals behind bars. She prayed for much more, for a long time.

+  +  +

In Little Haiti, Al was taking no chances. "Okay, listen up. We've put too much into this, and there's too much on the table to screw it up. We're going to have a clean distribution tonight, just like everything we've done before, but bigger. Way bigger. And then everything sits until further word."

He paused and looked over the three dozen men. Each one had substantial firepower, either a rifle or large caliber handgun. Most had both, along with extra ammo clips. Al wiped the sweat off his face and head, regretting the large, late, and hot Mexican lunch he had indulged in. He chewed a couple of antacids and continued.

"So, here's the deal. I asked you all to come here, come early, and come prepared. We don't expect any trouble. But you follow my lead. Got it? No one, I mean no one, fires off a single round without my specific direction. Not even a warning shot. Got it? Don't screw this up!"

They all nodded. He was the boss in Angelo's absence. And no one wanted to have to answer to Angelo.

+ + +

Jennifer glanced at the clock beside her bed for the hundredth time. It was 7 p.m. She nervously ate some snacks she had purchased from the hotel. Seven fifteen. She prayed again, for another ten minutes. She paced, stared out her window, fixed some decaf. Seven thirty. Prayed some more. By the time her phone went off at eight, she was a nervous wreck.

"Jennifer. Are you sitting down?" She had never heard that tone in Sam's voice before.

"Sam, are you okay? What's happening?"

"Jen, this could have been a brutal blood bath. I mean, we could have lost everyone. Hopelessly outgunned."

"Sam!"

"Bottom line, the raid was an overwhelming success. Not a shot fired. Everything confiscated, all done by-the-book. Should completely close down this operation and everyone involved. And we've got records. I found Jasmine's name and phone number."

"Hallelujah. But . . . you said it could have been a disaster. It turned out a success?"

"One casualty. Travis overheard some of the gang griping to each other. Seems the guy in charge had to go to the bathroom just before the FBI hit the place. Apparently, he'd been really tough on them not to use their weapons without his specific command. The FBI found him dead in the bathroom, apparent a heart attack. So? Everyone laid their weapons down. We're all in shock. Travis says he's never even heard of such a thing."

# 55.  NEW BEGINNINGS

"Commander?"

Garrett answered. "I'm on. I've also got Agent Jackson, part of our local FBI team. He'll relay information to Yuma."

"Got Clayton and Manuel's phones?" Sam asked. She and Jennifer were in Sam's motel room, listening to Sam's cell on speaker.

"Yep. Same gibberish." Garrett responded. "Dwayne, can you hear us?"

"Sure can," Dwayne replied. "Sam's got some news for us?"

Garrett said, "Yes. I asked everyone to conference in for two reasons. First, Sam's going to tell us about a world-class drug bust she and Jennifer helped orchestrate last night. Then, Jennifer's going to explain the code. It should be of direct help in Chicago. But there may also still be some benefit to tracking down similar activity in Yuma. They all used the same code."

For the next ten minutes, Sam explained how they used the code to first observe the arrival of a major drug shipment, and then intercepted the planned distribution. Jennifer then spent over an hour explaining the code and answering technical questions. She even had Garrett play back a couple of messages from Clayton's phone, which she decoded live, on-the-fly. She told Dwayne to play back two particular messages that he had played for her earlier, and from memory did the same thing.

"Any other questions?" Garrett asked. After a brief pause, "Thanks, ladies. Great work. Have a safe trip back and we'll see you in a couple of days."

"Let me see what Mia wants, then let's get some breakfast. I'm starved," Sam told Jennifer after they hung up. She re-dialed Mia, who had tried to call twice during the conference call.

Mia answered on the third ring. "Sam, just wanted you to know something that might help close out a huge missing piece of your report in Atlanta."

"Oh?" Sam asked.

"Yeah, you know in the report you brought down, it said that a man named JR appeared to be shot, then SWAT couldn't find the body when CSI arrived?"

"Right," Sam answered cautiously, glancing at Jennifer.

"Well, one of the guys we captured, guy named Marcos. He's cooperating, hoping for a lighter sentence. Said that he got a call from a guy they'd met briefly from Atlanta. Guy named Skylar. He told Marcos about the raid there in Atlanta and said that JR had died. Marcos had no way of confirming, but it helps close out your Atlanta report. And, he said that Al Fredrickson, the guy in our raid that died of the heart attack? That's why he called in all the extra firepower. Apparently, he thought that the organization had been compromised."

Sam smiled. "And he was so right, Mia. Thanks. If you can fax that to us, we'll add it to our report. See ya!"

"Will do, girl. You and Jen are welcome down here anytime. I'll personally take you out to dinner. Thanks for helping save my Miami."

"JR is dead? So?" Sam raised her eyebrows.

Jennifer looked wistfully at the ceiling above her friend for a moment as her smile grew. "So, Ed and I get our lives back."

+   +   +

"Uh, hello?"

Jennifer smiled at the voice on the other end of the call. She had first identified her as Voice Two. Later, as one of her captors and tormentors. But she came to realize that Lanora had been her strongest advocate and helper during her imprisonment. Now, she thought of Lanora as a friend.

"Lanora . . . " she slowly and sweetly drew the name out.

"Jennifer! Honey! Oh, I'm so glad you found my number. Jasmine's gonna be coming home! Thank you, thank you, thank you!"

"You are so welcome. Soon as she gives her statement, I'm told she should be cleared to head back. I haven't met her, but if she's anything like her mom . . . "

"Oh, honey, now don't wish that on the poor girl!"

"Well, don't go into details about our little secret, but you can tell her that I've got a temper, maybe that I know karate or something. Tell her I'll come put a hurt on her if she doesn't treat you right. Okay?"

"Aw, Jen. You're an angel."

+  +  +

Sam and Jennifer took their time getting back to Atlanta, taking an extra day in Miami and three days visiting attractions in Orlando. They made it back to Sam's office mid-day Monday, ten days after they had left.

"So, commander, what do you think?" Sam asked Garrett behind closed doors. Jennifer sat quietly, wringing her hands.

He walked around his desk and sat on the edge, thoughtful. "You know, it comes down to this. I really don't know what to advise. A week ago, we just knew of four remaining people who could be a threat to your secret, Jennifer. I don't think there's an issue with Julian or Lanora. And like I told you when we talked Friday, when we finally tracked down Edgar, we found that he'd committed suicide. Who's left? JR. But SWAT believes he's dead. Even if they were wrong, and somehow that he escaped on his own, we now hear indirectly that he did, indeed, die."

"So, just maybe Ed and I can go back to living normal lives? At least, whatever normal may look like for me now?"

Garrett smiled. "Maybe in time. Let's keep watch for a little while longer. Maybe we'll get proof that he's dead. Me? I'd sure like to see you as a police investigator. Or at least as a consultant, an analyst, something for heaven's sakes!"

He blushed profusely as the beautiful young blonde grabbed him and lifted him off the desk in a bear hug. Sam laughed so hard her sides hurt.

+  +  +

Encouraged, the ladies drove back to the safe house. They had big plans for the night.

At 7 p.m., they met the guys at a popular casual steak restaurant outside of Atlanta. They all hugged. Mick and Sam just hugged a little longer, as did Ed and Jennifer. There was plenty of background noise, and their table was off in a corner, so they talked freely about Sam and Jennifer's adventures in Miami.

Finally, after dessert, Ed shared his one remaining frustration.

"So, if maybe everything's cleared up, what am I supposed to do now that I've got rid of half my stuff, put half of what's left in storage, and have to clear out of my place in a couple of weeks?"

"You could become a monk," joked Sam.

"Or a male stripper," added Mick.

Jennifer laughed, yet even though she was immersed in their conversation, she remained fully aware of everything happening around her. That ability had been disconcerting for a while, but she was getting used to it. There was an argument in the kitchen, a person several tables away ordering one too many Margaritas, a couple in a separate dining area celebrating an anniversary. Several televisions were playing simultaneously on different channels.

One TV behind Jennifer and to her right, was playing a network news channel. Nothing special, just a commentator interviewing a former Congressional candidate. Jennifer didn't pay it much attention, but as with everything else, she couldn't fully ignore it either.

"So, Mr. Matthews, it's been weeks since you suspended your campaign," the female reporter continued. "And this is your first interview since that initial announcement. Can you tell us where you plan to go from here? What's next?"

Sam was making another joke about Ed hosting a radio call-in program for people who survived UFO abductions. They all laughed again.

"Martha, it's like this," began the candidate's reply to the reporter. His voice was warm, sincere, captivating. "There's a unique, higher calling on my life. You'll be a part of making that happen. I won't let anything get in the way of my destiny."

Jennifer caught her breath, dropped her water, and stumbled out of her chair. From the floor she gazed at the TV, shaking. The man's body size and proportions, his voice, his facial expressions . . .

Ed jumped to her side, checking for choking or some other medical emergency. She waved him off. Other patrons were staring as Ed helped her back to her chair and knelt beside her. For all appearances, she'd suffered a seizure.

"Jennifer," Ed said. "What is it? What's wrong?"

She grabbed his hand.

"Sorry," she whispered as she lightened her grip. "I'm so sorry," she repeated loud enough for all her friends to hear. "We need to leave. I don't want to cause more of a scene, but sooner rather than later. Like in the next few minutes. Who has the largest car? Ed. Let's get into your car and I'll explain."

Within five minutes, Ed had paid their bill and they had casually left the restaurant. They were in Ed's sedan, engine and AC running.

"Okay. This is not a joke. You've got to believe me, and it's heart-attack serious. Ed? JR is alive. He's Jason Matthews."

## 56.   GOODBYES

They made it back to the safe house after midnight. Garrett authorized it, but it took time to collect everything they needed for another few days. He was adamant that if possible, they should all have at least those last few days together.

The next morning, Ed and Jennifer were in his office behind a closed door. Sam and Mick had not been invited.

"This is something I've had to do several times in my career," he said, pacing. "It's never easy. And it's never been this personal. Jennifer, when Sam called last night, I checked back on Edgar. Talked directly to the coroner first thing this morning. His suicide? Questionable."

"Oh, no!" Jennifer exclaimed, then added, "We've got to warn Lanora."

"You're right. I'll have Sam do that. I'll make sure somebody tells Julian as well. But now we need to talk about the two of you. I can't promise how long it will take to get this man. To eliminate him as a threat."

"There's the other issue, Steve," Jennifer said softly. "I'm severely constrained in what I can do. I'm your main witness. But if I testify . . . "

He stared at her, at both of them, for a long time, then resumed pacing.

"I understand. Take out one threat, and risk international attention a hundred times worse."

"Or a thousand," added Ed.

"I'll help however I can, it just has to be in the background," Jennifer said.

"Agreed." Steve Garrett stopped pacing and sat at his desk. "I'm afraid the two of you will have to plan this out for the long run. Perhaps for the rest of your lives."

For the next two hours, with several breaks, he force-fed them everything he could teach them, all the techniques to establish new identities and disappear into society. He ordered lunch for them and continued as they ate.

At 3 p.m., he wrapped up the day. "So, I can use my resources and contacts to help you, exactly once. There won't be a do-over."

They both nodded in agreement. Garrett stood and began pacing again.

"There's a final point I feel I have to make. It's personal, and I certainly wouldn't force this on you. But I believe, well, I believe it will increase your chances."

Ed spoke up. "We need to be married."

Garret stared at them and remained silent.

Ed turned and looked at Jennifer so seriously it startled her. "Jen, I can't think of anything I want more." He grabbed both of her hands and knelt before her. "I owe you my life, and whatever's left of it, I want us to be in this together. If you'll take an older man? Please. Please marry me."

+  +  +

Ed and Jennifer promised each other that if possible, they would someday have a full church wedding and Christian celebration of what should have been the most exciting day of their lives. Each realized, however, that such an event could be years, perhaps decades, away. Or it might never happen at all.

Still, standing before the magistrate judge in the small, private ceremony, Jennifer couldn't think of a single living person she'd rather have as part of their celebration than Sam, Mick, and Steve Garrett. Ed felt the same way. They only regretted that even the legal documents had to be witnessed by strangers, as they couldn't afford to leave any trail back to their friends.

There was one change that Jennifer did request, however, and that day the judge made it happen. Her legal name would no longer be Jennifer Karen Lane. It became Karen Lane Richardson.

"Jennifer represents the old me," she explained to Ed and their friends. "But I am a new creation, in more ways than one. The old has passed away."

Their reception was no more than the four of them, plus Steve Garrett, getting together at the safe house that afternoon. That was also where they began their honeymoon, as Sam and Mick had already returned to their apartments that morning.

Alone, standing in the living room, holding each other tightly, Karen remarked, "I wouldn't have it any other way. It was at that other safe house that my life changed. I went in there as a narcissistic jerk. I became a Christian. I grew up and became a woman." She pulled away just far enough so she could gaze intently at Ed. "And now I'm in this safe house as a wife," she smiled, and they kissed again. "I can so get used to this," she said as they embraced again. "Even if I may never actually be able to use my married name after today."

She said the same thing even more enthusiastically the next morning, after very little sleep.

+  +  +

Karen had said goodbye to Jennifer. For better or worse, she and Ed had said goodbye to their single days. Soon, as they continued clearing out their apartments over the next few days—under close guard—they would say goodbye to Atlanta and perhaps even Georgia. They would also have to say goodbye to their friends.

+  +  +

Jason had said goodbye to his long-time alias, where he had gained his clandestine wealth. It's also how he had honed many of his management skills, not that they would ever show up on a resume. Skylar had announced the death of JR to each of the teams in Yuma, Chicago, and Atlanta just over a week ago. Now? Jason was excited to say hello to his future.

Jason followed a tall, slender thirtysomething brunette who called herself Valerie, down the long hall to the meeting. As Vasilly Dvorak had said, these meetings were rare, carefully planned well in advance, and highly secure.

The old but marvelously restored mansion in Breckenridge, Colorado oozed opulence, power, and secrecy. The latter was further ensured by multiple personnel, mostly large, muscular stern-faced men, who were clearly not part of the considerable wait staff. The facility definitely wasn't open to the public.

Jason dressed in the manner he preferred for all his public appearances. Turtleneck, either a sweater or a lighter material depending on the weather; and matching pants and sports jacket, both custom tailored. And expensive leather shoes and belt. Very expensive.

*Got to be a better way to stay in touch,* he mused. *Code names? Really?*

Jason was as surprised as anyone concerning his remarkable recovery. His thinking seemed to be a little clearer, his memory sharper, and he felt somewhat younger and stronger. One critical fact remained hazy. Wasn't there something, something of utmost importance, that happened when he was shot? He just couldn't remember. Maybe someday. For now, no one would know that he had ingested an infinitesimal amount of the same fruit that had been processed and put into capsule form—and that both Bull and Jennifer had swallowed. His response was closer to Jennifer's than Bull's, yet without a timely exposure to pure oxygen.

They reached the heavy oak doors and Valerie knocked twice, then opened the one on the right and stepped aside. As Jason stepped inside, she closed the door behind him and stayed outside. Jason had already noted that her business pantsuit had a large bulge under her left arm that was not accounted for by her attractive figure. It appeared that her right pant leg also did not cling as tightly to that ankle as her left.

Vasilly stood. "Ladies and gentlemen, it is my honor to introduce to you Mr. Jason Matthews. The man who, for all practical purposes, is back to us from the dead."

## 57.  BALAAM INITIATIVES

After a few minutes of introductions, Jason began his presentation. He stood before the five members; not behind the lectern, but in front of it. Without notes.

"I'm grateful to finally meet each of you in person, as well as to identify you by your true names and identities. Vassily told me the ground rules and that you have much to cover, so let me proceed directly to my strategy.

"In a previous century, Alexis de Tocqueville made a statement that was true then, and remains a problem now. It also implies our solution. I quote: 'America is great because she is good. If America ceases to be good, America will cease to be great.' We'll return to this shortly.

"First, a little history. I believe we are all in agreement that mankind came the closest to our destiny, to true greatness, when we were together on a plain in Shinar and began the noble task of building a city, and a tower that would reach to the heavens."

Everyone nodded in agreement.

"We were one people, one language. But you know there was more. This was to be a statement of allegiance to our great leader and his fallen ones, as we would figuratively join with him. We would ascend above the heights of the clouds and make ourselves like the Most High.

"So, what did our Enemy do? He scattered us, as we still are today. For all our generations since then, we have sought out and followed The Fallen One, or his leaders; Baal, Beelzebub, and others. Why? To bring us back together, to our rightful place of freedom, power, and control.

"Our Enemy and His weak-minded minions stand in our way. We make progress, but it's measured in decades, or in centuries. Even if we had FSAT today in a safe form to make us like our original Fathers? We would be dust before the world would be ready for us."

Again, everyone nodded in agreement. This time, solemn agreement.

"I, for one, am not willing to wait," Jason smiled. "The catalyst I propose, I call the Balaam Initiatives."

"Thousands of years after Babel, our Enemy grabbed hold of a pathetic group of mongrels and decided to waste His favor and protection on them. Their twelve tribes were in the plains of Moab beyond the Jordan opposite Jericho. Moab's wise king, Balak, knew that he couldn't defeat them. We never can. Not when the Enemy's hedge of protection is in place. So, he enticed Balaam to curse the Israelites. But the Enemy is devious, and each time Balaam opened his mouth to proclaim a curse, words of blessings to the sons of Jacob and curses against Moab and others emerged instead.

"But did you realize that even so, Balaam didn't completely fail our cause? Did you know that he brought about untold destruction against our enemies for years to come? In the final chapter of the Accursed Book, you'll find it: In one of the final churches, there are some who will still hold to the teaching of Balaam. What, you ask? What did Balaam do? He kept teaching Balak to put a stumbling block before the sons of Israel. He taught them to eat things sacrificed to idols and to commit acts of immorality."

Jason registered the surprise on their faces, but he didn't acknowledge it. *So, they have not heard of this tactic, and its continued success over the millennia.*

"Yes. The Balaam Initiatives. Take away the 'goodness' of America. Make them odious in the nostrils of our Enemy. Tear down His hedge of protection, of favor. We're already doing this through evolution. We teach them that they are products of chance and time. No purpose, no accountability. That's led to atheism, drugs, abortions, immorality, all manner of perversions, pride, and more. But let's throw away the simple-minded goal of godless anarchy. Sure, that's what we'll eventually need so we can declare martial law and subdue the United States and bring her into our world community.

"But no. Our greater goal is to remove the hedge. Take away the goodness? The greatness is gone. The hedge comes down. That is the catalyst we need to make everything else come into place.

"Specifics? Look, none of us like to get into the accursed Book. We know it's blatantly one-sided. Yet I challenge you. Stand firm, cut through the crap. Go for the meat. All that you see prophesied about the so-called end times? Those should specifically be our goals! Evil will become worse? Yes! Persecution will increase? Yes! False teachers, people becoming lovers of self, irreconcilable, prideful, all the rest? Absolutely! Bring about complete moral schizophrenia. Save the whales, kill the babies. Hug trees? Euthanize grandparents.

"Your primary vector, of course, is gaining control of the free news media. Free, of course, only in appearance. We intentionally weaponize disinformation. They must maintain that appearance and even believe amongst themselves that they are professional and unbiased. But totally sold out to our world view, without even knowing we exist. Think of four D's: Distract, deceive, divide, and disarm. Like the "newspeak" or "doublespeak" that George Orwell refers to in his novel, *1984.*

Jason gave a slight nod toward Vasilly, who returned the nod.

"Orwell described using euphemisms to obscure anything meaningful. We can so twist and neutralize any true discussions, any critical thinking, that we can say and do virtually anything without repercussions. To paraphrase an old American idiom some of you may be familiar with, we'll get folks so distracted trying to strain gnats—like confusion over using the pronouns 'him' and 'her,'—that we feed them truckloads of elephants. They won't even see us getting in progressive judges to legislate from the bench.

"The Balaam Initiatives should be applied to every country, of course. But especially to the U.S. Think about it. I foresee a time when abortion, our blood sacrifices that our Fallen Ones so enjoy, will be accepted for any reason, up to birth. Even after birth. Men and women will marry whoever they want; even their step-parents and siblings. We will have complete gender and sexual confusion and force it on the youngest children. Shared bathrooms and showers for children starting in primary school, all the way up. The demons of hell will be ecstatic . . . and empowered, like they are in so many Third World countries. Marriages will crumble, families will disintegrate, and churches? Everyone will go just to be entertained and get their ears tickled.

"Oh, what wonderful chaos that will be. For now? We keep throwing everything against the wall and seeing what sticks. Whatever happens, we blame guns. Conservatives. Capitalists. Christians. Home schooling. Founding fathers. Open borders to refugees and immigrants who won't assimilate. Do it all; doesn't matter. Just always keep them on the defensive. Ladies and gentlemen?"

He paused for effect, looking intently at each one of them.

"Ladies and gentlemen, we can't lose."

+ + +

Two hours later, Valerie knocked on Jason's door. "Mr. Matthews," she said in a commanding voice.

Jason opened the door.

"Dinner will be served in thirty minutes, sir. You will be our guest of honor," she said simply, then turned and walked away.

Jason smiled. He liked the mind games they played. He assumed that she was there to either assassinate him if they had voted not to bring him into their group, or to invite him to join them for dinner if they had voted in his favor. He was correct on both counts.

The next morning, as he awaited his flight in a private jet back to Atlanta, he knew why he had been raised up in such a time as this. More, he had finally found—or had been found—by like-minded men and women who understood the times. They were brilliant, powerful, and as a group, they were rich beyond measure. They literally had the ability to buy out any but the top three world economies.

And he had them right where he wanted them.

## 58.   HIDING

Karen looked at Ed. Everything was ready. At least everything that she and Ed and Sam and Mick could do, along with Major Garrett in his official capacity and otherwise. Now? It was time.

She knew the threat was not academic; it was existential. The previous day, Garrett had solemnly reported that Dr. Julian Winfred had joined Edgar in what "appeared" to be a suicide. Garrett promised Karen again he would contact Lanora to warn her, and that he would advise how she and her daughter could go into hiding.

Then, Garrett called Sam and Mick to cancel the going-away meal they had all planned. It was too risky, and Karen knew they needed to protect their friends.

With tears in their eyes, she and Ed got into a used Dodge Caravan paid for in cash and registered to "Ed Miller," and drove south on I-75.

"So, any more thoughts on what we should do? Where to go?" Karen asked as she stared out the window.

"You mean, other than survive, and other than drive south?" Ed glanced at her and smiled. She didn't even notice.

"Sorry. Guess that really isn't funny. But, yeah, I do. It's bottom-line stuff, like approaching this from a triage and emergency room perspective."

That got her attention. She shifted in her seat to face him.

"See, the bottom line for anything from now on, is we have to intentionally commit ourselves to honor God. In the third chapter of Proverbs, the Bible says, 'In all your ways acknowledge Him, And He will make your paths straight.' They may not be straight from our perspective, but they are from His. I hate that we have to be somewhat deceitful with different identities, yet that's to protect others as well as ourselves."

"Yeah, and possibly the world as we know it," Karen added.

"Yep. So how do we acknowledge Him? Of course, studying the Bible, prayer, worship, all that. And by asking the right questions."

"You lost me," she said flatly.

"Think about it. I'm married to the hottest, the most beautiful, intelligent, and strongest woman alive today. And she's only two-thirds of my age. You think I don't ask questions?"

Now she was smiling, at least a little. "Alright, so flattery will get you somewhere, old man. What does this have to do with acknowledging God and figuring out where to go and what to do?" she demanded.

"Jen– Karen, that's the point. You are absolutely unique in the world. Why did God allow that? Why did He keep you alive, and bring us together? Bluntly, what's in it for Him?"

She looked back out the window. Ed let her think as the minutes and miles went by.

"It's a God thing," she said quietly as she turned back to face him with a look of amazement. "In the safe house. It wasn't you, or Sam, or Mick. God led me to do what I did, then He saw me safely through it. This trip? It isn't you and Sam, or Mick and me. I'm different. You're the researcher. We're the Christians."

Ed smiled and nodded, as he took the fork to stay on I-75 down to Macon. "Bonus for me? We're married!"

"So, it has to be for us to take what God's done with me, and isolate anything good out of it that can help others!" she exclaimed.

"Without weaponizing it."

"Exactly. Hmm . . . " She paused. "Several things. Other than survive and drive," she chuckled.

"Tell me your thoughts, and let's compare."

"Okay, we'll need funding. For our protection, we need income that doesn't require eight-to-five work around a lot of people."

"Agreed. Suggestions?" Ed asked.

"You'll think I'm crazy," she stated.

"Other than for marrying me? Not a chance."

"You can make it up to me tonight. And tomorrow night. And . . . "

"Good grief," he broke in. "I've created a monster!"

"Admit it. You love it," she teased.

"Guilty. So, what's your suggestion?"

"You know I told you how I can look at things, and just see patterns? Same with numbers, which is sort of ironic 'cause I was terrible in math. Well, things just kinda jump out at me."

"Things? Now I'm not tracking," Ed said.

"Things like, like the stock market."

"You're kidding!" he exclaimed.

"Wanna bet on how quickly I make our first hundred thousand?"

"Soon, I hope, since I've only got six thousand left to our new names. Okay, where?"

"Jacksonville, Florida."

"Really?" he asked.

"Out of Georgia. A big enough city we can get lost in. And," she emphasized, "my dear husband, lover, doctor, and personal researcher?"

"Yes, my queen?"

"We should have good access to medical equipment."

"Jacksonville it is. I spent a lot of time there while I was growing up. We lived down around Cape Kennedy. We can pick up I-16 out of Macon, head east, and hang a right at Savannah. Or stay on I-75 to I-10 and hang a left. Preference?"

"Yes. Savannah. You don't want to fight all the I-75 construction in South Georgia. And," she put her hand on his knee and smiled, "let's stop in Savannah tonight. I don't want to wait till Jacksonville."

+  +  +

"It's time," Jason said to no one in particular. He started his Cadillac and drove away a final time from the place that had been his home.

Jason's departure from Atlanta was in every way different from Ed and Karen's. He had packers professionally move everything. He left by himself. And he went north on I-75, then northeast on I-85. For now, he was moving to northern Virginia. He looked forward to cooler weather, and easy access to anywhere he wanted to go, which would include the Washington Beltway. That was his mid-term goal, not as a representative, but as a senator. That's what he and the Five . . . now, the Six with his membership . . . had agreed upon. He would pursue their various objectives in the United States for the next fifteen years or so, and then rise to a prominent position in the Senate once other initiatives had matured.

Other differences? He had no concerns about funds, and never would again. He would have personal access to several million dollars each year, no questions asked. With just a little justification, which he planned to have within a few years, that figure could rapidly jump by three more zeros.

That was his first goal, to identify top-of-the-class students who could be molded, mentored, and used to implement the Balaam Initiatives. Unknowingly, of course. They would be recruited into secret or even not-so-secret societies, aided by considerable grants, and strategically placed for maximum impact. As Jason had briefed, the primary goal was to back-fill retiring journalists. He adamantly agreed with William James, a quote that he loved: "There's nothing so absurd that if you repeat it often enough, people will believe it." Hitler and many others had proven the effectiveness of that philosophy, and he would as well.

Still, his overarching goal would always be to recapture Jennifer, capture Dr. Richardson, or preferably both of them. He needed FSAT. If it suited his purpose, he would also share it with the other members of the Six. Much of the rest of his "allowance" would be directed to finding . . . buying . . . a world-class research team to continue analysis and tests using Jennifer's blood and marrow that had been stored off-site.

"So much to do," he mused as he continued through Greenville, South Carolina.

Jason had already identified and secured a premium condominium in a secure, gated community and was anxious to move in. There was one aspect of his former "JR" life, his latest, that he planned to continue with Skylar's assistance, and that would be a nice location for his personal enjoyment. The young man seemed astute and loyal enough to carry on the lucrative benefits of the human trafficking operation, and he would be allowed access to the benefits himself.

"I'll be settled in within a few weeks, Skylar will have a place and be productive within a few more. Fall in northern Virginia. Nice," Jason thought out loud as he drove toward Spartanburg.

## 59. WORD OF CONFIRMATION

Ed and Karen Miller, according to their detailed new identities, enjoyed a long lunch at Steak and Ale in North Macon, then Karen took the wheel as they continued on to I-16. Ed asked if she minded him turning on the radio. "I listen to Christian talk shows when I can and when one's available. Taken together, that's exactly, almost never," he quipped.

"Go for it. This'll be a first for me," she replied.

He scanned the AM band and in a few moments the radio locked to a station broadcasting *Point of View.* Marlin Maddoux and Kerby Anderson were interviewing a guest who immediately caught their attention.

"Imagine," he said. "We are all concerned about First Amendment Christian rights. And we should be. Challenge, challenge, challenge and then we fight, fight, fight. But there are two dangers."

"Dangers. In fighting for our Christian rights to free speech. How so?" Marlin challenged.

"You're seeing it already. Apathy. We fight so often, on so many issues, we become tired. Then numb. Finally? Apathetic."

"Good point," Marlin agreed.

"What's the second danger?" Kerby asked.

"More subtle," the guest responded. "And this could take years. But it's coming. We fight tooth-and-nail for Christian rights. And other so-called faiths take advantage of that. They come in and use our freedoms against us."

"How so?" asked Kerby.

"Here's one example. You'll say it won't happen. But I'm telling you, if we don't establish clear laws that protect the Judeo-Christian foundation and legal system of the United States? What if Islam continues to grow worldwide, and they decide to target the U.S. Not through Jihad, but through a systematic, planned overthrow."

"An invasion?" Asked Marlin.

"Not necessarily. Most immigrants wouldn't have the slightest negative intent against us. They would simply want a better life for their families."

"So, what's the problem?" Marlin challenged.

"Some would assimilate. Some may even become Christians. But others attend mosques, and might be taught to remain separate, demand freedoms, run for public office, and promote Sharia law."

"You're saying that could happen here?" asked Kerby.

"I'm saying it will happen here," replied the guest.

"Turning our own freedoms against us."

"That's just using Islam as an example. I'm just saying, just like communities need to pass solid, well-thought-out laws against the so-called 'adult entertainment' clubs . . . "

"The strip joints opening up along the interstates?" Marlin interjected.

"If they don't pass those ordinances in advance, it will be far more difficult and exorbitantly more expensive once one opens up at your town's exit. We need government to codify laws to mandate that no other law, be it Sharia, a World Court, or United Nations ruling, will have jurisdiction over this country."

Karen shook her head as the program took a break. "I could really see that happening."

"It's a dangerous world we live in. I believe we're in what the Bible calls the end times; the end of this age," Ed replied. "Far more is going to happen, it's going to happen faster, and it's going to get really ugly."

The station gave its call letters and city, Warner Robins, along with a brief forecast; hot, humid, with a chance of afternoon thunderstorms. *No surprise there,* thought Ed. *August in Georgia.*

The announcer continued. "More of *Point of View* in a moment. This is station manager Bill Bruton. We've received a lot of prayer requests about all the challenges and changes people are facing. Join us for Prayer Time at 8:30 each weekday morning. And let me encourage you with this. Nelda and I can tell you from personal testimony: If you're in God's will, He will provide. Now, Back to *Point of View.*"

Ed reached over and turned off the radio. He looked at Karen.

She simply said, "Uh, wow."

"That, my dear, doesn't happen often. I take that as a specific word to us," he said.

"It ties right in with the Scripture you quoted, 'In all your ways acknowledge Him'."

"And if you're in His will, He will provide," Ed said, adding Bill's testimony.

+ + +

I-16 heading east toward Savannah is long, flat, and boring. After they stopped for gas in Metter, Georgia and got back on the road, Ed resumed driving.

"Gotta confess something," Karen said. She'd been staring out the window for several minutes. Now she looked at Ed. "I had every intention of getting a cab and going over to Little Haiti for the FBI raid. You know, just in case. And, honestly, I wanted to do anything I could to hurt JR."

Ed glanced at her. "Really? But, you didn't."

"That's the thing. Stronger, faster, smarter, all that. But I was calling for a cab, and I just suddenly felt that I was supposed to pray."

A few seconds passed. Ed glanced at her with a quizzical look, his head cocked slightly. "Karen. That was when, Wednesday evening?"

"6 p.m. I just hung up and started praying. I guess off and on until Sam called at eight."

Ed slowly nodded. "Amazing. And Sam told you that the bust went down better than anyone expected? Not a shot fired?"

"Right. They also learned it could have been a disaster. She said they had a small army there. I think she used the phrase, 'loaded to the teeth.'"

"Karen. I'd just gotten back to my apartment. I started supper and was going to do some more packing. I turned off the stove, went to my desk, and started praying for all of you. At 6 p.m."

"Wow. Okay, this is all new to me. So, this was another 'God thing?'" she asked.

Ed hesitated, collecting his thoughts. "A lot of Scriptures come to mind. Some are warnings. The Bible warns that pride comes before a fall, and that the Lord reserves vengeance for Himself. Others teach important perspectives about trust. One says that deliverance is not by might, nor by power, but by His Spirit. Another, that some boast in chariots and some in horses, but we will boast in the name of the Lord. Honey, I think this was not just a 'God thing' for that specific circumstance. I think God is teaching you something critical for the rest of your superhuman life."

Now she pondered, looking back out the window as the miles passed by.

"What God has given me, is not for my own vengeance. And it's never to take the place of depending on Him. It's really that simple, isn't it?"

"Sounds about right. As you study Scripture, watch for those kinds of admonitions that apply to you. That's how the Spirit takes His word and makes it alive to our specific lives and circumstances. Another thing to watch for? Throughout the Bible you'll see a lot of references about waiting patiently on the Lord."

"Like, I want patience and I want it right now," she quipped.

"Yep. Or the person who brags about being twice as humble as anyone else." Ed glanced at his wife, before looking back at the road. "God knows how to build patience, and by definition, it takes time. He also knows how to knock us down if we start thinking too highly of ourselves."

"And too little of Him."

## 60.  ROOTS

"**M**orning," Ed yawned as he walked to the kitchenette and poured a cup of coffee. "Up long?"

Karen smiled. "Oh, since, uh . . . about four? I only need around four hours anymore. Wide awake."

"Amazing." He smelled the aroma and took a sip. He walked over to her chair at the small dining table, leaned over, and they shared a long kiss.

"Second best morning of my life," he smiled.

"Better than the morning after our first night? Really?" she teased.

"Cumulative. I'll say the same thing years from now if I can keep count."

"How sweet."

"So, what's up?" He nodded at the newspaper on spread out on the table. It was a free morning paper that had been left outside their motel room.

"Well, most important is not this. It's that," she said, pointing to the new Bible he gave her as a wedding gift. "I read all the way through Genesis. Ed, we need to talk."

"Are you feeling a connection?" he asked, noting her sudden serious tone.

"Do I! I mean, didn't you used to debate this? It's real. I guess I'm living proof. I felt like I was researching my genealogy. Do you think this is from the Tree of Life?"

Ed nodded. "Honey, yes. I really think it is. God planted it there in a perfect environment. Under those conditions, our understanding is that it would have given physical immortality. Would they have to keep eating it, like once every decade or century? Don't know. But after sin entered the world and with the continued degradation of our genome after the Flood? Well, you saw that it normally kills. And for you? Maybe just an extra forty years or so. But the genetic reboot? Who knows how strong and intelligent those first generations were!"

She sipped her coffee and stared at the Bible. "What do you think the flood was like?" she asked.

"Terrifying. Many scientists and Bible scholars believe there had been a clear water vapor canopy high in the atmosphere. When it collapsed, all but the small amount we now see as clouds fell to earth. Removing trillions of tons of water significantly lowered the atmospheric pressure. Reduced pressure and the new clouds caused temperatures to drop, which soon led to multiple ice age cycles, along with cyclical warming and cooling of various parts of the earth. We've had cycles of climate change ever since.

She looked up at Ed and nodded. "Cycles. Now that makes sense."

He continued. "The earth's crust broke apart, releasing subterranean pockets of water, which along with the water pouring down from the atmosphere formed huge oceans. The crust itself broke into various tectonic plates, and the portions that rose above the waters became continents and mountains.

"It's not referenced in the Bible, but we've seen massive crater impacts on the earth. God may have allowed a swarm of comets to slam into the earth's atmosphere and impact the crust as his judgment on the sin of mankind. Water and dust from the comets could have precipitated the collapse of the canopy. Meteorites could have been what cracked the crust."

Karen just stared. "Unimaginable. What was it like on the ark?"

"Did you know that last century, studies were done to determine the most stable ratio of height, width, and length for ocean barges? Guess which design was by far the best?"

"You're kidding . . . "

"Nope. By far, the exact God-given proportions used for the ark. It must have been tossed around violently. But it protected its occupants from unimaginable cataclysmic worldwide upheaval."

"All those animals. How many?"

Ed walked over to a window, opened the curtains, and looked out.

"Nowhere near as many as most believe," he answered. "Remember what you read this morning in Genesis Chapter 1. All the animals were brought forth, 'after their kind.' With the pure genetic pool, all 'cats' that ever existed and ever would exist were genetically available in one pair of, well, whatever came on the ark. Over the centuries, they would mate and their genetics would produce lions, tigers, panthers, and kitty-cats. Dogs? Wolves, coyotes, and hundreds of different dog breeds. All the genetic material was already there; nothing new evolved, and everything mated and reproduced after its kind."

"Noah, his wife, their sons and their wives? Their genome was still pure. Brothers and sisters could marry, cousins . . . ?"

Ed sat down at the table across from her.

"For many, many generations," he agreed. "Even well after the Tower of Babel days. But without the vapor canopy, ultraviolet light and higher frequencies of the electromagnetic spectrum, not blocked by the ionosphere, could descend to the earth's surface. Gradually, over the centuries, their cumulative effects on human and animal DNA shortened lifespans and increased hereditary defects. Similar degradation of fruits and vegetables meant lower levels of antioxidants and other nutrients. The effects were very slow, over thousands of years. And irreversible. In His law to the Israelites, God forbade marriage between close relatives."

Karen walked to the coffee pot, refilled her cup, topped his off, and sat back down. "Everything on the earth, all people, animals, birds, and many sea creatures as well, perished. Unless they were on the ark."

"Think of all the carcasses, along with trees and plants. Everything got stirred up in the flood waters as currents formed, storms raged, and earthquakes pummeled the planet. When the waters receded, everything was deposited in layer upon layer based on buoyancy. Under pressure and as minerals permeating the sediments, they were quickly fossilized, even on many rising mountains. We've witnessed that happen in years; it doesn't take centuries or millennia. As the earth continued to shift from earthquakes and volcanos, some lower layers of sediment slid up above higher layers. Remember the 1980 Mount Saint Helens eruption? It's given us a scale model of the Grand Canyon, and it happened in a decade! A canyon has been carved out of soft sediment by a small river."

"And, the Garden of Eden," Karen commented as she sipped her coffee. "Destroyed."

"Along with the Tree of Life, not to be seen again until the new heavens and earth at the end of the age."

"But for some reason . . . " she said, looking deep into Ed's eyes.

He set his cup down and gently held her shoulders. "For some reason, my dear, God chose to preserve a small portion, for you, for now, for such a time as this."

+   +   +

They prayed together, fixed and ate breakfast, and planned out their trip. Then Ed motioned to the newspaper. "What are you thinking, young lady?"

"Well, I'm fascinated with the stocks. I know so little, yet I see patterns. I'm watching for trends. I need to buy some books or something. Maybe go to a library. I've got to see how we can earn money legally, keep enough of it liquid, pay taxes, and not draw attention."

Ed nodded. "I was thinking as I dozed off last night. You'll soon be able to do anything I can do, even the medical research, and better. But you can't do everything at once. So, here's the deal. Choose the areas you want to pursue, like fundraising, and likely our identity security and all that, and I'll focus on, well, on you."

Karen giggled. "Why, you dirty old man!"

And they kissed. Again.

"I already put the 'Do not disturb' sign on the door, and checkout isn't till eleven," she whispered in Ed's ear.

## 61.   COMPROMISED!

K aren was excited for her friend, and she was unaware of significant circumstances developing around her. Specifically, above her, as she drove east on Atlantic Boulevard toward Atlantic Beach. She and Ed had chosen a small, modest apartment there because of the high population turnover, what with the beach, Naval Station Mayport, and the University of North Florida. Easier to hide in plain sight, Ed said.

Now, being so close to the base was about to be an issue. According to investigation reports, a TA-4J Skyhawk jet trainer had departed Naval Air Station Cecil Field half an hour earlier, flew to Mayport, and the student was performing touch-and-go's. After one approach, the cockpit filled with smoke and the intercom went dead. Not knowing whether external radios were still online, the Instructor Pilot shook the stick to indicate that he was taking over the aircraft, initiated cockpit clearing procedures, and broadcast a Mayday and inflight emergency.

Still heavy on fuel, the IP began dumping as he tried unsuccessfully to loop back around to Mayport. The investigation determined that the twenty-three-year-old aircraft had suffered a significant hydraulic system overheat. Circuit breakers had opened and flight controls quickly degraded. He pulled engine power, lowered flaps, and tried unsuccessfully to lower landing gear. The last thing he was able to do was aim between buildings, down a major road off of Atlantic Boulevard.

The Skyhawk impacted the crossroad not more than a hundred yards in front of Karen, fuel still spilling from the dump valve which was stuck full-open. It slid down the road on its twin external wing tanks, eventually clipping a telephone pole with a wingtip. That threw it into a violent ground loop and slammed it against one of the few vacant buildings in the area, a store that was being remodeled.

Without hesitation, Karen turned and followed the aircraft, checking on cars that had swerved to avoid the jet. They had, at the cost of multiple secondary collisions. None appeared serious, so she kept following the trainer. She slammed on the brakes and put the van into park just thirty yards from the aircraft. A trail of flame followed the aircraft, which was moments from being completely engulfed in the fire, with the pilots still inside.

Karen often discussed with Ed how they could discretely determine exactly what she was now able to do, over a year after taking FSAT. Today would be that day, although it was anything but discrete.

She sprinted the thirty yards in world-class time, despite the shorts, spaghetti-strap blouse, and plain sneakers she was wearing. She knew nothing about jets. She quickly read all the warning and caution placards on the fuselage as she ran, so she was able to identify and pull the "Emergency Only" handle to blow off the cockpit canopy.

The men were conscious but dazed from being slammed around in the violent crash. The heat was becoming unbearable and the craft would explode at any moment. She jumped up to the top edge of the cockpit and leaned down, figured out how to unstrap the men from their safety harnesses in one second, and then freed each of them in two more. She then grabbed each man by his flight suit, stood, and lifted them cleanly out of the cockpit. She jumped to the ground and immediately ran another sprint around the building to shield the three of them from the blast, which came exactly as she turned the corner. Only then did Karen carefully lower the men to their feet. As they tried to gain their balance, she ran just far enough to glance around the building and make sure the van was engulfed in flames. Without looking back, she then ran a good mile in a pattern to throw off anyone who might try to track her, yet slow enough not to draw too much attention.

Finally, she slowed to a walk in a safe neighborhood and pulled out her cell phone.

+ + +

Early that evening, Skylar was straining through his last he reps of presses, finishing up his final set on the weights. Not the machines. He preferred the old-fashioned iron, and he'd just increased his personal best by two more pounds.

The considerable background noise in the gym was interrupted by a stream of profanity by a woman in the far corner. Something on the large TV had caught her attention. Exclamations continued as eight men and four women quickly worked their way over to see the still image on the screen. Skylar was the last to join the group. His mouth gaped open.

A grainy picture filled the screen. A young blonde woman, appearing to be in her early twenties, stood on a crashed Navy jet, flames and smoke all around. She was only wearing sneakers, shorts, and a skimpy summer blouse. She held one man in each hand by the front of their flight suit, just below the collar. Skylar shook his head in amazement. She held them both in the air above the aircraft, about to jump to the ground.

Someone found the volume control. " . . . is there anything more you can tell us, Bob?" a female voice asked. The picture changed. Now the young woman was on the ground, running away from the burning aircraft, dragging the men on either side as if they were large stuffed animals.

A man's voice replied, shaky. "I tell ya, I haven't had a drink in a week. Tonight? I'm getting' wasted. Like, she sprinted around the side of the building, dragging both of those dudes!"

The picture changed again, showing the woman running around the building.

"Look, I played high school football. Ribault. I was a wide receiver. Man, I could run. But not dragging two full-size guys behind me! One in each hand? Come on, now . . . " his voice trailed off.

The screen now showed a close-up of the reporter, a redhead in her late thirties.

"So, you've heard it from four eyewitnesses now, and you've seen the pictures from the only person who caught the action on their Instamatic camera. At this point, there are far more questions than answers. Alien? Classified Navy experiment? Female Nephilim? Wonder Woman? For North Coast News, this is Jane Thompson. Back to you . . . "

Skylar was already out the front door. Ten minutes later he made his second call and immediately had Jason's undivided attention.

"Where?"

"Jacksonville, Florida," Skylar answered, "near one of the beaches. Big news story of a Navy jet crashing, and this young woman sprints to the plane, blows the canopy, pulls both men out—one in each hand, mind you—jumps to the ground and runs them around a building just before the jet explodes. Somebody snapped a couple of grainy photos."

"It's her." Jason said, flatly. "How soon . . . "

"I've alerted the team. Randall's checking on flights now. I'll let you know as soon as I do."

"Do that. Get a reservation for me, too," and he hung up.

"Hello, Jennifer. Or Karen. Or whatever your name is. See you soon," Jason said, smiling.

+  +  +

"Gotta say it. Always had a thing for redheads. And you, my dear, are a knockout!"

"You're so sweet," Karen replied to Ed, twirling a lock of her reddish-blonde wig. Actually, their new identities were now Rhonda and Tom Halford. The pictures of her were poor quality because of the distance, from shaky hands and the burning fuel's smoke. Still, they would air for days, as if she were the final proof of aliens among us.

"Think it's enough?" she asked, as they left the Huddle House off of an I-10 exit near Tallahassee, Florida. It was 2 a.m.

"For you, for now? Yes. My baseball cap? Not so much. We are only concerned about one person, and he has pictures from a year ago. From now on, we both need better disguises. Maybe even colored contact lenses. Now that's a thought . . . "

She groaned softly as she slid in the passenger seat of the six-year-old Honda Civic. They had just paid for it, in cash, and drove it out as the dealership was locking up for the night. All their "take with us" stuff was in the back. Everything else would stay in the apartment, where it would be picked up by a local Christian ministry. They had worked through the process months earlier, and they would continue to improve on the details each time they had to move over the years. But for now?

"How are the burns?" Tom asked.

"Down to a mild sunburn. Should be back to normal in a few more hours."

The pilots had been protected by their fire-resistant flight suits and helmets. Karen, in the lightweight shorts and top so perfect for a hot summer day in Jacksonville? Not so much. But the second-degree burns were quickly healing.

Tom merged back onto I-10 West and glanced over at his wife. For the tenth time in as many hours, he shook his head in amazement. "You are incredible! We talked about what we were going to do when we left Atlanta, and we agreed to honor God and put Him first in all our decisions. You did that. You risked your life to save those men, and they were able to go home to their families tonight."

She lovingly patted his knee, then held his free hand for several moments. "Did you hear what the one guy said? He said that whoever I was, it was divine intervention that I was there when it all happened. He's taking his family back to church Sunday."

"Wow. No, I missed that. But God didn't."

"They may end up at the one we attended. Sure going to miss that."

"We'll find another one. Absolutely," he agreed, and sipped the strong, black takeout coffee he had brought with him. "You know, I really like this Civic," he smiled.

"And I always wanted to visit Huntsville. Or, at least, I have ever since we left Jacksonville."

They chuckled. They were heading west on I-10 to catch U.S. 331 North, and then I-65 to Mooresville. Finally, I-565 would get them to their destination by early afternoon. They chose that route rather than the construction on I-75 and the early morning Atlanta traffic of that alternative.

Tom reflected on their unique situation. Sure, they were madly in love. But that could, and probably would, come and go. They had been through some tough times, and not a few very strong disagreements. But their commitment to honor God first, and then each other, is what held everything together.

Rhonda glanced at her husband, so handsome, so compassionate and understanding. Their situation was unique. She was one-of-a-kind, and he was the only person in the world that she wanted, that she trusted to help her cope. If possible? To also harvest any possible bene-fit to mankind. But if not, to keep those with evil intent from capitalizing on her condition.

Lost in their own thoughts, they reached the same conclusion.

*We're different. God brought us together. He has a purpose for our lives. It will involve sacrifice and commitment. But finding and following that path is not only our purpose; it's also the journey to our ultimate fulfillment.*

Without a word or a glance, they reached over and held hands.

Rhonda, aka Jennifer Karen Lane Richardson, realized how profound that conclusion actually was. *It's true for everyone, even without FSAT.*

# EPILOGUE

Jason Matthews continued his assignments to the delight of his new organization, which he suggested they refer to as "One World Peace Now," or OWPN. Their ultimate goal was for him to secure a high-level Senate seat at some point in the future. That was the organization's goal; for him, it would simply be the next step toward his ultimate ambitions.

The Eight, then Nine, increased its membership at his recommendation. One noteworthy addition was a Spiritism adherent, but one who believed that the "Supreme Intelligence and Primary Cause of Everything" was not the Biblical God of Abraham, Isaac, and Jacob. Jason believed the man would be instrumental in uniting world religions, when the time was right.

What OWPN didn't know about Jason, and what he himself was not able to explain, was the slow but notable improvement to his thinking, memory, and overall well-being. Oddly, it seemed to be accompanied by a lustful desire for more power, more control, and more physical gratification. It seemed to have begun when he survived the gunshot wound. If only he could remember . . .

+ + +

Skylar? After turning up empty-handed in Jacksonville, Jason's direction was simple: "I want a larger team helping you track them. Florida, Oregon, France, China, I don't care where they go. We will find them. And we need a strike team ready at all times. Your top priority."

Skylar's mind whirled with the possibilities and he followed his directives relentlessly. He continued to learn the latest computer tech, the expanding capabilities of something new called the World Wide Web, and made more contacts throughout the news media. Cell phones would help the media—and him—track stories faster than ever before, like they did in Jacksonville. And if "the lady" was all that?

Dragging a couple of grown men out of a burning aircraft and carrying them, actually running while she carried them, to safety? He significantly increased his time at the gym and his martial arts training.

They got away this time. They may do so again. Maybe many times. But each time, it would get more personal.

Jason would have his superwoman and her doctor husband.

And when they got the formula right? Skylar would be more than happy to be their test subject. Oh, yeah.

+ + +

Ed and Karen Richardson became known by many names and stayed in many locations over the next fourteen years. They never stayed anywhere more than a year.

The potential for FSAT to cure diseases and literally change the world was enormous. But, despite their combined best efforts, it continued to be just that: potential. Even as they quietly developed new technology an order of magnitude better than any that existed commercially, they could not extract beneficial antibodies apart from the FSAT genetic reboot that would cause a crisis, then death. And that was just with lab animals. They weren't about to conduct experiments on people. Still, they never gave up.

They continued to remain aloof, always watching out for any compromise that could put their identities at risk. Skylar came close, in some cases within just hours, of carrying out his goal. After each escape, the couple learned new tricks to hide and evade. But Skylar also continued honing his team and resources to track them down and prepare for their capture. He, too, would never give up.

Many couples exist together for decades, yet they never really live.

Ed and Karen Richardson were together as husband and his exceptional wife, for fourteen years. He continued to grow older. The effects of FSAT reduced her apparent age down to eighteen years, after which she appeared to age very slowly. In the latter years, to reduce unwanted attention and to honor her, Ed would treat her as his daughter in the rare occasions they were together in public. When they stayed in hotel rooms, he would ask for a room with two beds. But in private?

They were in every way a loving, committed married couple. And more. They didn't just exist. They lived!

In years to come, unusual events would continue to bring together an unlikely team, who would risk everything to hold off the prophesied, ultimate evil as long as possible.

Karen Lane Richardson was the first.


**Did you like <u>Five Score and Ten</u>?**
*Please leave a review!*


*Don't miss <u>Book Two</u>:*

# *The Guardian Collection*

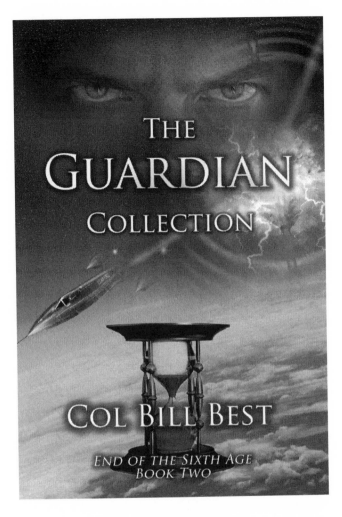

Book Two, *"The Guardian Collection,"* brings us up to date on Karen's struggles in 2020, and the One World Peace Now countdown for world dominance by the mid-2020s. It all comes together in the "Guardian" novellas, as more lives are changed forever. Will the planet be destroyed by World War III? Will every country be crushed by an authoritarian one-world government? Will there be any time left for each person to make decisions with eternal consequences?

## Links at BillBest.net/My-Books

*Unusual circumstances bring together an unlikely team, who risk everything to hold off the ultimate, prophesied evil as long as possible.*

Next? Book Three: "**Reflections of a Shadow.**" Now in the late 2020s, the unique team fights the growing forces of darkness, hell-bent on ushering in a one-world government, the Antichrist, and the "End of the Sixth Age!"

*Dedication:*

To those on the front line: Christian pastors, missionaries, and those serving in parachurch ministries.

You preach, teach, encourage, lead by example, and serve in countless ways. Your impact is eternal!

## *Want More?*

- How did Karen and Roger meet?
- How did Roger lose his family and the use of his legs in 2020?
- Why did he choose to join DPI and become the driving force behind the Guardian hypersonic manned interceptor?
- Finally, were the events in Roger's life a specific answer to prayer? Was he uniquely positioned, " . . . for such a time as this?"

Free eBook Novelette at **BillBest.Net/Free**

# ABOUT THE AUTHOR

Colonel Bill Best (B.S., MBA; USAF, Retired) began writing as a culmination of many interests and careers.

Bill read every Science Fiction book in his school libraries.

After college, he served as an Active Duty Air Force officer for nine years. He continued an additional twenty-one years as a Reservist while serving at AM and FM Christian radio ministries around Warner Robins, Georgia.

As a broadcaster, Bill interviewed hundreds of Christian leaders such as the late Dr. D. James Kennedy (Coral Ridge Ministries) and Dr. Duane Gish (Institute for Creation Research). He also interviewed Joni Eareckson Tada, Herb Shreve (founder of Christian Motorcyclist Association), and Dr. Tim LaHaye (co-author of the incredible Left Behind series)!

Bill's interest in computers and Science Fiction, his military background, experience as a Program Manager for a Department of Defense Contractor, and years in a Christian radio ministry have led to a unique writing "voice" and perspective.

His "End of the Sixth Age" series combines today's headlines with tomorrow's technology, as the world inevitably moves to the prophesied One World Government and Tribulation.

Bill and his wife, Barbara, live in Middle Georgia. They have two daughters and – currently – four grandchildren.

Follow Bill at **BillBest.net**.